Mama Sadie

A Quaker Cafe Novel

Brenda Bevan Remmes

This is a work of fiction. Names, characters, organizations, places, events, and incidents are either products of the author's imagination or are used fictitiously.

ISBN: 9781976891571

Cover art by Karen Slama

Published by Amazon.com

www.KDP.com

Printed in the United States of America

For Bill,
my moral compass and 3:00 a.m. friend
for forty-five years

"Heroes are not giant statues framed against a red sky. They are people who say: This is my community, and it is my responsibility to make it better."

—Studs Terkel

Chapter One

A small Christmas tree sat on a side table inside the Quaker Café. Multi-colored lights blinked on and off. Sadie watched as her eighteen-month-old grandson Gabe picked up first one and then another of the plastic pieces in the manger scene under the artificial branches. She grabbed a Kleenex out of her pocket, wiped his nose and pulled back a wisp of hair from his mouth. His curls, with that lovely red tint, were his father's. Already he was beginning to freckle.

Sadie tore open the cellophane on a pack of saltines, handed one of the crackers to Gabe and placed an order for three fried chicken dinners and some chicken nuggets. Miss Ellie, the café's aging proprietor and the model of gentility, bent down and tweaked Gabe's cheek. Her floral dress could have been worn any day of the year. On this afternoon she'd added a red wool sweater that matched her lipstick and as always, she wore heels.

"Oh, such a honey," she said before taking Sadie's order back to Teensy, the cook. "I hope the next one is just as beautiful."

A shiny gray Mercedes Benz pulled into one of the five parking spots in front of the café. Sadie watched with interest. Locals didn't start arriving for dinner before five. She pushed the sheer curtains aside to get a better look—sleek, maybe one of the newest '96 models equipped with those navigation systems everyone talked about. She didn't understand the big fuss. You'd have to take it all the way to Raleigh or Virginia Beach for service. No dealer in Northeastern North Carolina would know how to repair the gadget. How much better could it be looking at a tiny screen on a dashboard instead of a larger map in your lap?

Two men in identical black suits and dark glasses stepped out of either side of the car. They stood beside their doors and surveyed Main Street. Their dress, the sedan and the timing felt wrong. Sadie scanned the dozen store-fronts and knew that everyone in the two block downtown had these men on their radar now. They didn't look like the typical travelers who'd wandered off the beaten track.

The taller man reached into the backseat and pulled out a leather briefcase. Together they walked into the café.

"Mrs. Cartwright?" One man removed his sun glasses and looked at Sadie.

"No." Sadie glanced down at Gabe and slipped her hand into his. "She's in the kitchen. She'll be out in a minute." Sadie should have welcomed the strangers and asked where they were from, but she sensed something fishy and remained cautious.

The kitchen door swung open. Miss Ellie walked into the room. She stopped. Her back straightened. Her chin tilted.

"I believe you have a meeting room reserved for us?" the taller man said. In a quick glance, he surveyed the ten empty oak tables. "A room in the back, maybe?"

"Oh," Miss Ellie said, as if an electric shock had just restored her memory. "A woman called. I was expecting a woman." She walked over to the cash register and pulled a slip of paper from under the counter. "A Miss Caren Drake?"

"That's right."

Miss Ellie stepped towards the door that led down a short hallway. "Let me show you what I have." She picked up two menus and walked them to a room with an extended table that could seat twelve. They pulled out four of the steel folding chairs stacked against the wall.

"Just coffee," one said.

"I don't suppose you have a Scotch and soda?" the second asked.

Miss Ellie shook her head.

"Then I'll take a Coke."

When Ellie returned to the dining room, Sadie hoped to be told what was up. Having owned the grocery store next door for thirty years, she prided herself on knowing everything that went on in town. "What's that all about?"

"Don't know," Ellie said, not nearly as forthcoming as Sadie wanted. But Ellie had always been like that—not one to carry tales. Sadie, in contrast, felt a moral obligation to intervene in her neighbors' personal lives. She believed that small towns thrived on the premise that everyone needed to look out for the well-being of the community. Friends took care of friends.

"Where they from?"

"Raleigh, I think," Miss Ellie said as if it were normal to have folks from Raleigh conduct business in her back room.

"Why are they here?"

"Didn't say."

Ellie took the coffee and a can of Coca Cola with a glass of ice to the two men before heading to the kitchen. She needed to help Teensy get ready for the senior crowd. Retirees arrived early and often hung around to chat with the moms and dads who stopped to get take-out after work. Younger couples and bachelors tended to show up towards six.

After Sadie sold the family store to her son Dutch and his wife Ada Lynn, she'd planned to fix them home cooked meals every night. Her good intentions diminished as the café not only provided better food, but also an active social life. All but Sunday evenings and Mondays when the café was closed, she could walk in any time between seven and seven and get an invitation to sit down with entertaining company.

Her husband Coen's death five years ago hit her hard. Thirty-four years had been a long time with the same man working side-by-side. Theirs had been a good marriage—the kind that you know what each other is thinking without having to say it. He had a head for numbers and loved her and their boys in a quiet and gentle manner. She, in turn, thrived on the daily encounters, the local scuttlebutt, and the countless ideas of how to improve the business. Plus, she put her back behind her words. She knew about hard work.

The Cedar Branch Grocery was a family business, originally started by Sadie's mother and father. Coen had grown up in a neighboring town and when they'd married, they saved until they could buy the business from her parents just as she hoped her boys would do from them. But as an adult their oldest, Hammie, wanted no part of it. Dutch worked for several years at Smithfield Packing Plant making good money. After his father's death, Dutch had a change of heart and decided to come home and brought with him a wife and baby.

A small town grocery is a good business to support one family but not two. Sadie delighted in the fact that she could transition the business without any regrets, although there were financial hurdles to work through. She needed to sell the business in order to retire. Dutch and Ada Lynn took out a loan to purchase the store and Sadie moved out of her house to let them live rent-free until they could afford to build something more to their liking. She rented one side of a duplex a few blocks away and turned over the keys to the grocery.

She started to read again, volunteered to deliver Meals on Wheels, thought about what she could do to help her community grow, and ran for mayor. She lost. Her defeat came as a bit of a blow, especially since she'd grown up in Cedar Branch and she considered the man who won an outsider, even though he'd lived there eighteen years. The inscription on one tombstone in the town cemetery said it all—*although not a native, he'd spent his last sixty-four years in our town.* Even the Quakers drew a line in the sand. You were either a birthright Quaker or a convinced Quaker, but you couldn't claim both sides of the same coin.

Sadie accepted her political defeat as a minor set back. She figured the town wasn't yet ready to have a woman at the helm, even though she felt she would be more open to public input than the colonel. Nonetheless, she refocused her energy and geared up for a batch of 1996 New Year's Resolutions. She'd lose that extra thirty pounds that clung to her like honey on biscuits and maybe do something different with her hair. She'd kept it short all these years so she could be at the store by six-thirty in the morning without a lot of primping, but now that she had the time, maybe she'd let it grow, color the gray, and practice using a curling iron.

Recently Dutch had told her that he and Ada Lynn were expecting another baby in July. Sadie wanted to help them out more. Unlike some women, her daughter-in-law didn't glow during the first three months, but paled at the smell of eggs and fish.

"Gotta pee," Gabe said, suddenly grabbing at his crotch and jumping from one foot to the other. There were only two restrooms in the café: one for the staff off the kitchen and the other for customers through the private dining room in the back. Sadie looked first towards the kitchen. She knew that Teensy would be in overdrive slicing, carving, chopping, flouring and frying to get ready for the dinner crowd. The kitchen was small. Teensy was big. Nobody invaded Teensy's space when she had a knife in her hands and hot grease on the stove. Sadie picked up Gabe and headed down the hallway. When kids gotta pee, they gotta pee.

"Sorry," she said as both men looked up. She pushed through the door. Sadie scurried in front of them urging Gabe ahead, stepped inside the bathroom and twisted the lock.

As she lifted Gabe onto the oversized seat, his eyes grew big and round. He stared up at his grandmother. Desperately, he grasped either side of the toilet seat with both hands and begged, "Hold it down."

They'd been through this before. As often as Sadie had tried to teach the child to take hold of his little johnson and point it down at the water, he wouldn't touch it. For Pete's Sake, what boy wouldn't hold it down? She knew he feared losing his balance. Sadie took her index finger and pushed the tiny penis towards the inside of the toilet bowl. Gabe let loose and a rush of urine drained out of him.

"I gotta poop, too," he said.

Her chin dropped. This additional little detail required time and patience. Gabe liked for someone to read to him while nature commenced, and if you encouraged him off the pot too soon, he'd have an accident in his pants. Sadie had seen the shameful tears that ran down his cheeks if his daddy found out. She wouldn't let him be embarrassed. She sighed. "Can you wait?"

His curls bounced with the back and forth motion of his head.

"Okay, hon," she said and slowly knelt down on her knees. The ceramic tiles felt cold and hard and she knew she'd have to struggle to get back up. Her joints weren't as supple as they used to be. Years of helping move boxes of goods around the store left her on a daily dose of ibuprofen.

"Put your hands on my shoulders, darling," she said. "You're not going to fall in, I've got you."

She'd been unaware that someone else had entered the private room next to them until now. The silent waiting between her and Gabe alerted her to the muddled conversation on the other side of the wall. In an effort to help the boy focus without the aid of reading material, she whispered in a playful voice, "Look at Mama Sadie's blouse and pick out all the little puppies." She wore a particular blouse he loved with patterns of dogs. He'd point to each one and say the name of her dog Smokey over and over again, even though none of them looked at all like her little mutt. Smokey, Smokey, Smokey.

As Gabe poked at her, Sadie caught bits of the conversation in the next room. "I can't sign this offer to sell that land without my client's authorization. I'll have to get back to you."

Sadie didn't quite recognize whose voice it was but the words sell and land got her attention. Selling land amounted to treason in small towns and selling to an "outsider" sent shock waves through the community. If overpriced, the tax base went up. If racially mixed, housing prices could plummet.

"Well, you're welcome to take as much time as you like, but…" one of the men began.

"It's a lot of money to put on hold," the second interrupted. "You need to know we're scheduled to meet with a dozen people tonight. We've given your client first option since all the land is together, but if we can get a combination of a few others to agree and they're willing to sign first, they'll get the gold ring."

"Done," Gabe announced with pride. Sadie wiped him, flushed and then steadied herself on the ceramic wash bowl. As she struggled to her feet the pain shot through her right knee. She lifted the child to wash his hands.

"Excuse me," Sadie said after she'd pulled a paper towel out of the dispenser and opened the door. She brushed by the three men. They looked startled. The room went quiet. The third one looked familiar, but she wasn't quite sure—a lawyer from Roanoke Rapids maybe. She didn't pay much attention to the ones who lived outside the county. He didn't shop at her store.

Gabe took tiny unstable steps. He stumbled. She lifted him to his feet, perhaps too abruptly and then pulled him by his hand as the men's eyes followed her. Sadie felt her cheeks burning.

Her four meals waited in Styrofoam boxes inside a plastic bag on the counter next to the register. Sadie grabbed it and nodded to Miss Ellie. The cost would be added to her tab. Five other people had come into the cafe but Sadie hardly noticed. She wasn't sure why, but whatever had just happened felt threatening. She wanted to get Gabe out of there.

"Sadie." She heard Cliff Lyons call her name. "Aren't you going to have dinner?"

"Back in a minute, Cliff." She acknowledged him and wasn't sure why she said she'd be back. Force of habit. They ate together frequently.

Sadie walked the few steps between the two businesses and set Gabe behind a make-shift play area that Dutch had built for him next to the front window. She handed him a toy fire engine and entertained him for several minutes while Ada Lynn finished up with three customers at her register. Two cleared their accounts with Social Security checks. Ada Lynn peeled out hundred dollar bills in change.

Running a "tab" was part of commerce everywhere in Cedar Branch: the café, the pharmacy, the gas station, the hardware store, the barber shop, the Stitch and Sew Boutique and the one little antique shop. If you didn't have an account, you couldn't even cash a check at the bank, which meant Dutch and Ada Lynn kept large amounts of money in a safe in the back for folks who came in to settle up. The only places that wouldn't run tabs were the Post Office and the bank. Seemed once government got involved, it took the friendly out of doing business.

"Something's going on next door," Sadie said after the three customers left.

Dutch stepped away from the bread rack where he had repositioned all of the loaves that had been pulled and pinched. Immune to cold weather, he wore a tee shirt that revealed the muscles he'd earned at the packing plant. His red hair showcased the same curls as Gabe's...like Coen's. He marked down four bags of hot dog buns and then turned to acknowledge his mother. "Oh yeah?" he said.

"Two men from Raleigh over there offering to buy land, I think."

Dutch seemed unconcerned. He never got as caught up in the heated debates over who bought what. His generation didn't perceive the same threat as their parents. "Someone's getting a nice Christmas present," he said and turned his attention back to the hamburger buns.

"They didn't look like Santa Claus," Sadie said.

"If it's enough money they can look like Godzilla. Who cares?"

"Don't you want to know who's selling what and why?" Sadie asked.

"Doesn't concern us, Mama," he spoke over his shoulder. "We can't control every piece of land in town, not unless you got a secret stash you've been squirreling away for a rainy day. It don't look like rain to me." He winked at her.

Sadie didn't take lightly to his attempt to dismiss her concern. "You didn't see those men. They're up to no good, I swear. I'm going back over to find out what's going on." She put the take-out meals from next door on the empty counter and removed the one meant for her.

"Mama." Dutch stopped what he was doing, more serious now. "Don't go stepping in it."

"I'm just gonna sit down and have a bite to eat with Cliff. That's all."

Dutch eyed the Styrofoam boxes. "Thought you planned to take these to the house and eat with Gabe?"

Sadie winced. That was exactly what she'd planned to do. "I won't be but a few minutes. I told Cliff I'd drop back by."

"Un-huh," Dutch said. "Don't say I didn't warn you. You'll end up with stink on your shoes if you're not careful."

*****

The tables had started to fill up. Leaning on an oak walking stick, Cliff rose when he saw Sadie open the door. He pulled out the chair between him and Billie McFarland, the aging femme fatale in town. Known for her pink wardrobe, Billie never failed to brighten up a room, plus she always knew more about what was going on than Sadie did. Her knowledge made her a valuable ally.

Billie and her husband had retired to Cedar Branch from New York City fifteen years ago. Fortified by a generous trust fund, her husband painted unencumbered by societal expectation and took off frequently for shows and workshops around the country. Billie took his absence in stride and came and went as she pleased. No one thought the two of them would last more than a year in Cedar Branch, but Billie surprised everyone. She quickly became a tremendous asset as a ready volunteer for all kinds of community events and an unexpected expert at raising money. The woman could talk quarters out of a Coke machine.

"You've done something to your hair," Cliff said after Sadie sat down.

"Trying to hide some of the gray," she said, pleased he'd noticed.

"I like it," Cliff said. "You look ten years younger."

"Tsk, tsk. A woman should never tell." Billie shook her head.

Sadie smiled. It was no secret that Billie's own hair color transitioned through an array of shades from radiant auburn to rusty red on a regular basis.

"Ed Garner came in and went to the back room," Billie said and nodded in the direction of the door. "Everyone noticed, of course."

"Maybe he's using the bathroom," Cliff volunteered the obvious.

"No, I don't think so," Billie said.

Sadie knew as well as Billie that black men walked into the Quaker Café for take-out orders, but none asked to use the bathroom. The black community generally felt more at home dealing with establishments owned by black proprietors. They were around, but not easily accessible—someone's kitchen in the rear of their house, or an outback shack converted into a barbeque and fried chicken hut. Some of the best eating in the county wasn't on Main Street.

"I was back there with Gabe just a bit ago," Sadie said. "I overheard two men from Raleigh talking to someone about selling some land."

Billie pursed her lips. "Well, that's not a death knell. We bought some land."

"No," Sadie corrected. "You bought a house on a half acre. I got the feeling these men are looking at a lot of land."

Miss Ellie arrived at the table with chopped steak and fries for Cliff and a chicken-salad sandwich for Billie. "You decided to eat here?" Miss Ellie looked at Sadie's Styrofoam box. "Want anything else?"

"Just some sweet tea. Decided to come back and have dinner with Cliff and Billie."

Cliff patted Sadie's hand and winked at Miss Ellie. "My two favorite girls," he said.

Ed Garner reappeared before they'd finished their meals. Two of his neighbors walked into the restaurant with their heads bowed and edged past him. Ed shook his head and whispered, "Don't."

"Ed." Billie waved at him. "Come over here and tell us what's going on."

Ed was a big man just shy of eighty with stubble of gray beard and a pair of ears that stood out prominently. In recent years whenever he stepped out, he wore a white Fedora over his clean-shaven head. He owned a few acres just outside the town limits where he and his wife had raised a dozen kids, all of them grown and gone to Durham or Charlotte. Most of the year he drove heavy equipment for the highway department, but when the weather turned cold Ed used to butcher hogs. But Smithfield had pretty much taken over the slaughter houses. The South grew up on pork in one form or another and Carolina now competed with Iowa as the biggest hog producer in the country. Pigs and peanuts were the county's claim to fame.

Ed looked across the room at Billie. He seemed uncertain and he hesitated before accepting the offer. The whole town had learned quickly that Billie ignored the boundaries of racial etiquette. *There were just some things that weren't done,* she'd been told.

"Poppycock," Billie would say and go along her merry way doing whatever she liked. She volunteered in the black community at the senior center and delivered Meals on Wheels. She tutored at the public school where ninety percent of the children were black and she got acquainted with their parents. She knew the folks living on Skinner Row and Half Mile Lane better than a lot of the whites who'd lived in Cedar Branch a lifetime. Ed Garner liked her.

"You want a cup of coffee, Ed?" Billie asked.

"Well, if that wasn't the darndest thing," he said, giving a slight nod to the back room.

"What? Tell us Ed. What are they up to?" Sadie pressed. She pushed out the fourth chair at the table with her foot and he slumped into it.

"Those guys are from InCinoSafe. They want to buy our land for that hazardous waste incinerator the governor's been trying to shove down everybody's throat."

"You're kidding?" Sadie sat up straight. That was the last thing she'd thought of. Their county had been ruled out months ago as town after town had fought the siting in their community. "I thought the governor had given up."

"Guess not. They made a tempting offer. Someone's going to take it."

Helen Truitt had been sitting two tables over with the three friends everyone called the God Squad. She rose and walked over next to Ed. "Why Mr. Garner," she said. "How nice to have you join us this evening. We so rarely see you and your people here for dinner."

"What are they offering?" Cliff asked. He ignored Helen.

"They offered me about five times what my land would go for, plus an upfront bonus if I signed tonight. It'd make a nice retirement package."

"You won't do it, will you?" Billie caught her breath. "I didn't move to Cedar Branch to live next to a hazardous waste dump."

"It's not a dump," Helen said. No one paid her any attention.

"Nah," Ed said. "I'm not taking it, and they'd have to put together about six of us with land on that side of town to make it work. But, I'm telling you, there are people who'll jump at the offer."

Sadie bristled. "Christmas is two days away. What the heck? Why are they coming in now?"

"To take us by surprise," Cliff scowled. "They know exactly what they're doing."

"Is it really all that bad?" Helen asked.

"Bad? You're a county commissioner. You should know. Haven't you been following the protests around the state? It's terrible," Sadie said. She looked at Helen in disbelief.

"It's not up to the county commissioners," Helen stammered. "The invitation came from the town board. It's their decision."

"The town board?" Sadie gasped. "In God's name, when did the town board make such an offer?"

Cliff didn't wait for a response. "You're telling us the county has no jurisdiction over them? They don't have restrictions on hazardous waste dumps?"

"That's my understanding," Helen said, her foot now on a higher moral ground. "It's a private company making an offer to private land owners. It's in the hands of the town board."

Sadie felt her blood pressure rising. This whole palaver had begun well over a year ago when Governor Martin Dunnet had involved North Carolina in a pact with Tennessee, Alabama, Kentucky and South Carolina to share responsibility for the disposal of different levels of waste. Dunnet had promised that North Carolina would build a hazardous waste incinerator as their part of the deal. In response citizens had gone ballistic at every proposed site. Following multiple failures, it was rumored his efforts were dead. Now this.

"Well, the town board will have to just uninvite them," Sadie said defiantly. "We're all reasonable people. As soon as they understand that nobody wants this thing, they'll change their minds."

Chapter Two

Max Little sat in front of the television at his son's home in Great Falls, Virginia, with a pastrami sandwich, chips and a Bud on the TV table. A nine foot white flocked Christmas tree with blue frosted lights stood in the corner even though the presents underneath had been opened two days earlier. Kick-off time for the Buffalo Bills and Miami Dolphins would be in the next ten minutes, and he looked forward to a good football game uninterrupted by outside calls. His wife Millie had been right when she suggested that they extend their stay for a week during the holidays. There was no point returning to Cedar Branch right after Christmas and diving into work again.

Little's oldest son Keith had done well—a VP at a financial investment firm in DC. Little ran his hand across the leather upholstery, leaned back in the recliner and pulled up the leg rest. He glanced around the room with pride. His son had spared no expense in furnishing this beautiful home on a cul-de-sac off of Highway 7. The three story house had mahogany flooring throughout and showcased a family kitchen and den that alone surpassed the total square footage of his and Millie's home in Cedar Branch. But what he especially loved was the private office entrance on the first floor, and the large playroom on the third, that allowed space between the children and adults. Millie implied perhaps there was too much space.

The smell of chocolate chip cookies baking in the kitchen wafted through the den and he expected to soon have his two granddaughters on his lap feeding him hot morsels from their afternoon cooking project.

"Dad." Keith stood in the doorway, his hand over the speaker of a portable hand phone. "It's Miss Mary Law," he whispered. "Should I tell her you're not here? She sounds upset."

Little groaned and put out his hand to take the phone. He'd love to ignore the call, but Mary was on his town board and he'd known all along that she'd have trouble handling the pressure if anyone decided to make a fuss. The only one he expected might be a problem was that Quaker farmer, Phil Harper. Governor Dunnet had predicted that a group of environmentalists might descend on the town, the ones from up in the mountains calling themselves the Appalachian Farmers Land Protection Association. Little had never heard of such a group and doubted they would even find Cedar Branch, much less make the effort to cross the state. It was a long way from the mountains to Eastern North Carolina—a good eight hour drive. "Not to worry," he'd assured the governor. "I've got my finger on the pulse of the community."

"Colonel," Mary said when he answered. She always called him colonel. "I really hate to bother you but I've been getting phone calls ever since the newspaper broke the story about InCinoSafe. People are upset—some even angry. I can't walk out my front door without someone stopping me to tell me what a mistake we've made. One person accused us of taking bribes."

His face reddened. People should be ashamed of themselves. A nice old lady like Mary, the Methodist Church organist. Everything she'd ever done was to benefit someone else.

He let the leg rest snap down as he sat up straight. "Who's saying those things?" His voice had an edge. "I'll call the police chief. He'll go by and talk to them."

"No, no. Don't do that. I just want the calls to stop. I thought people would appreciate the fact that we'd recruited a new industry to town. They're supposed to be happy."

"Of course they are. No one expects criticism when they're working hard to do what's best for everyone." The last thing he needed at this point was for his board members to start second guessing their decision. He had promised the governor that they would stand firm.

Mary's voice sounded muffled and he feared that she might be crying. He couldn't be sure if people had figured out yet who was selling the land. If they had, the pressure would intensify.

"When are you coming back?" Mary asked.

"I'll be back midweek. We're going to answer everyone's questions in a timely and organized fashion." He breathed in deeply through his nose, letting the air fill his lungs before he continued. "We've got a town board meeting

January tenth. The governor's sending someone from Raleigh to provide factual information and correct any misconceptions people may have." He waited a minute to try to tell if she sounded better, but she said nothing. "They're confused is all, Mary. They're being told lies. We'll get everyone up to snuff and they'll be thanking you, I promise."

"And until then?"

"Why don't you go visit your daughter? Where is she? Edenton? Ask her to drive over and pick you up."

There was a moment of silence before Mary said, "You're right. I think I'll do that."

*****

When he retired from Ft. Hamilton, NY, Colonel Max Little and his wife looked for a quiet little town with three components: they needed to be able to live on his pension; the winters had to be shorter and warmer; traffic jams should be things of their past. Millie added a wish. If possible, she wanted to live near water. He often told people that they attached their snow plow to their SUV and drove south until someone asked them what that thing was on the front of their car.

They found a house twenty-five miles east of Interstate 95 beside the Potecasi Swamp in Eastern North Carolina. "Water," Max had said. Millie smiled. Not exactly what she had in mind, but the town was lovely and people welcomed them.

Later Max and Millie realized that Cedar Branch had a strong Quaker history and a number of Quaker residents. Although he disagreed vehemently with the idea of conscientious objection, he tactfully engaged in small-talk on the rare occasions they socialized together. If nothing else, he learned Southerners were polite and the Quakers seemed a quiet group not likely to be confrontational.

Max Little began his retirement by doing some substitute teaching. Principals liked the way he ran a classroom—with emphasis on discipline and respect. In deference to the challenges of his military career, which he described in detail at the beginning of every new school year, the students called him

Colonel Little. Inevitably, he became just "Colonel" and he let the nickname stick. It had never helped that he was barely five foot four inches and his last name matched his physical appearance. He had endured the teasing of kids his age until he joined the army right out of high school and did two tours in Vietnam. He worked and fought hard to prove that stature had little to do with his manhood or courage, and after a tour of duty in Korea he received silver eagles on his shoulders. That proved to be the end of any smart remarks. The only ones who didn't adhere to his title were the Quakers. True to their beliefs that titles should never elevate one person over another, they continued to address him using his first name, Max.

Since 1986, Cedar Branch had elected Colonel Max Little to be their mayor in four consecutive two year elections. His only opposition was in 1994 when the retired owner of the local grocery, Sadie Baker— a likeable woman, but alas a woman, got an itch to challenge him. She was unsuccessful. He admired the wisdom of the electorate.

"Millie," the colonel called past his son, "bring me that new cell phone you got for Christmas." He needed to touch base with the other town board members just to reassure them if they had been receiving calls similar to Mary's.

"You can just use that," Keith said indicating the phone his dad held in his hand. "Just dial out."

"No." the colonel didn't expect his son to cover his business expenses. "Might as well try out that one you gave your mother."

"I'll get you a phone, too," Keith offered. "You said you didn't want one."

"I don't." The mere idea of lugging around such an appendage on his hip seemed a contradiction to manhood. Who in his right mind would saddle himself to a telephone? He got up and headed to the office Keith had off the den. To indicate his intentions, he nodded in that direction.

"Sure, of course. It's yours for however long you need it."

"Won't take me long. I'll be out in time for the kick-off."

Chapter Three

At six o'clock on the evening of January 10, 1996, Andy Meacham, the police chief in Cedar Branch, stood at the door of the town hall. An announcement posted at the entrance read *Meeting reserved for citizens of Cedar Branch. Sign with your name and address. All others are asked to remain outside.* Objections came fast and loud. The town clerk's lips locked as tightly as a child refusing to eat spinach. Chief Meacham tactfully moved people aside and explained there were rules.

Cliff poured on his charm. "My lovely lady, I have a guest who knows a lot about hazardous waste," he said turning to acknowledge a smartly dressed woman in a navy blue pants suit. "Mrs. Elmore has driven all the way over from Lee County to address the board. She's here with data that proves we do not want a hazardous waste incinerator in Cedar Branch. Surely you'll give her the courtesy of a seat."

"I'm just following the mayor's orders," the town clerk said. Evidently the lovely lady comment didn't impress her. "There will be a public meeting in two weeks. Guests will be allowed to speak at that. Step aside, please."

Cliff leaned on his cane and pivoted towards Chief Meacham the best he could. He'd lost the agility he once had but he and Meacham shared similar backgrounds. Cliff had been a police chief in a much larger and more dangerous place called Atlantic City. At one time in his life he roamed the back alleys to collar criminals and ultimately took a slug in his hip that sidelined him. After his wife's death he returned to Cedar Branch with high hopes of rekindling the memories of a sleepy little town void of vice and corruption. "Andy," he said, "you can't deny access to a public meeting."

"Fire codes, Mr. Lyons."

"Well then hold the damn meeting some place that will seat more people," Cliff snorted.

"Yes sir. They will next time. They had no idea this many people would be here tonight."

"Like hell, they didn't. Haven't any of them been answering their phones?"

Standing in line with Billie, Sadie stepped forward. "I'll sign in and Mrs. Elmore can take my seat instead," she said although in reality she wanted to be front and center to confront the colonel herself. She'd never trusted him, being from New York. Now, here he was making deals with some waste industry from Baltimore. He'd turn their town into a dump.

"Not allowed," the town clerk said. Her left eye started to twitch and Sadie thought at first she might be sending her a secret code, sort of like special sign language, but that was not the case.

"You got something in your eye?" Cliff was back in her face. "A LOG maybe?"

"Mr. Lyons, please." Andy was by his side. A homespun boy younger than many of the citizens surrounding him, Andy lived by the golden rule and tried his best to enforce the law in the same vein. For the most part, it worked. "This is not an unreasonable rule, sir. The room will only accommodate so many. The mayor is giving priority to those living within the town limits."

"You think water contamination and air pollution stop at the town limits?" Cliff snarled. He turned to see a reporter a short distance back. He tugged at Beth Elmore's arm and waved his cane to clear a path in that direction. Andy radioed the sheriff's office and asked for reinforcements.

By six-fifteen more than two hundred disgruntled people skulked outside. A local reporter fresh out of East Carolina with a degree in journalism listened intently and took copious notes. He was on the fast track learning about hazardous waste and why county after county had rejected it, despite Governor Dunnet's attempts to build the facility in North Carolina. Opponents proclaimed that it exposed citizens to contaminated air, soil and water.

"I want you to meet Beth Elmore." Cliff shoved the petite Sunday-school-looking lady in front of the reporter. "She knows more about hazardous waste incineration than all the buffoons on that board put together. Listen to her for a minute."

Inside, folding chairs faced an oak table with seating for six—five for the board members and one for the mayor. The box-like room had been carved out of the corner of an old warehouse with a smaller room for a town clerk. Maintenance equipment and two vehicles were stored opposite the rear wall. Sparse in design and void of any decorations, the accommodations mirrored a small town's limited budget.

At seven-fifteen the door to the town clerk's office opened and the mayor and town board members filed in. A stunning blond accompanied them and sat down next to the town clerk at a small table to the right of them. Heads turned. Eyebrows shot up. People mouthed, "Who's that?"

Sadie rose to her feet with what she considered to be a reasonable request. "It seems to me as there are so many people who want to hear what you have to say, the board should move this meeting to the school auditorium."

"Request denied," the colonel said without even a glance.

His curt response startled several in the room. This did not appear to be the beginning of an informal discussion among friends. The colonel sat down and called the meeting to order with a snap in his voice. He immediately took up the first item on the agenda—approval of the past minutes.

"Please read the minutes from the previous meeting out loud, so that we all might hear," Phil Harper interrupted.

The colonel had anticipated this meeting might become testy and decided ahead of time to run it on a tight agenda without public debate. He'd considered that Phil Harper might be a problem. He lived by a moral compass that always pointed due righteous. The colonel leveled his gaze like a gun dog. "You're out of order, Mr. Harper. Our minutes are distributed to board members prior to each meeting in order to save time. If you'd like a copy you may request one from our clerk."

"I did first thing this morning," Phil said. "I was told to pick them up in five days. Why does it take five days if they've already been published to members?"

The colonel banged his gavel. "If you check, you will find that we've always required a week to respond to requests. As you know, our town clerk only works part-time. She can't jump up and down to attend to every request that walks through the door."

Phil sat back down in his seat, crossed his arms over his barrel chest and waited while the board members slogged through a routine list of maintenance needs and budget items. In general, the responsibility of these elected officials was a thankless job that required someone to ensure that taxes were collected, trash got picked up, the sewer and water operated without fault, and local ordinances were enforced. To do this the town employed a part-time clerk, two maintenance people and a policeman who all reported directly to them.

People began to become restless as mundane reports dragged on. Abruptly, Phil stood. “It's obvious that everyone is here to find out what the deal is with ICS. It appears to me that you might give us the common courtesy of addressing our concerns.”

The colonel banged his gavel. “Chief Meacham, please remove anyone who speaks out of order again.”

Chief Meacham looked startled. This was highly unusual and he could see that the citizens were becoming annoyed. Billie waved her hand in the air. The colonel briefly looked in her direction and then ignored her. Sadie got up from her chair and moved to the back of the room to stand along the wall. Three people left. Three more replaced them, including the local reporter.

Finally, the colonel announced, “Since I've lived in this town, the one thing I've heard people complain about over and over again is the lack of opportunity for their children. Young people are leaving in droves for the cities. People have asked that the town board seek out business and industry in hopes of keeping our youth closer to home. With that concern as our focus, I am proud to report that an agreement has been reached for a new industry to build here. InCinoSafe plans to operate a facility that will create as many as three hundred new jobs starting at eight dollars an hour. This is the beginning of a turn around in our unemployment problems...good-paying jobs and steady incomes. Citizens should be thrilled.”

“Who's selling the land?” Sadie called from the back of the room.

“Not really any of your business, Miss Sadie.” The syrup dripped off of the colonel's tongue as he spoke. “It's a private sale between a company and a landowner. It is not the board's prerogative to discuss details of the location. It is up to the company to make the announcement when all contracts are finalized.”

“So you're saying nothing has been finalized?” Phil asked.

"No," the colonel said sharply. "A lot has been finalized. But the company must meet certain state requirements before they can begin construction."

"Such as?" Phil persisted.

"Such as..." the colonel raised his voice, "will be revealed at an information meeting scheduled in two weeks."

"When was the agreement reached to invite a hazardous waste company into our town?" Phil remained standing. One of his eyebrows arched upward underneath a full head of jet black hair. His voice remained respectful, but nonetheless, his body language implied he did not intend to sit down quickly. "Was it done in an open meeting and if so, was there any research as to the potential harmful effects it might have on the surrounding land and residents?"

"Colonel." Sadie waved her hand in the air along with several other people. "I am reading reports that eighteen other counties have fought to keep ICS from building near their homes. Will you explain why we should want it here? I have grandchildren who live in this town. I don't want them breathing in toxic fumes."

"Everyone sit," the colonel demanded. He had no intentions of letting this meeting get out of order. He lowered his chin and raised his eyes as if he were speaking to a classroom of children. "I am aware that there are environmental extremists who have their own agenda. I will not allow lies to become part of the discussion. The board has studied the risks and reached a conclusion that is beneficial for everyone."

"What if the majority of the citizens in this town don't want an incinerator built here?" Phil Harper squared his shoulders. "What if we have information that contradicts yours and indicates that this incinerator may destroy our farmland or threaten the health of our children?" Phil locked eyes with any board member who cared to look in his direction. None did.

"Mr. Harper, sit down or I'll ask that you be removed." The colonel ignored Phil's question and addressed the board members directly. "We have been elected to make decisions for the welfare of this town. It is important to move ahead and not be swayed by a few outspoken protesters."

He continued, "Before this meeting gets completely sidetracked, I'd like to take this opportunity to introduce everyone to Miss Caren Drake. Did I pronounce that correctly, Miss Drake?"

"It's Car-n. Like the automobile with the sound of "n" afterwards. Car-n." She smiled.

The colonel nodded in approval and noted the room had quieted down. This pleased him. "Miss Drake is here to help us through the permitting process as ICS prepares to meet the state requirements to build. She will make herself available to answer many of the questions that you have this evening. Therefore, we won't spend more time on them tonight."

Up until this moment Miss Drake had followed the proceedings as if she were being read the Ten Commandments.

Annoyed by how the colonel had just sidestepped any discussion, Sadie shouted, "Who's paying her salary?"

The colonel closed his eyes and muttered as if the question hardly merited a response, "Her salary is covered under a grant. Her services aren't costing the town anything."

"What grant?" Sadie pushed, but got no response.

Phil jumped in. "I have attempted to get copies of the minutes from the meetings in which the town board did preliminary research on the impact of InCinoSafe on our town and the motion to invite them. Perhaps Caren Drake would expand on the extent of your research."

The colonel's voice ripped through the room like a whip. "Mr. Harper, *I have said* we will address these concerns later. Now, if you would allow, I'd like to use what little time we have left to let Miss Drake introduce herself." He nodded in Caren's direction. She rose, looked around at the crowd and then directly at Phil Harper. He sat down.

Caren was poised and professional. She had on an ash grey tailored suit. The jacket opened to reveal a peach blouse with a tiered ruffle neckline that dipped low enough to create interest. She brushed a strand of hair away from her eyes and tucked it behind her ear. In her three-inch peek-toe patent leather pumps she stood just shy of six feet. Sadie groaned.

Caren faced the crowded room. She'd been forewarned to expect opposition and had been painstakingly coached. "Mr. Harper and all of you here, I understand your concerns. Of course, I'd be concerned too if an organization had received bad press similar to that fabricated against InCinoSafe by environmental extremists. Why if we followed every rule they want to impose, none of the ladies here would be wearing lipstick because of mercury contents or feeding your children peanut butter because of the aflatoxin content. Now really! We all aren't that naïve about what could harm us, are we?"

She paused, raised her palms together at the tip of her chin prayerfully and held the poise. She wore no rings. The room went still. "We are all intelligent individuals who want what is best for our community," she said. "That is why I am here. I have been hired to be your advocate. I promise to make myself available to answer questions, to calm your fears and to investigate any concerns you may have. I want the same long-term benefits for Cedar Branch as you do. I want to provide a healthy environment for future generations and help create good-paying jobs. I am here for you."

"What training do you have in hazardous waste?" Phil blurted out.

The colonel banged his gavel. "Do I have a motion to go into executive session?"

"I so move," said Mary Law, who immediately made an effort to rise and extract herself from the increasing hostility. She stumbled. Two board members jumped to her aid.

The colonel spoke gently to her, "Mary, the others are going to leave. Stay seated and we'll continue as soon as we clear the room."

"Would everyone please leave?" the colonel asked. "I have a second and we have voted to go into executive session."

Several people got up, but others barked out their disapproval. Chief Meacham politely directed the crowd to the door. Most people were compliant, but a lone voice from the middle of the room asked, "For what purpose?"

Few people even heard him. "For what purpose?" came the voice, louder this time. Those remaining stopped and turned to see Phil Harper staying firmly in place.

"Mr. Harper, we have town business to discuss in private."

"I believe you are out of order," Phil crossed his arms and leaned back. "Town business must be discussed in public."

"Chief," the colonel said. "Please escort Mr. Harper from the room."

"Phil." Chief Meacham stretched out both arms, palms up in an unspoken plea. The two men knew each other as friends. "I need to ask you to leave the room, please."

Phil didn't move.

"Mr. Harper, don't make me do this. Let's go outside and talk this over."

"You got the wrong man, Andy," Phil said, not relinquishing his glare on the colonel. "I'm not the one breaking the law."

Nodding for the county deputies to help him, Andy asked one more time. "If you don't leave, I'm going to have to arrest you. I don't want to do that."

Phil didn't move. He didn't argue. He didn't get up. He simply refused to cooperate. Billie and Sadie had been sitting behind him. When Phil began challenging the colonel, both Billie and Sadie applauded. Sadie knew Colonel Little would try to dismiss her, but Phil Harper wouldn't be as easy.

Although he was at least twenty years older than Dutch, in many ways Phil reminded Sadie of her own son. They were both Paul Bunyan types who worked the kind of jobs that built muscles and strained backs. Their size alone could be intimidating, and yet she'd rarely seen either of them lose their tempers. Sadie tugged at Billie to get her to stay and they backed against the wall. Phil would need witnesses.

Andy motioned to three of the county deputies. They approached. Phil resisted in the only way a Quaker could. He became dead weight. They'd have to carry him out. Two deputies took Phil's arms and Andy and the third officer took his feet as they dragged him through the room. Folding chairs collapsed and were kicked aside. Those who hadn't yet left gawked in disbelief. Mary Law searched frantically through her pocketbook and pulled out a pillbox.

A couple hundred people were alerted that there was a stand-off going on inside.

The deputies lugged Phil down the steps and handcuffed him.

"Hey, you can't do that." Cliff Lyons moved towards them, his cane swinging wide like an unhinged screen door.

"Stay back, Mr. Lyons," Chief Meacham warned. "If you have anything to say, you can speak to a judge."

Opening the rear door of the cruiser, they heaved Phil into the back of the police car with the same effort as a vet might use to load a large sedated animal onto a short flatbed.

The reporter scrambled from one side of the patrol car to the other clicking his camera in hopes of getting some statewide coverage.

"I'm calling the magistrate," Cliff shouted. "I'll meet you at the county jail."

"We'll bring bail money, Phil." Billie shouted. "Come on." She tugged at Sadie. "I need to stop by the house and get cash." She grabbed Sadie's hand and tried to pull her towards her Land Rover.

Sadie couldn't move. She stood among the others and watched as the flashing red lights pulled away. An adrenalin rush seized her—triggered more by anger than fear. Who did the colonel think they were—a bunch of yahoos? She had no intentions of stepping aside and letting this monstrosity be built. For Pete's sake, her children and grandchildren lived in town. How would it affect their lives twenty years down the road? She could feel a fight building... like a log splitter cutting through the heart of Cedar Branch dividing the town in two.

Chapter Four

By ten o'clock the next morning the colonel was on his way to Raleigh to meet with the governor. Cliff had called in details of the arrest to a talk-radio show, and Sadie had a thousand newly printed posters in her car and was headed from Westtown back to Cedar Branch. Billie McFarland theatrically rehashed the town board meeting at the Quaker Café to an attentive audience.

"What did *you* hear the colonel say?" Billie asked Sadie as soon as she walked through the door in the same sweatshirt and pair of denim slacks she'd worn the night before.

"When?" Sadie asked, a little self-conscious that her hair hadn't seen a comb in twenty-four hours. She looked around the room grateful not to see Cliff.

"What did the colonel say when he called for an executive session?" Billie raised her hands to quiet the others. "I'm talking here," she called out above the murmurs. "This is important."

"He asked for a motion." Sadie's mind was a bit fuzzy. She'd been up 'til three in the morning, first with Billie over at the sheriff's office, and after Phil was released she'd spent the rest of the night making lists in her head…lists of how to mobilize the town against ICS. What was Billie getting at?

"Did he say for what purpose?"

Sadie shook her head no and dropped a box of eight-by-twelve inch cardboard signs on one of the tables. Each sign had NO emblazoned across them and *Hazardous Waste Incinerator* in smaller letters at the bottom. Miss Ellie moved like a mannequin from one table to the next, her expression frozen.

"Just as I said." Billie applauded. "That's what Phil said, too. An executive session is only legal if it's called for specific reasons and those reasons have to be stated in front of the public. I called a lawyer and he said Phil was right not to leave the room. It's the colonel who's going to have to explain."

Sadie started to hand out the NO signs in batches of twenty. In her mind she'd already moved on to a different project. "Put one of these on everyone's front door. Staple them up and down the telephone poles. I'm going to get some larger ones. We want the colonel to get a clear picture of how many people are opposed to InCinoSafe." She picked up a roll of tape and casually glanced at Miss Ellie. "Can I put one up front here, Miss Ellie?"

Miss Ellie put down the coffee pot and straightened herself. When she did not reply, conversation slowed and then stopped. Sadie hesitated long enough to look back over her shoulder. With coffee cups not yet to their lips and forks in suspended motion, even those with food in their mouth stopped mid-chew.

"No, you may not."

Diners exchanged glances.

"You want a hazardous waste incinerator in our town?" Sadie asked. "A fifty-thousand ton incinerator…the second largest in the country?"

"I didn't say that," Miss Ellie said. "My restaurant has always been a place for everyone to gather. You are my guests. Colonel Little is my guest as are the county commissioners and town board members. The colonel hasn't been here for the last week because someone verbally attacks him every time he walks through the door. If you come into my restaurant, I expect everyone to be polite to one another. Those are my rules."

Sadie lowered the poster. She paused. "Ellie," she said, "you and I have been neighbors for more than thirty years. The more I read about this incinerator the more it scares me. I can't bear the thought of my grandchildren growing up under that cloud of smoke."

"I know that," Miss Ellie said, her tone more gentle. "I'm just asking you to take your disagreements elsewhere."

"What about the back room?" Billie asked. "Could we meet there?"

Miss Ellie hesitated but then nodded without much enthusiasm. "I suppose, as long as you use good taste. Remember your manners. Remember we're all friends here."

"Thank you," Billie said and eyed Sadie. "We'll disappear quietly into the back room."

Those who already had posters slid them between the newspaper folds of their copies of the *News & Observer* and returned to their breakfasts. Miss

Ellie continued to refill coffee cups amid muted conversation. Sadie gathered up her things.

Helen Truitt sat nursing a cup of decaf and nibbled on dry toast at a corner table. She pinched her lips together and raised one finger for a refill. "Thank you, Ellie." she said appreciatively when Miss Ellie came her way. "That's exactly what was needed...a bit of civility. Although, I think letting them use the back room is a bit much." She ran her hands over the few wrinkles in her polyester skirt and tilted her chin upward.

"Well, Helen." Miss Ellie poured hot coffee into her cup. "I let the men from ICS use it several weeks ago. I can't play favorites."

"You have no idea how many people in town are thrilled about the prospects of a new industry coming," Helen said. "Sadie and her friends will calm down once they bother to consider the benefits. Lord knows, Cedar Branch is long overdue some good job opportunities and now we have them. We're lucky."

Helen sipped her coffee and nodded with the air of a duchess to the other patrons in the café. She'd become a fixture at this particular table, sometimes alone, sometimes with her Methodist friends, most often with Mary Law. As a county commissioner, she considered it her obligation to stay in touch with her subjects. The Quaker Café served as her court.

******

"Absolutely not," Dutch said without hesitation when his mother walked into the grocery and showed him the NO posters. "Not here."

Sadie bristled. "I'm not asking for the cash box. Just give me a little credit for knowing what is best for our town. Do you know how many trucks will be coming through every day carrying all of the poisons they're talking about?"

Dutch shook his head. "Mom, the thing is the bank still owns more of this store than I do. I can't afford to take sides. You're the one who taught me that—you and Dad. Don't you remember? We never sponsored one homecoming queen over another. We don't allow posters for political candidates in the windows. If we let the March of Dimes have a slotted dime collector on the counter then we had to also put out the jars for Breast Cancer and the

Veterans. Things got so cluttered there was no room for groceries. You decided to write each charity a personal check but not allow any of them to ask for donations in the business. That was your rule and now it's mine."

"*The thing is!*" Sadie pushed harder. Her son had made a good point, but this was different. "If the town board realizes how many people are against this from the start, there's a chance they'll rescind their motion at the next meeting. We could stop this nonsense before it goes any further. Signs would come down in two weeks."

"I'm not getting involved. If you want to fight this thing, then go ahead. But, please not in here." Dutch took a deep breath. He seemed more intense this morning. Unlike his older brother, he'd never been one to pick a fight but instead used his size and evenhanded approach to encourage peaceful resolutions. Sadie said he had Quaker blood in him from her great-grandfather.

Sadie stared at him in disbelief. "It's your children who will have to grow up with this monster in their backyard. Are you bothering to listen to what people have said in the other counties who have opposed it? The incinerator will spew out tons of toxic gases every year."

"You don't know that. It's an incinerator. It burns the waste up. The hazardous part is destroyed."

"You think so?"

"Until someone proves otherwise, yeah, I believe that."

"I don't believe I'm hearing this." Sadie dropped the box of posters onto the counter with a loud thud. Several shoppers stopped mid-aisle and listened. "Didn't you read the newspaper article on why other counties didn't want it? Lead, mercury, arsenic from all up and down the east coast will be coming out of the stack."

"Look, Mama. I don't want to duke it out with you here in the middle of the store. Everyone has their own agenda. Those folks have their agendas and you've got yours. But I can't be a foot soldier in your army."

Dutch indicated the conversation was over by redirecting his attention to Ada Lynn at the register. "Someone sliced into these." He handed her a plastic bag of Pampers. "They'll need to be repackaged. I'm working produce now."

Ada Lynn set Gabe down in the play area. He coughed. She wiped his nose before pulling out some Ziploc baggies from under the counter. They had trouble with the disposable diapers…people cutting open the package and stealing one or two.

"Sorry," Ada Lynn mouthed to Mama Sadie.

Sadie, somewhat bewildered, let her shoulders sag. What if all the other business owners told her the same thing? "Gabe's pulling at his ear again," she said. It was one of those things she always noticed and repeated like a mantra. "Everyone in and out bringing the latest cold virus with them. Better take him to Dr. Jane again."

"He's okay," Ada Lynn said. They'd had this discussion a dozen times. "I'd have to wait all day. I've got some cough syrup."

"Nonsense, she's new in town. Probably not as booked as you think….not yet, anyway."

Sadie didn't want to nag. When Ada Lynn didn't reply, she picked up her box of posters to leave. If she'd thought, she would have realized Tuesdays weren't good. It had been the wrong time to say something to either Dutch or Ada Lynn. Sales for the week started on Wednesday so Dutch needed to rework the produce, cut off wilted pieces of broccoli and cauliflower; check for bad apples, oranges, bananas to be pulled and marked down. Fresh produce would come in this afternoon.

The weekly orders from Nash-Finch distributors came in on Tuesday and Friday mornings. They'd be restocking the shelves, rotating cans and pulling off anything that had exceeded shelf life. Their contract guaranteed a minimum $10,000 weekly order, which was a challenge for a small town grocery. It was important to have the staples available that people bought on a regular basis. Dutch had perfected the task of sticking the high-ticket items on either side of the sales products where they'd be seen. These so-called *wing products* paid the bills.

Ten to twelve additional trucks would arrive from individual wholesalers between Tuesday and Friday bringing bread, dairy, chips, Hostess Twinkies, candy bars, cigarettes, over-the-counter drugs, beer, and soft drinks. Tuesdays were always hectic.

Sadie pushed her back up against the swinging glass door and marched across the street. Within the hour several NO signs went up in the front window of Hoole's pharmacy. Chase Hoole was a chemist. He understood full well what could happen, and he promised Sadie he was *all in*.

*****

Afternoon staff came in at one to take over and give Ada Lynn time to get everyone's lunch, put Gabe down for his nap, get the vendors' checks written and take care of the accounting.

Billie walked in just before Ada Lynn left. "Want any NO signs?" she asked.

Ada Lynn shook her head. "Don't," she whispered.

Billie noticed Gabe whining to get out of the playpen and picked him up. "Come here, little fellow," she said. "Dear me, still got that cold? She pulled a handkerchief out of her pocket and wiped his nose. Let's give your mama a break for a few minutes." Putting Gabe in the grocery cart, she wheeled it around to check out any mark-down produce. From there she took Gabe to the back of the store where she had her weekly chat with Marvin the butcher, who put in special orders for her. Marvin started work right out of high school with Sadie's mother and father, and honed his skill quickly. He was built to be a meat cutter—short, stocky with broad shoulders and muscular arms. He knew his meats and fish and which distributors delivered the best quality. His friendly demeanor and broad smile earned him the trust of many households and he had developed a following of customers who came to get his recommendations every week. Already in his late sixties, Dutch hoped Marvin would be around for a dozen more years at least.

Billie returned to the counter with some oysters along with a clove of garlic and four lemons. She continued to joggle Gabe in one arm. She pulled an Almond Joy off the candy rack next to the register.

"Have you seen what Phil Harper is doing to his house?" she asked as Ada Lynn rang up the sale.

"What?"

"He's painting an enormous NO on the roof." She stifled a laugh. "It's ghastly, but it does make a statement. He's pretty worked up. He's invited some farmer from the other side of Asheville to help brainstorm on what to do. His town went through the same thing. You should come hear what he has to say."

Ada Lynn reached across the counter and took Gabe from Billie's arms. She gave his nose another wipe. "No, thanks. This really isn't my thing."

*****

Phil put the last stroke of black paint on his metal roof and climbed down the ladder to admire his handiwork. He wasn't an artist, but he was enough of a mathematician to get the size of the lettering exact. As far as he was concerned eight-by-twelve inch posters didn't hack it. The town board members needed to be reminded every minute of the day that citizens would not subject themselves to the threat of this incinerator.

After he surveyed the twenty foot N and O he'd finished painting on the slant of his A frame, he put away his art supplies and felt a pang of regret that his son was at NC State this semester and not home to be in this fight. Understanding how to challenge injustice was an important part of a young person's education.

A 1985 Ford Escort pulled into his drive. A gangly Mark Twain look-a-like with a dark bushy moustache and unruly hair to match got out of the car and took a step back to admire the roof. "Like the statement, my friend," he said.

He was exactly what Phil had expected. "My wife thinks I got carried away." Phil approached him with a wide grin and an outstretched arm.

"Nah, I think it's just about right," he said, introducing himself. "Stu Ricks. Nice to meet ya." He put down a guitar case, shook Phil's hand and looked up for a second view. "The governor can see it from the air in case he flies over."

They exchanged a look of appreciation. "You play this thing?" Phil nodded at the case as he helped to unload two boxes out of the back of his car.

"It comes in handy now and then. Something to entertain folk when they aren't allowed into public meetings." His eyes danced with mischief. "You play?"

"A little." Phil smiled. The man looked like every environmental activist he'd seen on TV. "Thanks for helping us out. I didn't think anyone from the mountains would make such a long trip, but Beth Elmore told us you'd come."

"Those of us who've been on this wild ride before know what you're up against. We don't interfere unless we're invited, but when you called, I knew at once I wanted to help."

Phil picked up the guitar and led the way into the house.

"I'll teach you a few songs and then we can make up some more," Stu added.

Daily newspapers sat on the table, the most recent with a front page picture of Phil being dragged from the town board meeting. Tossed to the side were monthly bills, advertisements from feed stores, ag-extension letters, and shopping lists. Stacked in one chair were a pile of photocopied sheets on hazardous waste.

"Sorry about the mess," Phil said. "My wife's a teacher. She's at work and there's a PTA meeting tonight so you won't meet her until later. She left some soup and cookies."

"Smells good." Stu eyed the information sheets from Greenpeace and his own environmental group. "See you're doing your homework."

"There's a lot." Phil looked at the clutter and stood with his hands on his hips. "You want to eat first or freshen-up?"

The aroma of beef vegetable soup and warm whole wheat bread filled the room.

"Let's eat. This *outsider* is hungry and the house smells like my mother's kitchen," Stu joked.

"They're bringing in their own outsiders," Phil said as he pulled out two bowls and handed Stu a ladle. "Ever heard of Caren Drake?"

"Good Lord," Stu laughed. "What's CAR-n doing here?" He emphasized the first syllable of her name. "She was working out of Senator Ian Lasker's office, last I heard."

"Really? He's not my favorite politician. She know anything about hazardous waste?" Phil asked as he dished up chunks of beef, carrots, and potatoes.

"About as much as she knows about nanotechnology. She's a pretty face. Degree in marketing from Appalachian State as I recall. You got an election coming up?"

"As a matter of fact, all of our board members and the mayor are up for re-election in November."

"Whoa, that's unusual. Not many town boards all go on and off at the same time," Stu said not hiding his surprise. "Lucky for you."

"Sort of a quirk in the town by-laws," Phil said. "But I'll accept anything that you consider luck at this point."

Stu swallowed a spoonful of soup and then nodded as if everything had just fallen into place. "She's here to guide them through the election. They must be worried."

"That's almost a year away." Phil sat down across from Stu. "I was hoping we could toss these folks out long before then."

"Maybe," Stu said.

Lights flashed across the kitchen window as several trucks pulled into the driveway. "Folks coming. They know you're here." Phil got up to open the kitchen door while Stu dipped a crust of the bread into his bowl to sop up the juice.

As a small group gathered, Phil greeted each one with a handshake. Introductions were made. Extra chairs appeared as Henry Bennett and several other peanut farmers arrived. Included in the gathering were Sadie Baker, Billie McFarland, and Clifford Lyons.

Henry got right to the point. "So, tell us how you got them to leave."

"Wish I had a silver bullet," Stu said. "Basically, the last man standing wins. Eventually one of you will give up."

"What's the fastest way to get them out?" Cliff asked.

Stu tilted his chair back on the hind legs, then reversed his posture, leaned forward and apologized. "Sorry, bad habit. Drives my wife crazy. Best bet is to get your town board to change their minds and renege on their invitation. The board has the ability to implement and enforce zoning and environment ordinances that would make it impossible for ICS to build. If that fails," he said, "you might stumble onto something else that nixes the plan…an endangered species, a school or hospital too close to the site, water table's too high. But," he warned them, "it's hard to get sympathy from permit agencies and the media when the community *invites* the industry into their town."

"WE didn't invite them, our town board did," Phil blurted out.

Stu cocked his head to the left in an empathetic squirm. "That's not the way the governor reads it."

"As far as I'm concerned the community had nothing to do with the invitation. This sits squarely in the colonel's lap and it was all done in secret—behind closed doors," Sadie added.

"That might be your ace," Stu said. "Get a judge to overturn the vote because it violated the open meetings laws."

"Our school would be right under it," Billie jumped in. "There are at least two-hundred and fifty kids at that school, plus a day care program."

"Our water table is pretty high, not much clay in the soil," said Henry. He shuffled through a pile of papers he'd brought with him. "I thought the state had already eliminated this site because of potential spills into the aquifers."

"Not to mention our crops." Phil eyed the other farmers. "Seems to me that's enough of an issue right there. One buyer over at the peanut plant reacted immediately when I told him about the possibility. He said if there is some kind of fallout from this incinerator that creates a problem with selling our peanuts, then it would have severe implications for both the growers and their company. Our land would be worthless. Peanuts are the mainstay of this county."

"I'm just wondering," Billie said, "and I want to be very cautious in how I say this, but do you suspect there has been any money exchanged or promises made in return for this invitation from our town board?"

Stu laughed as several other eyebrows arched. "Without a doubt, but not necessarily illegal."

"Such as?" Sadie asked.

"An increase in their local budgets. A new staff person. A bump in pay scale. Some counties have been promised roads, health facilities, contracts to certain businesses. For example, the governor may be asking for budget money to increase the funding for the schools or recruit more doctors into the county."

"Is that bad?" Billie asked.

"Depends on the trade-off. A hazardous waste incinerator is for life. A bump in funding is as good as the end of that annual legislative budget."

"Sounds like bribery to me," Cliff said.

"Or politics," Stu said. "We've learned not to be surprised by anything."

There was a lull and for a moment a plate of chocolate chip cookies and coffee sat untouched.

"You make it sound impossible," Sadie said. "You telling us it can't be done?"

"Shucks no. I'm telling you Rowan, Iredell, Caldwell, and Granville Counties have sent them packing. Those communities all rose up and kicked the SOBs out. The difference between you and them is that their folks all came together in strong opposition against the company and the governor. It appears to me your town is splitting in two."

"Unfortunately, yes," Billie admitted.

"What about the research?" Sadie asked. "Colonel Little says everything we say is lies."

"I've got articles by William Sanjour with the EPA and Paul Connett, a chemist who's done extensive research on hazardous waste. They not only cite failed regulations, they question the technology." Stu got up from the table to retrieve the box he'd carried into the house. He began to distribute pounds of paper: documents, reports and photocopied news clippings.

"The state agencies will try to assure you that no harm can come from hazardous waste incineration." He talked as he passed around various documents. "You need to be prepared to present the other side of the story. At least one of you needs to be able to quote credible research to the contrary."

"Damn," Sadie said. "This is a lot of stuff."

"Probably too much for most people. Break it down for them. A pound of lead is a pound of lead. It doesn't disappear. Emissions that include heavy metals can be washed into the river, or blown into the air, or dropped into an ash pile, but they can't be destroyed. That lead then enters the food chain – your peanuts, for example and the drinking water. So it goes with all the other metals and toxins that are dumped into the incinerator. Remind people that requirements to remove lead from gasoline and paint were done for health reasons."

They exchanged somber glances around the table.

"Do you think we need to hire an environmental lawyer?" Sadie asked.

"Eventually, if ICS gets to the permitting stage. We'll give you names of lawyers who have helped us a lot, but keep in mind the lawyers won't win it for you. They can put up some roadblocks…help stall. But this stuff right here"—Stu tapped the picture of Phil being dragged out of the town board meeting in handcuffs—"this is the most powerful exposure you've got going for yourselves. Photos demonstrate what people are willing to sacrifice to defend the health of their children and their property. The media will eat it up. And that radio talk show this morning…who was that?"

Everyone pointed at Cliff.

"I listened to that on my drive over. That was magic. Cliff, you're a natural. You have a knack for entertaining and informing the public at the same time. Honestly, it's all about theater." He stopped and stretched out his arms and put his hands on the table. Leaning forward with his weight he repeated, *"It's ALL about theater.* Whoever puts on the best show wins."

"What about facts?" Billie asked.

"I repeat: *It's all about who puts on the best show* with one exception."

"What's that?" Billie asked.

Stu stood up straight, took a long swallow of coffee and then when he had everyone's eyes riveted to him he added, "You guys may be in for a long haul. You've got to pace yourselves. Have a little fun. Support one another, and under NO circumstances can you let violence become a part of your strategy. The minute someone gets hurt… you lose."

Chapter Five

The colonel sat across from Caren Drake. His wife Millie poured coffee and placed a bottle of Korbel Brandy next to him and then excused herself. "I've got bridge club tonight," she said. I'll leave you two to talk business."

"Thank you, sweetheart," he said. He watched his wife leave the room. "She may be just a pint of peanuts, but she's my rock." Colonel Little raised the bottle almost as a toast and then turned to Caren. "It's aged in oak barrels."

"I'd love some." Caren shifted her weight in the Queen Anne chair.

"A gift from my son," he said as he poured a finger into each of the two snifters and handed her one. He took a sip with obvious appreciation. "That training session was well done."

"I think everyone will handle things better now," Caren said. She couldn't help but remember she'd offered them that option weeks ago, but the colonel hadn't felt it necessary. It had been Millie who had talked him into reconsidering after the last town board meeting.

"That guy who pelted them with questions was very good. Acted like a real pro," he said.

"He *is* a pro." She made an effort not to sound sarcastic. "He works as a news broadcaster out of Virginia Beach. That's why we hired him."

"We probably should have done that sooner," he said. He seemed to miss the irony.

The governor's chief of staff had told Caren she'd be working with a pretty unsophisticated group, but she'd hoped the colonel would be better at following her advice. Typical of the men she knew, he wanted to run the show, but she had far more experience in public relations. She wanted to say *I told you so*, but she asked a question instead. "Do you think everyone can speak with conviction now? The board members must appear to have earnestly studied the pros and cons and reached a unanimous decision that benefits everyone."

"Mary's our weak link," the colonel said, "but she's heavily invested."

Caren took a sip of her brandy and leaned forward, revealing a bit of cleavage. "I can't stress how important it is for the board members to repeat the same phrases over and over, regardless of what charges are hurled at them. *The technology is safe. The technology is clean. The industry will provide jobs and bring money into this county.* Always talk about safety first and jobs second. Otherwise you get accused of sacrificing people's health for money."

"I think we're all on message," the colonel nodded his head in assurance.

On message she thought. At least he was picking up the lingo. ICS had prepared her for the controversy that might arise. Lord knows, they'd been through the same battle several times before and had the videos to show. But this was different. They'd learned from their mistakes. She'd been brought in to put a new face on the industry. They'd found a town with few environmental restrictions that could be reworded to fit their needs. The governor's office had courted the county commissioners and town board members in advance and invited them to submit a "wish list". They emphasized what a contribution their town would be making to the state economy and promised that the state would reward them in-kind. Caren thought this little god-forsaken crossroads should be on their knees with gratitude.

Now that the story had broken, Caren needed room to spin it. She could only do this effectively if the colonel would give her the reins and let her do the talking. But his ego got in the way. He enjoyed the attention of the governor and other state muckety-mucks.

"We need to encourage our supporters to become vocal," Caren said. "You're so good at that sort of thing." She could charm him, she knew. A bit more cleavage appeared. "The news coverage so far has focused on those people who don't want InCinoSafe in town. The press needs to hear from those who do want their jobs and tax benefits."

"I'll make some calls," the colonel said. He began to rattle off names starting with those who'd been guests in the governor's office. "They need to stand tall and speak up. After all, several of them will benefit." He sipped on the brandy and scratched the ridge of his nose. "Write these down."

"Oh," she hesitated. She wasn't being paid to be his secretary. She needed to clear that up as soon as possible without bruising his ego. "I can't even read my own chicken scratch and I don't know these folks yet. Maybe you could find someone else to work on that list?"

The colonel looked at her momentarily confused and then agreed. "I suppose Helen Truitt would do that. She's dying to be more involved."

"She'd be excellent." Caren jumped on the idea, pleased that it had come out of his mouth first. They needed to give that woman something to do or she'd become a ball and chain. "Perfect. She's a county commissioner—has already met the governor—is a member of the Methodist Church. I'll bet she'd be willing to work with Millie on setting up a women's group. Women have to be visible. They're powerful proponents. Their support shows they see a positive future for their children in the industry."

"And she loves the sound of her own voice," the colonel smirked. "Put her in front of a camera and she'll pontificate until the icebergs melt."

"What about the black community?" Caren asked. "Wouldn't it be wise for us to go ahead and set up a meeting with some of the black ministers and the president of the local NAACP? Surely you've worked with them before."

"Yes, of course I have. I got elected, didn't I?"

Caren knew he hadn't really needed the black vote in this town to get elected. The majority of the black population lived outside the town limits. She took his assurance with a grain of salt. "Good, then I'll talk to the governor's office to see if they'll give us some additional support."

Caren stood and walked to the other side of the room. She wanted more control. "I think we need a few private meetings," she said. "I'd like to do some training and help proponents with a few phrases to use with the media. Again, it's all about sharpening the message."

"Okay," he agreed. "We could do one here at the house, say Thursday evening?"

"That's good," Caren said. "Maybe invite a few people who're sitting on the fence—hopefully convince some others to switch sides?"

"We could have several gatherings," the colonel said, feeling like they were getting some momentum. "The majority of locals have been too unnerved by the opposition to speak out. We need to meet with our supporters in a safe place without the constant heckling." He waved his hand as if delegating chores. "Can you handle the money and order some refreshments."

"Colonel," Caren cut him off. "I'm not here to take notes or cater food. I'm being paid to handle the press, assist in gaining legal and financial help and insure that ICS gains the support of the majority of the voters in this town. You and I both have our connections in Raleigh. You need to use my expertise in ways that help the town the most. I don't think you want me ordering refreshments."

"Why of course. I know that." The colonel looked slightly embarrassed. This was new for him…letting a woman take the lead. "I'll talk to Millie," he said as a way out. "She always has ideas about these things, but I can't be billing everything to the town. Already the opponents are talking about law suits. Where's the money coming from?"

"That's the sort of thing I'll deal with," Caren reassured him. "Leave it to me." She'd made her point.

*****

Sadie poured a cup of Kibbles and Bits into Smokey's bowl and scratched the top of his head. Next to Gabe, he was the best thing that had happened to her since she'd retired from the store. She believed there had to be some Jack Russell terrier in him, but not enough to make any high-handed claims. He was a black mutt with a gentle disposition. Dutch found him three years ago rummaging through the garbage behind the store and brought him to her for foster care. Despite her initial insistence that she'd only keep him until they found the owner, the dog won her over early. He'd been house broken and trained by someone. He sat obediently. He begged for food with his tail wagging furiously back and forth, but never attempted to grab and run. Within a few days she was calling him Smokey. She figured his owner would eventually show up to reclaim him. After two weeks she hoped that they never would.

"I'll be back in a bit." She patted Smokey's back and talked to him like the live-in companion he'd become. Piles of reading sat on her table. It would have to wait. "Gotta go find Miss Mary."

After unsuccessful attempts to get Mary Law to answer her phone, Sadie was surprised when she knocked on the door to the house and Mary opened it. Sadie could tell immediately Mary had been expecting someone else. She was dressed for town. Sadie, in contrast, looked as if she'd just unloaded the produce truck.

"On your way out?" Sadie asked.

"Sadie." Mary appeared startled.

Sadie considered some humor about expecting a gentleman friend, and then thought better. "May I?" she asked indicating her desire to be invited in. "I won't be long."

Mary hesitated, but then gave into that old bug-a-boo that dictates good manners—Southern hospitality. She stepped aside.

"How are you doing?" Sadie asked with as much sincerity as she could muster. In all honesty, she hoped that Mary lay awake at night in fitful dreams over her decision. What must she have been thinking to let the colonel talk her into voting for this albatross? The woman had bowed to a rooster as fast as a dog could tree a coon.

"So-so," Mary said. "I've been deeply hurt by the personal attacks. My husband spent his life dedicated to making Cedar Branch a better community. All the sacrifices we made… I thought people would have more respect."

Amazing, Sadie thought, here was Mary living in one of the grandest homes in town, and she felt her life had been a sacrifice. Ninety-five percent of the town would gladly change places with her. Sadie, in comparison, had retired to a one bedroom duplex so that Dutch and Ada Lynn could have the house. No yard man or maids for her.

"Maybe I can explain that to you," Sadie said. "Could we talk a minute?"

Mary led her to the living room. A teapot sat on the mahogany coffee table next to a small plate of shortbread cookies. Sadie guessed they were a Christmas gift that probably had arrived in a fancy tin. She eased herself into a navy blue armchair next to Mary. She reached for a cookie and leaned closer to Mary. In response, Mary stiffened.

"I don't need a lecture," Mary muttered.

"This isn't a lecture. I want to tell you about my concern for my grandchildren."

"I have grandchildren, too. Four. One is quite ill. Did you know that?"

Sadie had forgotten, but Mary's words triggered a memory. It had been mentioned in a pastoral prayer. *Pray for Mary Law's little granddaughter who is in the hospital*. Sadie had assumed the child was having her tonsils out.

"It's a brain tumor," Mary's lower lip trembled. "Can you believe that—a child so small having to face cancer? It breaks my heart."

Sadie whispered a quiet "Ohhh, I'm so very sorry. Where is she being treated?"

"There's a new type of treatment at Mass General in Boston that is showing good results with children…proton therapy. But it's expensive…daily doses over an extended period of time. The travel and hotel costs alone are more than my son can afford. Then of course, time off work." Mary trailed off. "But parents will do anything for their children, won't they?"

"I hadn't realized how serious it was."

"We just pray. Of course, I'm trying my best to help them financially."

The doorbell rang and Mary rose quickly. Sadie didn't want to get derailed in a discussion of Mary's granddaughter, but now that the subject had been raised, she felt more compassionate than when she'd first arrived. She needed to let Mary talk.

She heard a quiet exchange, a woman's voice that she didn't quite recognize at first. Sadie realized who it was only seconds before Caren Drake entered the room in her three inch heels.

"Mrs. Baker, what a pleasure to find you here." Caren extended her hand and flashed a set of orthodontically aligned incisors. "I've been hoping for the opportunity to speak with you one-on-one. That town meeting got a bit out of hand."

"For good reason," Sadie said. This was not the person she'd been expecting. "Maybe I should go," she started to rise. Whatever conversation she'd planned on having was now side tracked on two fronts. "This probably isn't a good time."

"No, no, no," Caren insisted. "If you don't mind, Miss Mary, I think this would be wonderful for us to all sit and get to know one another better. After all, Miss Mary has invited me to settle into her downstairs guest room while I'm here in town. Such a lovely gesture as the only motel is twenty-five miles away. I'm most grateful."

Sadie couldn't decide whether to view this as a blessing or a curse. So the blonde-haired viper would be living just around the corner in the home of a town board member. Sadie wondered whether this had been intentionally planned to keep Miss Mary in line? She'd been outmaneuvered already. Perhaps it would be best to eat another cookie and leave.

Caren settled opposite Sadie. Mary went to retrieve a third tea cup. The room felt heavy—ceiling to floor lined satin curtains pinned back to the windowsill with sheers running from frame to frame. Upon her return, Mary poured each a cup of tea and offered them lemon and sugar. Sadie took both. Caren asked for Sweet n' Low.

"Tell me about the house, Miss Mary. Have you lived here all your life?" Caren asked, the saccharin sweet on the tip of her tongue.

"I moved here as a bride," Mary said. "Forty-two years ago. This is actually the house my husband grew up in."

"Real..lee?" Caren hit a high E that resembled a squeal. It crossed Sadie's mind that she'd be good at calling pigs for their slop. "It's beautiful," she said, turning her head to admire the Barcelona front bookcase that protected various collectables behind glass cabinet doors. "When was it built?"

Mary relaxed a bit. "1896...a hundred years old this year." Sadie knew by heart the history lesson that was coming. Mary enjoyed talking about her late husband's prominent family—the land, the acreage, and the farm.

"His father farmed over two thousand acres. Planters came from miles away to buy the seeds that produced the finest corn in eastern North Carolina." A shadow fell over her face. "Of course, he had his share of bad years, too."

Sadie had heard it all, how the landowners who inherited land one generation to the next talked about *hard times* and blamed it on taxes, the lack of cheap labor and the weather. There was either not enough rain, or too much rain. If the crop was good, the insects were bad, and if the pesticides worked, the equipment broke down. The land was only worth the crop it produced until someone finally sold their inheritance. Sometimes there had been too many bad years in a row, but more often a descendant wanted to escape Cedar Branch by cashing in. The younger folks seem to have no sense of family history while the older generation considered selling the farm akin to patricide. With the loss of the land, so went the family name.

The truth hit Sadie like a shock from a jumper cable. Hard times, land, her granddaughter's illness. She couldn't help but wonder if Caren had moved in as a guest or a boarder? No doubt there was grant money for rent, too. It was Mary's land that was the proposed site. She owned two hundred acres on the edge of town where the county had wanted to build a consolidated high school. Mary rented out the land to Henry Bennett to farm peanuts and still did. The Board of Education tried to pass a bond that ultimately failed.

"And you, Mrs. Baker?" Caren's voice broke her train of thought.

"Sorry?" Sadie asked.

"Do you have children?"

"Two boys. Both married. The oldest is in Westtown with two sons. Dutch, my youngest owns the grocery store. He and his wife have a boy and another on the way."

"Oh, how nice. So they live closer than Miss Mary's children. I'm sure that's lovely for you. What does your older son do?"

"Hammie's a supervisor at a tool and die factory." Sadie was still processing her thoughts. She didn't really want to get trapped in small talk.

"Hammie?"

"My maiden name was Hamilton. Everyone calls him Hammie."

"And you, Caren. What's your background?" Mary asked.

"CAR-n," Caren corrected the pronunciation. "The first syllable sounds like a car."

"Oh, sorry," said Mary. "Everyone just calls you Karen. That's more familiar."

"It doesn't matter," Caren said. *Of course, it mattered. She felt like they did it on purpose, just to annoy her.* She swallowed her pride and retreated to the original question. "Not so much to tell. I graduated from college and got a job in Raleigh where I've been for the past several years. Grew up in Winston Salem."

"And you studied what? Chemistry? Engineering?" Sadie asked.

Caren tilted her head slightly and leaned in to take a cookie. "I've done a lot of on-the-job training. I imagine you did much the same when you started your grocery business."

Nice hand-off, Sadie thought. "Word is out that you'll be speaking at private home meetings."

Caren appeared a bit surprised but rebounded. "That's correct," She took a second cookie, then a third.

Aha, Sadie thought. *A nervous nibbler.* There was a good chance they could fatten this skinny gal up before she left town. "I haven't been told where I could attend one of these meetings. Several of us would like to come. You know Cliff Lyons? He can be very helpful about getting information to the public on that morning talk show. We could help you spread the word."

Caren strained a tight-lipped smile. "Actually, they are by invitation only."

"I thought your job was to help us all learn more about ICS…Caren," Sadie said with a special emphasis on the first syllable. Mary shifted in her chair uncomfortably.

"It is," Caren acknowledged the inflection of her name with a wicked smile. "Some people seem more interested in knowing the truth than others."

"You know, however, that we have a petition signed by more than six thousand people in the county, a hundred and eight of them are farmers asking the town board to reverse their decision. Obviously people are interested."

Caren deflected the remark with a wave of her hand. "I've never put much faith in petitions. I think people sign them just to make the person who's asking feel good. They have no idea what they're signing. Besides, it's not a county issue. The decision lies with six hundred people here in Cedar Branch."

Sadie's jaw tightened and she felt her blood pressure rising. "Really? You don't think people who live five or ten miles away should have any say-so? You don't think people know whether or not they want a hazardous waste incinerator?"

"No, I'm just saying Miss Sadie, that since they do business with you, they'll probably pretend to want whatever you want. It's not a very scientific way to do things. Hardly unbiased."

"And your research is unbiased?" Sadie's tone had sharpened. "It appears that all of your research is in marketing. We actually have a few scientific studies that should interest you. In all fairness, you should take your turn listening."

"And I will," Caren's tone matched Sadie's to show that she could give as well as take. "At the information hearing next week."

"If we invite you to one of our meetings, would you come?" Sadie asked. "We're told that you're being paid to educate everyone, not just those who support you."

"If you'll be respectful and open-minded," Caren said.

"I'm sure we can be just as open-minded as you. How about next Monday or Tuesday before the Thursday night public meeting?"

Caren hedged. "All right, a small group—no more than fifteen people. Where? What time?"

"How about at the Harper's house? Seven o'clock. You know where that is, don't you? The house with NO painted on the roof."

Caren flushed and curled her lower lip hard enough to make the pink lipstick pale. "Rather hostile territory, don't you think?"

"Not if your information is better than ours," Sadie said. "We're all reasonable people."

"I'd be delighted." Without looking Sadie in the eye she picked up a fourth cookie and took a bite.

Mary glared. Sadie knew immediately that she had offended her. Mary had opened her doors to her and Sadie had shown poor judgment in picking a fight with a soon-to-be houseguest.

"I don't think there's any need for people to get nasty over this," Mary said. She ran her hands across her skirt and leaned down to retrieve the cookie plate. "Maybe you should go, Sadie."

"Probably so," Sadie said. "I didn't mean to start an argument. I just came by to express my concern for the health of my grandchildren. I'm hoping you'll take that into consideration when the town board reconvenes…the health of the children in this community. We all want what's best for them."

Mary looked stricken. "Of course," she said. "I have grandchildren, too."

"I know, but yours don't live here in this town."

"And I wish they did," Mary said. "Because who knows where children are safe anymore? Mine live in a community without all the horrible things you're imagining and that hasn't kept them safe, now has it? Don't go telling me what causes these diseases, Sadie Baker. You don't know any more than I do."

Sadie lowered her eyes. "I'll let you ladies enjoy your tea. I have some work to do." Her visit had turned into a social blunder, but she'd learned a few things she hadn't known before.

Sadie left and headed straight to the café to find Cliff. She needed to tell him everything that had just happened. More and more she'd come to depend on him to be her confidant just like he'd been fifty years ago when she was the Tomboy that challenged him in hoops after school.

She'd been somewhat surprised and even more pleased at how easily she and Cliff had slipped back into those roles when he'd retired to Cedar Branch three years ago. Except this time, the best she could challenge him to was a game of Chess. Still, she was grateful for his company. Coen's passing had left a hole. Cliff eased her pain. Strange how people drifted apart and then back together later in life...as if they'd stepped into a different room for just a moment to change clothes, but returned and the only difference was a new outer garment.

Cliff needed to know. Mary was the one who'd signed options on her land to help cover the medical costs for her granddaughter. It was a guess, but Sadie felt sure she was right.

In turn, when Caren Drake left Mary's house to retrieve her things, she stopped first by the colonel's. She wanted to include Hamilton Baker on their list of potential supporters and ICS needed to make sure they had a contract with the tool and die factory in Westtown.

Chapter Six

Leland Slade opened his casket and removed a quilt. Underneath he had stored an old pair of boots and a vintage cast iron Dutch oven that didn't fit on his shelf. He had long ago made all of the arrangements for his own burial, figuring as long as he'd built the casket he might as well get some practical use out of it while he was still living. He placed the items on the floor and stepped away.

Henry and Phil stood to one side looking on. "Sure you don't mind?" Phil asked. We could always talk to the funeral home. I think they'd let us borrow one."

Leland shook his head. "Bring it back is all."

"Sure. Just need it for one night… a prop at the information meeting. You know…a little bit of theater."

A Quaker of few words, Leland had a reputation for being a bit eccentric, but basically he practiced simplicity and thrift as a guiding testimony to his faith. He nodded and picked up one end of the coffin to help load it in the back of Phil's pick-up.

The distance between Leland's and Phil's was only a half mile. They'd drop off the casket there where their wives were at work on a mourning cloth with *Cedar Branch* stitched on the side.

"She coming tonight?" Henry asked Phil as they drove.

"Caren won't show. I'll lay you ten to one. Her answers are all canned. She's afraid of anything that hasn't been rehearsed." Phil flipped on the radio. "If our timing is right we might be able to catch Cliff."

Cliff Lyons had become a bit of a celebrity on the talk-radio show out of Westtown. He called in every morning at nine sharp to update people on what the scumbags from ICS were up to. His language was colorful without quite crossing the bounds of censorship. He'd start with a joke, or a revealing tidbit about a local, which would get retold numerous times. People would listen just to see if the joke was on them. Sooner or later he'd take a swipe at ICS or the colonel or the governor…sometimes he'd say something newsworthy, other times he'd just bedevil the incinerator supporters.

Cliff loved to spin a good tale, if not entirely truthful, always entertaining. He had an infectious cackle that rumbled around in his belly before breaking loose into a boisterous ear buster. Even Zan, the disc jockey, couldn't contain his own laughter on air. He counted his lucky stars to have stumbled onto a comedian who had expanded his morning audience twofold. Zan's biggest challenge involved keeping the station from being sued for libel.

"Hel..LO, Clifford," Zan said. "How you doin' today?"

"Well, I'm doing okay, I guess. You know I've been having a bit of a rash on my leg, right up there behind my knee. It itches like crazy."

"Poison-ivy maybe?" Zan asked.

"Thought it might be. I was at the Quaker Café the other day. That new lady doctor we got, Dr. Jane McCabe, was having lunch there, too."

"Ooh, you got a lady doc now?"

"Yep, kind of young, but she's a looker…red head. We're getting used to her."

"You been in for a visit?" Zan teased.

"No, not yet. I try to get as much free medical advice as I can first. So, the other day when she walked into the café during lunch, one of the fellows suggested I go ahead over to her table and get her to write me a prescription… save the expense and time of an office visit."

Listening in the truck, Henry and Phil began to groan.

"So did you?" Zan asked.

"Sure, I figured what did I have to lose? I walked on over to the good doctor and said, 'Hey Doc, let me show you something.' Pulled over a chair and stuck my leg on it so I could roll up my pants leg."

"You did that during lunch?" Zan asked, and listeners could see the smiles through the radio wires.

"Yeah, lunch it was. I gave her a good look-see and said, 'What do you think that is?' Doctor Jane, she leans in close, all serious, and then she says as loud as she possibly can, 'Looks like Herpes to me. Better come around to my office and wear clean underwear.'"

Over the radio Zan let loose a howl.

"Everyone at the café is slapping the table and heehawing at me."

"I bet."

"So, I'm just saying, I get the feeling she don't take lightly to giving out medical information during lunch time."

"We've been warned," Zan said before regaining control. "What else you got for us today? Any news on ICS?"

"Folks pulling all of our signs off the telephone poles."

"You mean those NO signs you all got plastered from here to Kalamazoo?"

"Yeah, we got plenty more where those come from. Some puny attempt is being made to put up YES signs now by the colonel's friends."

"I imagine you're out there pulling those down."

"Who me? Limping around on a cane like I do. I couldn't even if I wanted to. I do have some other news, though. We figured out who sold an option on their land."

"Really? Who?"

"It's Mary Law, the church organist. Can you imagine that? She's a town board member. Now there's one hell of a conflict-of-interest. That'll show up in court in a law suit."

"Well, I'm sorry for her," Zan said.

"Don't be sorry. There's two million dollars coming her way if the permit gets approved. I hear she got thirty-five thousand just for signing the initial agreement."

Zan whistled. "Dang, that's a nice piece of change for a promise and your John Hancock. I might be tempted to sell too, if I had any land."

Phil turned off the radio and looked at Henry. "Damn, that's bad."

"What was Mary thinkin'?" Henry asked.

"No, I mean bad for us. A lot of people are going to be upset Cliff went after Mary on the radio show. She'll get a lot of sympathy."

"What she did was illegal. She's a town board member. She can't make deals that line her pockets while in office. She should be sued," Henry said.

Phil sighed. "She probably doesn't even know what she did was wrong."

*****

Sadie's phone rang and she considered not picking it up this time. It never stopped, and so many calls were just folks calling to argue. Smokey lay at her feet, his head alert waiting for her to acknowledge the ring. She read the next line on the county's environmental zoning restrictions strewn across her kitchen table. It appeared that the county had strong requirements. In comparison, Cedar Branch had only a weak one that had been modified within the past two months. In every instance, the word "regulate" had been changed to "review." Sadie could feel her temperature rising…*those conniving jerks*. Could it really be possible that the town did not have to comply with the country regulations? They had intentionally weakened the restrictions to accommodate ICS. She finally gave in to the incessant buzz and picked up the receiver. A thunderous shout greeted her.

"Sadie Baker, you should be ashamed of yourself. You have reached a new low as far as I'm concerned, and I should have you prosecuted."

This was not the first nasty call Sadie had gotten, but it was the first one from the colonel screaming at her like she was some redneck recruit who couldn't even shine his own shoes. He didn't intimidate her.

"Who put starch in your shorts?" she asked with no attempt to mask her annoyance.

"You fed Cliff Lyons that information, and now he just broadcasted it across three counties. You have no proof."

Sadie hadn't been listening to the radio and she didn't have a clue what the colonel was talking about, but she had no doubt that Cliff could provoke him. She savored the moment.

"Proof about what?"

"That Mary Law has signed an option on her land."

"Oh, is that what Cliff said?"

"You know damn well that's what he said. You put him up to it."

"I don't have to put Cliff Lyons up to anything. He says what he wants," Sadie shot back. "If it's not true, Mary Law can deny it. She can dial the number to the radio station as fast as Cliff can. I'm sure everyone would love to hear from her." Sadie slammed down the phone.

It rang again almost immediately. "Phil here. Did you catch Clifford on the radio?"

"No," Sadie said, "but the colonel did, and I've already heard from him."

"Me too, along with a call from Caren Drake. She's refusing to meet with us tonight. Claims we'll twist her words into a publicity stunt. She doesn't trust us."

"Easy out for her, isn't it?" Sadie said, not the least bit surprised. "Do you know that she and the other board members had intentionally weakened our local zoning ordinances in advance of ICS purchasing land?"

"No kidding," Phil said.

"Can't we sue them for that?" Sadie asked.

"I don't know. Depends on whether or not they gave public notice. Henry tells me that several farmers have called to say they weren't allowed to sign up to speak at the information meeting on Thursday. Evidently the town board has decided to limit the number of people who can actually say anything to fifteen speakers in favor of ICS and fifteen opposed," Phil added.

"What?" Sadie snapped. "God, they make me madder by the minute. What if there are five hundred opposed?"

"Equal time for equal sides."

"Can they do that?"

"Evidently, they can. There's a sign posted at the town hall announcing that the maximum number of slots available for speakers is already full."

"Damn," Sadie said. "Damn, damn and double damn."

*****

The crowd at the school was twice as large as the one at the town board meeting. People from around the county had become more involved. Three media trucks and several reporters took pictures of a six-by-eight foot white sheet hanging from an upstairs balcony with *ICS HAS GOT TO GO* spray-painted across the front. When Chief Meacham tried to get to the second floor he found the doors to the stairwell locked. The keys had disappeared from the janitor's closet.

"I don't know, Chief. They were right here when I left the building this afternoon," the custodian said.

Meacham had little time to argue, but obviously someone at the school was in on the tomfoolery.

Inside, the crowd chanted, "Hey, Hey, Ho, Ho, ICS Has Got to Go," in a filled auditorium of hand-held NO posters. A few brave souls kept YES signs close to their chest. Helen Truitt moved from supporter to supporter to build their courage and pointed an accusatory finger at others.

Colonel Little drove slowly past the school with an escort from the sheriff's department. He scowled at the banner and immediately turned to Caren seated beside him. "Get that damn thing down."

Caren hardly blinked. "The police will take care of it." Her mouth twitched.

Several naysayers spotted the police car and followed it around the building. They were mostly farm hands in jeans, jackets, and farm hats—men who worked and ran the chicken and pig farms, grew the peanuts, cotton and soya beans. These were no longer small family farms but agricultural industries run by the likes of Perdue and Smithfield. Some of the men carried signs that they pumped up and down at the car window, most referring to the peanut industry. *Hands off Our Nuts* was the most prominent.

"Colonel," one yelled when the car door opened. "You sold us out."

Caren climbed out the door on the opposite side of the car and a few wolf whistles were heard. The colonel cupped his hand to the ear of one of the sheriff's deputies who shook his head. "Keep moving, Colonel," Caren walked up beside him. "Just ignore them and go inside."

The insults came fast and furious particularly from three or four voices.

"Caren, who's paying you?"

"Who's getting paid the most? You or our mayor?"

"You two screwing each other or just us?"

The deputies had formed a barrier around Caren and the colonel, but the colonel wasn't about to take the taunts without a response. "Get lost, you thugs, or I'll have you arrested," he yelled shaking his fist.

"For what? We ain't done nothing. You're the one who should be arrested for selling us down the river," one young man shouted back.

"Can't you do something?" the colonel scowled at a patrolman. "I don't recognize any of these people. Someone must be paying them."

"Freedom of speech, sir. They're not breaking any laws."

Caren didn't give the crowd the satisfaction of a glance. "Inside, Colonel." Caren grabbed his arm and tried to pull him behind her. "Let's just get inside."

"Hey Hey Ho Ho, Colonel Little has got to go." The chant started and alerted those inside that the colonel had arrived. The crowd in the auditorium joined in. The colonel pushed his way past Caren and bolted through the back entrance to the stage.

Behind the curtains, four of the town board members huddled. Chief Meacham entered from the opposite door that led into the main hallway of the school. "Get that goddamn banner down," the colonel yelled at the chief as soon as he saw him.

"I can't sir. The stairwells are locked and no one can find the keys."

Rod Palmateer, a thin and bookish-looking board member, adjusted a pair of wire rim glasses that kept slipping down his nose. As the others waited, he finally stuttered through what sounded to the colonel like the beginning of a concession speech. "This is perhaps a huge mistake. If the community doesn't want this …."

"Oh no, you don't." The colonel raised his chin like a llama about to spit. "We talked about this. We knew there could be opposition. We agreed this would help the town in the long run." He glared at the four lowered heads studying the floorboards. "Where's Miss Mary?"

"She's not coming. Said she was afraid of what people would call her now that they know she signed the land option," Rod said.

"You didn't tell us Mary signed an option." Lucy Woodright's voice was shaking. "This is a conflict of interest. We could all be sued. I agree with Rod."

"Colonel," Chief Meacham interjected. "We have another problem, sir. You need to take a look."

The colonel turned sharply, feeling disgusted at the lack of spine he'd just witnessed. Had these people never experienced adversity? Trying to maintain a Norman Rockwell image in this economy was self-destructive. The local businesses were already on life supports.

The colonel pushed back the side of the curtain and a jeer arose when he appeared. The chant got louder. He looked at Chief Meacham, who in turn nodded to the table and chairs that had been arranged on the stage to seat the town board. The table was covered with a black cloth with *RIP Cedar Branch* stitched along the side. Atop the table was a pine coffin.

"Get that out of here!" he demanded. The color started to rise above his shirt collar.

"I tried, sir. It's filled with rocks. We can't lift it."

"Call the funeral home. Tell them to come and take it back the same way they got it in."

"I tried that, too, sir. It's not theirs."

"Then whose?"

"I don't know, sir. Nobody is claiming it."

"That's it," the colonel said sharply. "I don't have to put up with these shenanigans."

From the front row someone threw something at him and then ran out the side door. The colonel raised an arm to protect himself and a handful of coins rolled across the stage.... quarters.

"Judas, Judas, Judas," began a second chant.

"What was that?" the colonel barked.

Rod raised his eyebrows. "Thirty pieces of silver?" he whispered.

The chief took chase, but he had the stage stairs to contend with and the crowd created a webbed path which hindered his access to the prankster. "Sorry, chief. Oh, sorry," each said moving at first in front of him and then slowly to the side.

Fuming, the colonel headed to the backdoor. "Go home," he shouted at the other board members. "This is nonsense. We won't play their games."

After fifteen minutes when the board members failed to appear, Sadie, Cliff, Billie and Phil could be seen with their heads together. Finally Phil took the stage and picked up the microphone that rested on the coffin. The microphone squawked. People flinched. He shrugged apologetically and tapped the mic a few times with his finger to test it. When he was satisfied the pitch was appropriate he said, "I think our mayor and town board members left."

A roar went up in the room. They had accomplished something. No one was sure what, but it felt like a win.

"The board members are refusing to listen to our concerns, but the building has been reserved for an information meeting and we intend to have one. We'll give anyone who wants to speak the opportunity to do so." A cheer echoed through the room, even though a group still holding their YES signs appeared skeptical. They huddled together with heads bowed murmuring to one another.

"I think we all agree if we didn't feel blindsided, none of us would have bothered to come. But, like the old joke, we got a bucket of cowpies under the Christmas tree this year when we thought we were getting a pony." He paused and raised his index finger, centered the crowd and drew an imaginary line from left to right. "You and I all know Cedar Branch does not want a hazardous waste incinerator in our town. And in case you're not sure why, we've got some knowledgeable speakers who've joined us this evening to give you some facts."

"Stop right there, Phil." Helen was on her feet. "Not all of us agree with you. You said we'd each get a chance to speak. Don't tell us what we're gonna think before we've had our chance to present both sides."

A few "boos" could be heard, but Phil raised his hand for quiet. "No, no. Helen's right. Everybody gets a chance to speak. I'm willing to consider what she has to say. But first, I want to give the microphone to anyone who has travelled any distance to meet with us. They may have a long ride back tonight, and I want to let them say their piece and leave when they need to."

He waved at Beth to come take the microphone. "Beth Elmore is here from Lee County. She helped send ICS packing out of several other counties. We've also got a farmer, Stu Ricks, who's come all the way from over in the mountains to talk about the threat the incinerator could cause to farmers and Dr. Paul Connett a chemist from St. Lawrence University who has done extensive research in toxicology."

There was polite applause. Phil stretched his arms onto either side of the podium and adjusted his weight with his chin tucked down. Weathered by the sun and slightly bent from his labor, he towered over the podium and grabbed both sides firmly with his hands.

About fifty people stood to leave.

"Now wait. Hold on there," he called out. "We're going to let you get your shot at the microphone too. This is an information meeting and everyone gets to be heard." But the defectors could see they were outnumbered and the crowd had proven to be hostile.

From that point on speakers traded off the microphone. Paul Connett got his turn to talk about toxin pollutants, dioxins, furans, acid gasses, particulates and heavy metals and he left videos of other talks he'd given. Stu talked about two studies that suggested hazardous waste burners could contaminate crops and irritate the lungs of nearby residents.

Beth Elmore, professionally dressed in a black suit, spoke in a clear non-threatening voice. "It's not just what happens with these poisons in an incinerator. You also have to be concerned about the transportation to and from the site. Your county is filled with narrow two-lane roads that wind through fields of beautiful crops. You'd have as many as twenty-five trucks a day filled with unknown contaminants on these roads. One flat tire—one accident—one sleepy driver at the wheel could send tons of toxins into any field. The land would be unfit to use again for hundreds of years."

Helen Truitt took her turn at the mic and reminded the audience of how many times they'd begged the town board to come up with opportunities for new industry and jobs. "We're not the kind of place that can attract major business. Let's be honest with ourselves. Three hundred jobs is a goldmine, and we should be thrilled." She chided her neighbors for the behavior they'd shown to the elected officials who had tried to do as they asked. "Every job has risks," she said looking directly at the farmers. "You," she said staring down a few of them. "You know as well as I do what those pigs and chickens produce, and it's not honey."

Mike Warren rose to talk about the construction jobs this industry would initially provide. A likeable contractor in town, people listened to his arguments without interruption. Some even nodded agreement.

Katie O'Brien, who had recently completed her certification to be a real estate agent, rose and quietly asked people to consider how the housing market might improve if, indeed, three hundred new jobs were added to their town. She told of her own struggle when she returned as a single mother to Cedar Branch and had to move in with her brother because she couldn't find a job that paid her enough to afford housing. Eight dollars an hour would have made a big difference to her at that time.

When Sadie got her turn almost two hours had passed. She wasn't sure she had anything to say that was new, but Cliff encouraged her to get to her feet. "You're always good with a crowd," he said. He squeezed her hand. "Everybody's talking about the environment and the money. Tell them how it makes you feel."

Sadie relented and went to the mic. The crowd was beginning to thin and one by one the supporters of ICS had left. In a voice that began small, Sadie said "I've been encouraged to tell you how this whole mess makes me feel." She paused. "I feel like our town is being raped," she said.

Suddenly the room went still. Those who had been rustling in their chairs or talking with a neighbor stopped. Sadie looked out and saw a couple of her friends with their mouths open.

"I know," she said, "that's a harsh word. Let me tell you why I put it that way. Cedar Branch is my town. I grew up here. I've lived here all my life. I can't control all the things that happen in Cedar Branch, but all the things that happen in it affect me. Cedar Branch is a living breathing part of who I am and I've always felt safe here.

"The way that ICS was thrust upon our town was brutal. It was forced on us at a time of the year usually filled with joy. We were surrounded by family, getting ready to celebrate the holidays. We were in our homes, baking cookies, making fudge, decorating Christmas trees and wrapping presents and these strangers arrived secretly in our town under the cover of darkness. Without our knowledge. Without our consent. They came and made deals pitting neighbor against neighbor. They turned our holiday into a nightmare…a nightmare that has lasted every night since they arrived. I can't sleep."

She stopped a moment to pull a Kleenex from her pocket. "I feel like my town has been violated. My trust in my elected officials, people I have known for years, has been violated. My personal space has been violated. My right to be heard has been violated. My relationship with my neighbors has been violated and our humanity as a community has been violated. The town is being raped. I don't know any other way to put it."

Heads nodded in agreement and a few people shouted out "Yes!"

She continued. "Nobody felt we were important enough to respect our rights or to involve us in the decision process. No one felt we needed to know about the consequences to us or our families either in the present or long term. Our opinions became irrelevant, unrecognized, and undervalued."

Now there was applause.

"When people feel raped, there are only two things they can do. They can accept their misfortune or they can fight back. For me…I'm a fighter." Sadie's voice had risen by degrees as she spoke and now she began to shout. "I have no intentions of letting these outside forces surge through my town and force us into submission. Give us a vote and I'll live by the outcome. But without a vote, I will not lie down and take it. I will kick and scream. I will block trucks. I will picket state offices. I will disrupt public meetings. I will go to jail if need be. AND, I will not go quietly. If they want a fight, they've got one. I'm going to fight every inch of the way. And I hope you will, too."

A roar went up from the crowd. Sadie's son Hammie walked out of the auditorium.

Shortly thereafter the meeting ended with about half of the original audience in attendance and an additional seven thousand dollars in donations.

*****

Around three in the morning someone threw a brick through the front window of the town hall. Sadie awoke to the siren going off only a block away and she thought of Chief Meacham. He was young, inexperienced. He'd had a rough night and it hadn't ended. His parents were Sadie's friends. They'd be worried. She was, too.

Around that same time, the casket mysteriously disappeared from the stage at the school and the keys were returned to the custodial closet.

Chapter Seven

Stu Ricks stayed with the Harpers three days to discuss the next move. It was a long drive back to the mountains and he didn't know how soon he could return to Cedar Branch. Decisions had to be made about how to handle the money. They needed to incorporate as a non-profit, set up a board of directors, elect officers, open a bank account and decide on a name for this new entity.

After a minimum amount of discussion, they chose the name Citizens Against Pollution. The acronym CAP would be easy to remember and fit on posters. It allowed them to include all types of pollution and basically, they needed to come up with something quick and move on to more important things. The name would do.

"I could probably draw up the incorporation papers," Cliff volunteered. "I did the work once for the policemen's benefit fund in New Jersey. But I'll need a list of officers and objectives, an address, and a bank account."

"I know this all seems like nuisance work," Stu said, "but it's got to be done to keep you legitimate. Also, non-profit status gives you the ability to request donations from agencies and foundations. If this turns into a legal battle you're going to need a lot more financial help."

Sadie sighed. "I was so hoping we could end this in a couple of weeks."

"Still may happen." Stu sounded encouraging. "But might not, so spread out the work load. Set up committees. Don't force people, but let them join where they're the most comfortable. Not everyone will come to public meetings, but they may work a phone bank, write a letter, create a poster, or bake a cake for a raffle. If they're having fun, they'll keep coming back. The more hands digging the tunnel, the faster we'll get to the other side."

*****

Church services were somber in all three places of worship the following Sunday.

A new Methodist minister had arrived only weeks earlier. He'd walked into a hornets' nest and anxiously wanted to be embraced by his new flock. The public embarrassment and humiliation inflicted upon their organist had his congregation in a twit. He assured the members that the church would support Mary. Organists were a vanishing breed and losing theirs would be a disastrous way for him to begin his tenure.

Helen Truitt, a deaconess, was the most vocal and cornered the colonel and Millie as soon as they walked through the church doors. "You should have seen them after you left, Colonel. Basically a mob, most of whom had never been in our town before." Her voice escalated. "Radical recruits from Chapel Hill, Asheville, Greenpeace, God knows where else. Beards. Dressed like they'd walked out of the woods. A total lack of good manners…shouting and screaming like a bunch of spoiled children."

She dabbed at the corner of her eye with a handkerchief. "I can't believe what's happening. They spread lies. They defaced public property, vandalized the town hall and made a mockery of a public meeting. People like me, well-intentioned, honorable citizens who had come to learn the truth…they ran us out of the room. I fled, literally fled. I was afraid I might be assaulted."

Colonel Little listened, tried to reassure her that he'd handle everything. Then he turned to speak to someone else. But Millie stayed, took Helen's hand and whispered, "The world is filled with people who just don't know any better. We must learn to tolerate their poor manners."

"But Miss Mary? What about Mary?" Helen forged on. "She never realized she was doing anything wrong. She has a grandchild with cancer. Did you know that? I think she was hoping to be able to give them the money." She sniffed and wiped her nose.

"We'll help her get through this," Millie said and leaned in to embrace her. Helen went limp. It had been so long since she'd been held in anyone's arms that the tears flowed. While the colonel made small talk with others, Millie extended compassion and care to those around her and smoothed out the rough edges of her husband. He needed her to assume that role for him, and she did.

At the same time the Methodists rallied around Mary, the Baptist minister did his best to avoid any mention of events during the past week. He delivered a sermon titled *The Beginning of The End.* Those in attendance tried to discern whether he implied a double entendre or simply wanted to move their thoughts from hazardous waste to something more dreadful like death. Although Sadie's grandfather had been a Quaker, her mother married a Baptist and Sadie was baptized in that church. Sadie skipped the service completely. She had more important things to do: papers to read, editorials to write, for heaven's sake, and a television interview approaching. Since her talk at the public hearing, she'd received several calls from news media outlets inviting her to do a live interview.

Two blocks away Stu accompanied Phil and his wife to the Quaker meeting. Stu had attended Quaker meetings a few times and understood the importance of the silence. Before meeting, Phil introduced him to Nathan Hoole, a respected elder within the Quaker community.

But not all of the Quakers were in agreement on the issue of the hazardous waste incinerator and consensus had not yet been reached.

Three-quarters of the way through the service Stu felt moved to speak. He rose. "It has been a pleasure to be a guest in this small town. Even in winter time with the trees bare and the fields barren, I see the beauty in both the landscape and the hearts of those I've met. I pray with you that this splendor will never be destroyed by unwelcomed predators. I want the community to know there are those of us throughout this great state holding you in the light."

As soon as Nathan Hoole ended meeting for worship by shaking hands with the elder to his left, Homer Liston, who owned the Ford dealership in a neighboring town, walked over to Phil. Phil raised his hand to greet him but Homer said firmly, "Let's talk outside."

They had barely stepped through the front door when Homer turned with obvious agitation. "This is a place of silent prayer...a place where I come to seek solitude and comfort without the worries of the outside world. I've come here all of my life to find quiet inspiration. Today, I feel betrayed. You have brought your political views into our worship service, and I resent it."

"I said nothing during meeting." Phil kept his voice calm.

"He's your friend," Homer said nodding at Stu who had sensed something wrong and followed Phil outside. "You recruited that man to foist his personal agenda on our town. I am offended that you would deliberately insert such a dialogue into a worship service."

The elder Nathan Hoole appeared in the doorway. His stature within the meeting brought the exchange to a halt.

"I need to leave." Homer turned to walk to his car.

"What seems to be the problem?" Nathan asked.

"Homer feels that I deliberately invited my friend today to advance a personal agenda," Phil said.

"Did you?" Nathan asked.

"I invited a guest who was staying at my house to join us in worship," Phil said.

"Then he is welcomed," Nathan said.

"I must apologize if I said something inappropriate," Stu began, but Nathan stopped him.

"Our doors have always remained open to anyone who wishes to enter regardless of their religious or political beliefs. We encourage one another to be quiet listeners. Otherwise, we will never understand how far our neighbors have walked with painful blisters on their feet."

*****

"Mama." Dutch was on the phone. "Come on over to the house. Hammie's brought some barbecue and slaw and Ada Lynn's made a cake."

Sadie looked at the mess of papers on her table. The photocopied sheets kept multiplying like dust bunnies while she slept. Some came through the mail; others were simply left in large manila envelopes on her door step. She'd divided what she had into three stacks: problems cited with other incinerators in the country, scientific reports on hazardous emission, and reports on economic decline in areas with similar facilities. Every time anyone quoted Greenpeace their research was dismissed by the proponents as biased, so Sadie looked for other sources. Paul Connett had offered a lot of good statistics but reviewing the tapes took time.

"I don't know," she hesitated. "I've got a lot of work to do. You know I'm going on TV next week in both Raleigh and Virginia Beach."

"Yeah, we heard. That's sort of what we want to talk about."

"Is there a problem?"

"Dinner with your family. Gabe wants to see you. You haven't seen Hammie's kids for a month."

Normally, Sadie would have been overjoyed with the invitation and made a batch of cupcakes for the grandchildren. Today was different. Her mornings seemed to miraculously merge into afternoons that suddenly turned into darkness. Frequently she'd look at the clock only to realize it was past midnight, and she was still getting phone calls. The process had turned into something akin to a maze. One reference led to another, which then opened the door to a myriad of questions that immediately changed the configuration.

"I'll drop by," she said. "Can't stay long." Her mind swirled. She needed to figure out how to break down the scientific mumbo-jumbo into a few basic statements. The colonel had developed an annoying habit of telling the media that the process was too complicated for most people to understand but he had researched the information thoroughly to make sure health and safety issues were in place. That one statement drove her crazy because she didn't believe he knew squat. More and more, she began to think that a door-to-door campaign was needed. People should be able to sit across from someone and get clear and simple explanations without being made to feel stupid.

"Smokey, wanna go see the kids?" she asked. Smokey leaped from the sofa and bounded across the room. Sadie hooked the leash to his collar and began the four-block walk. The fresh air felt good.

She didn't bother to knock. She never did. Officially, the house was still in her name. She walked in and took a deep breath…the smells of spilt milk, Cheerios, and potato chips ground into the carpets assaulted her immediately, but beneath those were the comforting smells of a home she missed. The sight of her three grandchildren cross-legged in front of the television reminded her of how she really wanted to spend her time. The three boys were all beautiful: Gabe, the youngest and only redhead, and then Hammie's six and eight year old boys, Joel and Hamilton Jr., on either side—both blondies. She paused to admire them and give a silent blessing. They were watching *Toy Story* again. Hamilton and Joel looked up momentarily and waved. Gabe broke into a smile.

The clutter seemed worse. At some point she'd move out the rest of her furniture. She'd taken only a few things with her…her bedroom set and kitchen table, a couple of wing chairs. There just wasn't room in the duplex, and she couldn't bring herself to let go of the accumulation of memories she saw in every corner—the recliner she and Coen had gotten on sale at the auction house on his fiftieth birthday, the hutch that belonged to his mother, her mother's sideboard. The china, good Lord, the china…they'd collected it piece by piece until she'd completed the set. She pulled it down for Thanksgiving, Christmas and Easter. The joy, however, had been in their annual purchase, always on her birthday and their anniversary. She and Coen had toasted with champagne when they completed the set. She wondered whether either of her boys had ever noticed.

Smokey tore around the room and jumped on each of the children covering them with wet dog kisses. They pushed him away from their faces with their eyes still glued to the movie and then patted him in an effort to keep him still. The dog soon became more interested in the remains of barbecue buns and chips carelessly left on paper plates on the floor. Sadie could tell the children had already eaten.

"No, Smokey. Come over here." Sadie sat down on the recliner and patted her thigh until Smokey jumped up next to her. "Now sit," she said. The dog obeyed, nestled into her lap and wagged his tail.

Gabe picked up his stuffed rabbit and toddled over to her. Sadie lifted him up beside Smokey and gave him a squeeze. "Nasty old cold," she said taking the tail of his shirt and wiping his nose. The child coughed. Sadie kissed the top of his head. Poor baby caught every cold that blew through town.

"There you are." Ada Lynn popped her head around the door. "I thought I heard you. We're just about to sit down at the table."

Sadie eased out of the chair, leaving Gabe, Smokey and the stuffed rabbit together and went into the kitchen. She got a hug from everyone and was handed a bowl of coleslaw from the refrigerator and a bottle of hot sauce. Hammie's wife Cece filled the iced tea glasses and Dutch spooned out the chopped barbecue into a bowl. A bag of hamburger buns sat on the counter next to a chocolate cake with a thick layer of fudge icing…Dutch's favorite.

They blessed the food and passed around the dishes before Dutch asked, "So, Mama, did you hear what happened at the Methodist Church this morning?"

In reality, Sadie didn't care much what happened at the Methodist church. "What did I miss?" she said.

"They had a meeting after church about Miss Mary. Your name came up. They said you told Cliff Lyons to go on the radio and announce she'd signed an option to sell land."

Now they had her attention. "Well, that's not true. You know as well as I do that nobody tells Cliff what he can or cannot say."

Dutch continued, "Miss Mary is telling everyone that right after you visited her you went straight to Cliff and told him she planned to sell land to ICS."

Sadie looked confused. "I don't get it. Did she deny it? Call me a liar?"

"No," Cece spoke softly. "But people are feeling sort of sorry for her. She's embarrassed. After all, she's their organist."

"Well, do tell." Sadie sat back slack-jawed. "Did she think she was going to cash a check for a million dollars in this town and pretend the government had underestimated her Social Security?"

"Beeecause," Dutch let the first syllable linger on his tongue, "this is how it all starts. Remember my telling you to stay out of it. The Methodists are all upset at you and not one of them walked into my store today after lunch when they left the Quaker Café."

Sadie crossed her arms and reared back in her chair. "Dutch," she said. She made an effort to measure her response "One slow afternoon in the store isn't the collapse of the economy. I didn't start this. I'm responding the same way I think you would if one of your suppliers started sending you food that made your customers sick. You'd simply stop ordering from that supplier and you'd have other choices. Our town board has agreed to do business with a company that's going to make some of us sick and they're not giving us the option to do business elsewhere. The colonel's not offering us a take it or leave it deal. He's foisting this company on us against our better judgement."

Dutch closed his eyes and shook his head. "What if you're wrong? What if it's like going to the doctor and getting a shot. You know it's going to hurt. You don't want to get it, but in the long run the shot could save your life. What the colonel is offering may save this town."

"Mama Sadie," Ada Lynn stepped in. "What Dutch is saying is that even though we're trying to stay out of this, your being so outspoken doesn't help business."

"And the rape comment, Mama. That got a lot of attention. Pretty strong language, don't you think?" Dutch added.

"So that's what this is about. What do you want me to do?"

Hammie spoke for the first time. "You've done your bit. A lot of other people are involved who can take the lead. Why don't you take a break… stay involved in a less vocal way—maybe donate a little money or make a few phone calls. Just don't become the main attraction."

"What? Play my fiddle while Rome burns?"

"No, Mama," Dutch said, "but you're getting people worked up."

"I'm getting people worked up?" Sadie couldn't believe what she had heard. She looked at her boys. They both avoided any eye contact: Dutch with his lips curled, looking up at the ceiling—Hammie, arms crossed, studying something in the corner.

"You want me to cancel my television appearances. That's it, isn't it?" she said.

Hammie breathed out a loud sigh. "Let someone else do it. Cliff seems to enjoy hearing himself talk."

"Don't go bad-mouthing Cliff," Sadie said faster than she'd intended. Both boys exchanged a glance. "Look, I don't know how to explain how strongly I feel about this," Sadie said. "I am outraged." She stopped to consider her words. "I guess that's it… just outraged at the audacity of Colonel Little and the town board to assume they had the authority to invite ICS to Cedar Branch without finding out whether or not this was something the citizens would support. Not just any hazardous waste incinerator, but the second largest in the country. They're not talking about having a little wienie roast on the outskirts of town. They're talking about burning fifty thousand tons…one hundred million pounds every year and nobody has told us what happens to the ash that's left after the burn. Doesn't that concern you?"

She reached for her sweet tea and took a swallow to calm herself. Already she could feel the first bites of barbeque colliding with the acid in her stomach. She tried to moderate her tone. "In all honesty, if they had started out by saying the company wanted to build here and put it up for a vote, people may have voted for it. If they'd said here are the risks and here's how we're willing to compensate you, people may have gone along with them. I would have accepted that decision."

Her heartbeat accelerated. The more she thought about how devious the colonel had been, the madder she got. "The colonel…the town board members…they're all acting so arrogant, like they understand things better than we do…like they're smart and we're all dumb. And they've been underhanded in more ways than one…making decisions behind our backs in closed meetings, diluting the zoning regulations. It infuriates me. I'm not willing to let them get away with it."

Sadie crossed her arms over her chest. "The colonel thinks that he's some kind of visionary and he can make us believe he's serving up sweetbread when it's really horseshit. Well, you and I all know there are only going to be a few people who get rich on this. Who do you think is going to be buying your groceries when the school closes and families move away?"

"They're already moving away," Hammie said quietly. "At least this would be an effort to keep some of our young people around."

All eyes were on him. The silence hung in the air like an icicle starting to melt.

"What?" Sadie asked looking from one to the other. "Say it."

"I've been going to their meetings." Hammie's eyes were on Cece. She grimaced.

"Whose meetings?"

"The ones that the PROs are having," Hammie said.

"The PROs?" Sadie asked incredulously.

"The group supporting the incinerator. The PROs—Promoting Rural Opportunity. That's what they're calling themselves now." He made eye contact. "Caren explained the whole process to us. It's new technology. There's nothing but steam coming out of those stacks."

Sadie felt like her eyes would pop out of her head. "Are you kidding me? STEAM? You can't really believe that, not after what you heard the other night."

Hammie pushed back his chair and motioned to Cece. "Get the kids. We'll go."

"Oh, stop acting like a two-year old," Sadie scolded. "Sit back down and talk to me."

"Look, I'm just going to say it." He was on his feet. "They've offered my company a sizeable contract."

"They who?"

"ICS…the company building the incinerator. It could triple our business. We'd hire on at least fifty new employees…young men, men with high school diplomas who need jobs. I'd train and supervise a bigger team…get a significant raise. It'd be good for me, good for them."

"So, you're selling out?" Sadie's eyes had gone cold.

"No, I'm trusting the EPA regulators instead of your kitchen calculator and environmental extremists. We just have different opinions on what's best for the town is all." Hammie pulled his jacket off the back of his chair and motioned to Cece to do the same.

"They're paying you off. That's exactly what they're doing." Sadie was suddenly on her feet, the uneaten barbeque left on her plate. "You go on, all of you. Do what you have to do and I'll do what I have to do. Sit down. I'm leaving."

With Hammie still standing and Dutch hunched over the table with his head in his hands, Sadie left the room, gave each of the grandchildren a peck on the cheek and whistled for Smokey. She slammed the front door on her way out with enough force that everyone noticed.

The others remained motionless, until Ada Lynn finally got up and retrieved the dessert. "Come on kids," she called into the next room. "Put the movie on pause. It's time for birthday cake."

Chapter Eight

Sadie stormed down the six steps of her former house and tugged at Smokey's leash to make him move faster. He resisted, unprepared for the sudden departure. She yanked harder. A 1992 Dodge Spirit rolled to a stop beside her in front of the Quaker Café. Cliff leaned out the window, "Hey beautiful, going my way?"

"Oh, Cliff," she said. She stooped down to the car window. "It's not a good time."

"What's wrong?"

She nodded to the house behind her. "I've just had an encounter of the third kind with my children. They think I've gone off the deep end."

"You're not alone. I think we've all gone off the deep end," Cliff said. "How about a cup of coffee?"

"No really, thanks. I've got so much to do back at the house."

"You won't get any of it done now. You're too riled up. Come on, let's talk about it. We'll slip in there." He pointed to the Quaker Café.

"It's closed. Sunday, remember?"

"Good. Nobody will bother us. Light's still on in the kitchen. I'll bet Teensy will let us in while she finishes up." He pulled the white Dodge with two thin red racing stripes along the side into the empty parking lot and got out. Taking hold of Smokey's leash, he put his arm around Sadie's shoulders and led the way around the building to the backdoor. "Things are always darkest before the dawn," he said philosophically.

"You didn't make that up," Sadie said.

"Nope," Cliff squeezed her shoulder. "Some English guy. Makes me sound very high brow, don't you think?"

They knocked and then pushed open the screen door to the kitchen. The weather was still cold, but Teensy had stood over a hot stove all afternoon and they knew she could work up a sweat. As expected, Teensy was scraping the past week's grease and grit from the griddle. Every Sunday night she stayed late after the lunch crew left to give the kitchen a complete scrub down.

"Well, my soul, if it ain't Tweedle Dee and Tweedle Dum. We're closed," she said and returned to her work.

"Tweedle Dee and Tweedle Dum!" Cliff guffawed. "Is that what you call us?"

"You don't think half the town sees you two sittin' together all lovey-dovey in the café every day," she said matter-of-factly.

"Lovey-dovey?" Sadie objected. "We're just friends."

"Yeah, un-huh." Teensy flicked her hand like she was shooing a fly. "Whatcha want?"

"We want a cup of coffee and a quiet place for a few minutes. Miss Sadie here just had her clock cleaned by her young'uns and you know how that goes. Caffeine is a must."

Sadie cocked her head, stunned by Teensy's remarks. Surely the town didn't think she and Cliff were anything more than pals. "That's okay, I don't really want any coffee," she said.

"I got something better than that," Teensy said. "How about a shot of stump juice?" Teensy raised an eyebrow in a gesture that could have been either an invitation or a warning.

"You got some moonshine?" Cliff beamed. "You old fox, you. Sure, we want some."

Teensy went to the back shelf and took a canister of lard and two five pound bags of sugar off the front. She reached back and pulled out a dark bottle marked *flavoring*. Pulling two plastic juice glasses off the sideboard she poured each a quarter finger.

Cliff picked his up, sniffed and then took a sip. He let it roll across his tongue and then down his throat and smiled. "Damn, that's good. Who makes it?" Teensy scratched behind her ear, started scrubbing the griddle again and didn't say a word.

Sadie watched Cliff and when he seemed pleased, she tasted the poison. She gasped, tried to catch her breath and coughed. "Whoa…that's got a punch."

"Miss Ellie doesn't know, does she?" Cliff asked. He tapped the rim of his glass in hopes of a refill.

"And you ain't telling?" Teensy held the bottle mid air waiting for an answer before she poured.

"Cross my heart." Cliff made the x sign over his chest.

Teensy put another half finger in his glass and filled Sadie's to the original mark. Then she walked over and slid the flavoring back behind the sugar and lard. "Don't dirty none of my tables," she warned. "I need to clean the fryer. Be about another half hour."

Cliff and Sadie sat across from each other at a small table in the dining area near the kitchen wall. Smokey nestled in close to their feet. The curtains were drawn, lights out. All one could see from the street was the faint glow in the kitchen.

"Feeling better?" Cliff asked.

"Maybe a little," Sadie said.

"What happened?"

"My kids think my mouth is costing them customers. Hammie's company has been offered a big contract—to shut me up, I'm sure."

"OOOOH," Cliff cooed. "That's good news. ICS knows your name and they're trying to figure out ways to slow you down. You're making a dent."

"You think? Maybe I should back off a little…take a vacation?"

"You want to take a vacation? I've got a condo in Southport. We could leave right now."

"Together?"

Cliff mocked surprise. "Of course together. I'm the one with the keys. It's got two bedrooms, two baths."

Sadie started to laugh. "Most guys ask you out to dinner first."

"Dinner? We have dinner together every night."

"I was thinking someplace other than the Quaker Café." Already she felt better, the tension in her back slipping away.

"Okay, we could do that. Drive to Southport, spend a couple of nights, have dinner wherever you like. I'll pay or you pay, whichever makes you feel better."

Sadie picked up the plastic glass and took her time as she measured her response. She wasn't sure what to say. She still missed Coen, although it had been five years. She missed cuddling with him in bed every night, the wake-up kiss in the morning, the way he called her Love and never once criticized how she looked or dressed. It was the little things she'd taken for granted.

"You know, I loved Coen," she said.

"Of course, you did, and I loved Julia. We've both been lucky in marriage. Maybe that's why I'm not willing to give up hope that there's someone else out there that could make the magic happen again."

Sadie raised her eyebrows and straightened up. Since his return to Cedar Branch she had grown quite fond of her renewed friendship with Cliff and their daily meals together. He made her laugh. He valued her opinion. Since he'd left Cedar Branch as a relatively young man, he'd become more worldly. He talked about possibilities she'd not considered in life. Perhaps getting out of town was exactly what she needed. Every day was a constant barrage of new problems with no time to eat or sleep.

"Two bedrooms?" she asked. "Two baths? Dinner on you?"

"Yep," he said with a twinkle in his eye."

"What about Smokey?"

"We'll drive by your duplex, pick up a box of reading material and Smokey's gear and some god-awful flannel pajamas for you to wear, and we'll go! Could be there by eleven tonight. I'll have you back on Wednesday all refreshed and rehearsed for your first television appearance on Thursday. How's that?"

Sadie felt a sudden burst of adventure. "What about the kids?"

"The kids?" Cliff joked. "You told me you just had a squabble with the kids. It would do them good not to know where you are. Leave a note. *Took a vacation*, or some such thing. We won't be gone that long."

"Right," Sadie said. She could feel the warm glow of the stump juice gliding through her veins. She hadn't done anything silly since Coen had died. It was time to step off the grid.

As they headed out the back door, Cliff said, "Thanks a lot Teensy. We're taking off now." He stopped and pulled two twenties out of his pocket. "I'll give you this for the rest of that bottle up there." He eyed the bag of sugar.

Teensy looked at the bills, took her time lumbering to the shelf, her wide hips avoiding the handles of the clean pots so as not to knock them off the counter. She pulled down the local brew. "There you go, hon," she said. "If you go blind, I never saw the stuff."

Chapter Nine

"Clifford, how you doin' man?" Zan sang out over the air waves. "Hadn't heard from you in a couple of days. Where you been hiding?"

"Took some time off."

"Ohhhhhh," Zan crooned. "Got anything you want to share?"

"Did you hear about the break-in over the weekend in Cedar Branch?" Cliff started the entertainment segment of his banter. "Hoole's pharmacy across from the Quaker Café. We thought at first it might be in retaliation for all the NO signs they've got plastered all over their windows, but it ends up the crook was just after something he could sell on the street."

"So they got him, huh?"

"Well, there's a story to that."

"Somehow I knew there'd be." Zan sat back.

"Years ago when they closed the old jail, Chase Hoole, the pharmacist, bought one of the jail cell doors and installed it on the back entrance to his pharmacy. Seemed to think that would deter any thieves. Well, this airhead shows up in the middle of the night and attaches a chain to the axle on his truck and then to the door and he pulls the dern thing off. Then he simply backs his truck in and grabs all of the oxycodone, hydrocodone, morphine and codeine. Guess he was planning to whip up a few cocktails." Cliff is cackling and Zan is all smiles waiting for the punch line.

"He got what he came for, but he triggers an alarm in the process and panics. In an attempt to get back out the door, he forgets to unhook the chain. The jail door swings sideways and jams in the door and pulls the axle right out from under his truck. They said he was throwing bottles out of his window as fast as he could when the police arrived. I guess he thought the cops might not be able to prove he'd stolen anything if the evidence was lying in the ditch."

"I swear I don't know what's in the water down your way." The sound of Zan's laugh was loud and clear. "Anything new with ICS?"

Cliff hardly paused. “So the latest is that Mary Law has broken her contract with ICS and returned the earnest money.”

“End game. You won.” Listeners heard Zan slap the table.

“Boy, wouldn’t I like to believe that, but these folks are slippery. Caren Drake and the colonel have been back and forth to Raleigh a bunch of times this week. Met with the governor once. Course, it was a private meeting. We weren’t allowed in.”

“You guys tailing them or something?”

“We have our sources.”

“I’m sure you could liven up the conversation.”

“We try,” Cliff said. “There’s a town board meeting in another week and we’ve already heard that they’ve asked the county sheriff to send down a dozen men. They’re hunkering down into combat mode. Won’t allow any public comments.”

“Why not?”

“They say they don’t plan to discuss the incinerator. Of course, we’re going anyway. Don’t trust ‘em anymore. Come early if you want a seat inside.”

“You have something up your sleeve?”

Listeners could hear Cliff chuckle over the airwaves. “We’re serving up free hotdogs is all…maybe a little entertainment.”

*****

Sadie camped out on the town hall steps at five for the seven o’clock meeting. Another dozen people had joined her by five-thirty. A few had seen one of her television appearances and commented on how well she’d done.

Betty Tesh arrived early with dozens of homemade pamphlets listing possible problems involved in handling and disposing of hazardous waste. Betty had become an avid CAP supporter who had taken on the role of media coordinator. Looking like everyone’s favorite grandmother who spent her days in the kitchen, she’d emerged as a talented public relations dynamo. She simplified hard-to-understand facts and hounded the news media relentlessly. Every editor, reporter and television news broadcaster recognized her voice.

Phil Harper showed up with a loud speaker and his guitar. Phil tuned his guitar and warmed up with a few bars of several familiar songs. Pretty soon a banjo and fiddle player joined him.

Cliff arrived in a food vending truck which he opened up in the parking lot and began to grill hot dogs. A donation box rested on the hood of the van. A patrol car pulled into the drive and Chief Meacham approached him. "Do you have a vendor license, Mr. Lyons?"

"Not selling anything, Chief. Providing refreshments is all. No law against that, is there?"

"No sir, there's not." Meacham watched the crowd growing out of the corner of his eye.

"Want one?"

"No thanks," the chief said. "Keep it upbeat. No trouble, okay?"

"Who me? Trouble?" Cliff handed three more people hot dogs as he spoke and thanked them as they each put a few bills in the box.

Meacham and two county officers walked over to the town hall. The town clerk unlocked the front door and resumed her position at a table as head bouncer. Sadie was front and center. They had agreed that it might be best for Phil Harper to remain outside. No need for the media to see the same person harassing the colonel. Instead of a one-man show, they wanted the public to see the involvement of the community.

The music ramped up and the trio launched into the first of several verses played to the tune of *Where Have You Been Billy Boy.*

Where have you been
Colonel Little, Colonel Max?
Where have you been
cunning Colonel?
To Raleigh and back
with Cedar Branch in your sack
Did you sell us
for just a bit of money?

What have you done
Colonel Little, Colonel Max?
What have you done
cunning Colonel?
You can't look us in the eye
because you told a big fat lie
Come November
we plan to send you running.

Five more verses had a rhyme about each of the town board members and the grand finale was a repeat of the first verse. Most of the crowd appeared to enjoy the diversion. Others were not so amused. The news media got some footage.

From there the trio launched into the tune of *Tom Dooley* with the chorus repeated after each verse.

Hang down your head, Max Little
Hang down your head and cry.
Hang down your head, Max Little.
What else you gonna try?

You met with the governor
outside the county line.
Didn't want the public
to know what's on your mind.

You restrict public meetings.
Speaking out just won't do.
You claim to need protection.
But who protects us from you?

This time tomorrow while
we're shoveling up your mess.

You'll be smoozing with the governor
and the CEO at ICS.

You came here to retire.
Where folks are kind and life is slow.
You pulled one over on us.
It's time for you to go.

A cheer broke out at the end of each verse and pretty soon everyone around the minstrels sang the chorus with them. Cliff opened twenty packs of hot dogs and buns, passing them out as fast as they came off the grill. Captured by the mood, a few members in the crowd took off for the grocery and brought back ten more packs. A party atmosphere prevailed.

In the town hall, the colonel grew increasingly annoyed at the noise outside. He got up from the table and spoke privately to Chief Meacham. Sadie watched with some amusement as the chief shook his head no. It pleased her to no end that the music and singing were getting under the colonel's skin.

The reporters who had been allowed in the room gradually found the routine business mundane. The agenda didn't have anything referencing the incinerator issue. The only thing to note was that Mary Law's seat remained empty, which negated their opportunity to ask her any questions. Gradually, the press wandered outside where the interviews and photos had more viewer appeal.

Betty Tesh pounced on each of them, pumping them full of information. *What is hazardous waste? What happens to the parts that aren't destroyed? How much will be shipped to this plant? How does this affect the citizens?*

Inside, the town board finally got around to new business. Dick Evers, the longest serving member, ran his hand across the thin strands of hair above his right ear and stared at a paper in front of him. With his head bowed and no inflection whatsoever in his voice, he read verbatim, "I would like to recognize a request from six citizens for the noncontiguous annexation of a tract of land containing one hundred and eighty acres which is located two point eight miles southwest of town. I have in my hands a valid petition signed by the owners of the property. I make a motion that we turn this petition over to the town clerk to certify that all owners signed below agree to the annexation at which point the town board will set a date for a public hearing as required under the law."

All heads in the room shot up. Weary eyelids popped opened. Shoulders straightened. Colonel Little said, "I have a motion on the table, do I have a second?"

"I so second," said Wade Gorman, the fifth town board member.

"I have a motion and a second, is there any discussion?" the colonel asked, expecting none.

Rod Palmateer started to speak. He paused long enough for the colonel to attempt to ignore him, but then interrupted. "I'm having…" he cleared his throat a second time, his voice rattling, emitting a sort of frog croak… "I'm having second thoughts."

The intensity of the colonel's look couldn't be mistaken.

"Given the reaction from the community to ICS, I would like to suggest we take this annexation very slowly." Rod pushed his glasses up the bridge of his nose.

"Mr. Palmateer," the colonel's tone was a reprimand, "one does not second guess which way the train is going after it leaves the station. This train left long ago and you sir, have already bought your ticket."

Rod raised one eyebrow and tilted his chin to the left in response to the colonel.

"If I have no further discussion, I have a motion on the floor to review a request for a noncontiguous annexation of land outside our town limits. All in favor say aye."

Wade Gorman and Dick Evers both said aye and raised their hands. The colonel sat back hard in his chair and looked first at Rod and then over at Lucy Woodright.

"Nay," said Rod. The room went still.

"Nay," said Lucy in a whisper so low most people could only see her lips move.

A murmur began to build in the room. One person started to applaud, and then two.

The colonel hammered his gavel to stop the applause. With a clinched fist on the table top he said in a clear voice, "In the event of a tie, the mayor is allowed to vote. "Aye," he said and gaveled the table a second time. "The motion passes. Clerk, would you please verify the signatures of this request and inform the board of their validity at which point we will schedule a public hearing. Do I have a motion to adjourn?"

Without waiting for a reply, the colonel jerked back his chair, motioned to Caren Drake to follow and stormed from the room. One reporter scrambled to corral him, shouting, "Whose selling the land?" but it was useless.

The town clerk bolted to the side office and barricaded herself behind the door with the petition in hand while the four board members left through the backdoor with no comment.

Sadie shoved her way through the crowd in an effort to find someone who understood what had just happened. The throng buzzed. People turned to one another seeking an explanation. No one knew.

*****

"So Clifford, you all put on quite a show down in Cedar Branch last night. Been waiting for your call." Zan's voice echoed across the airwaves.

"They pulled a fast one on us," Cliff said. "I had to talk to a lawyer and the county magistrate to figure out what the board did."

"Okay, can you explain it to us? We thought when the land option with Mary Law folded you had won. So what's the deal?"

"Here's how it stands. ICS needs at least a hundred and fifty acres within the town limits of Cedar Branch because… and this is very important… ICS wants to be under the zoning and environment restrictions of Cedar Branch and not the county."

"Why is that?"

"Because Cedar Branch is less stringent. Every one of their regulations state that they can review but not regulate industry emissions."

"You're kidding. The town doesn't have to conform to the county restrictions?"

"Nope. Crazy, isn't it? The state and county can put in requirements on water table levels, gas emissions, proximity to schools, etcetera and if a local municipality invites a company to build and wants to exempt that industry from those same regulations, they can do so."

"Man, that makes no sense," Zan said.

"Sad but true," Cliff continued. "So what ICS has done is put together a land deal with six land owners outside the town limits. Now the mayor and board members have to approve the annexation to make if official. Then the land will fall under the environmental policy of Cedar Branch."

"These pieces of property don't even border the town. Am I right?" Zan asked.

"That's right," Cliff said. "That's why it's called a *non-contiguous* annexation. They're literally jumping over county property and incorporating a parcel of one hundred and eighty acres into the town zoning."

"I can't believe that's legal."

"It is," Cliff said.

"So what's next? What can you do?"

"Several people have filed a temporary restraining order and an injunction to stop the town from proceeding with the annexation. The town board has to wait for a ruling before they can take it any further."

"Will that stop them?" Zan asked.

"It's hard to say," Cliff said. "It's a stall tactic. Could take a month, maybe more if we're lucky. If it fails, the town still has to schedule a public hearing with thirty days' notice before they can vote on the annexation. That takes us until April or May. The closer we can get to the November election, the better off we are."

"So no chance of closing them down until the election?" Zan asked.

"I didn't say that. There's a better option. Two of the town board members are having second thoughts and might vote against the annexation. If we can get Mary Law on our side, they'd have a three-two vote against it. The mayor wouldn't have any say-so. It would be over."

"Then you could end it?" Zan asked.

"We think so."

"How did Miss Mary vote last night?"

"She didn't. She didn't show up," Cliff said.

"I'll bet she's a hot tamale about now."

"You bet. The mayor, neighbors, reporters, and state officials are all trying to talk to her as we speak."

"Do you know the names of those people who offered to sell their land? You just need one or two to change their minds."

Cliff shook his head. "I asked to see the annexation requests this morning. Per norm, the town clerk is sitting on them tighter than a goose on the golden egg. She told me I could get a copy at the end of the week."

"Should we expect more protests over the weekend in Cedar Branch?" Zan asked.

"We're discussing strategy now," Cliff said. "If protests would convince the board members to listen to us, then we'll protest. If what it takes is more personal one-on-one communication for them to appreciate our valid concerns, then we'll do that."

"Listen, let's schedule a time for you to come up to the station for a call-in. Maybe Caren Drake or Colonel Little will join us. Would you be willing?"

"Sure, I'll come, but so far they haven't shown up anywhere they don't have to."

After he hung up the phone, Cliff slumped into his chair. This weekend could be tense. What he knew but hadn't told Zan was that there was a high probability that the landowners on the outskirts of town were all black. That threatened to ignite an entirely different set of issues and possibly divide the supporters they had. When you added race to the mix, things got dicey.

Chapter Ten

Sadie sat across the table from Cliff at the Quaker Café and nursed her glass of sweet tea while they waited for their hamburgers and fries. He had picked the first daffodils growing across the street and placed them in a glass of water in front of her. The yellow lilies reminded her that even though another freeze might be just around the corner, Spring was on its way.

Billie walked in the door, sat down and spied the flowers. "Nice," she said. "Who picked those?"

"Cliff put them there. Pretty aren't they?" Sadie said.

"Anything going on between you two that I should know about?" Billie asked. "You're wearing lipstick lately, putting on skirts and blouses, letting your hair grow out."

Sadie blushed. "Just got inspired after my television interviews. I realized I feel better when I occasionally get out of my frumpy clothes."

The café had been somewhat neutralized by Miss Ellie's good-manners protocol. Both the CAPs and the PROs, had rearranged themselves at different tables. Conversation remained polite but strained.

"Afternoon, Colonel, how's Millie doing today?" Cliff asked when the colonel wedged through to the VIP table in the back. The colonel had taken a chair that had been reserved for a judge who had once eaten three meals a day in the café prior to his death. Hs table companions had appeared amused but tolerated the colonel's assumption that the chair was his for the taking.

"She's good," the colonel said in a monotone. He ignored Sadie.

Sadie wanted more than anything to yank his chair out from under him when he sat down. It had become harder and harder to even be in the same room, but she wouldn't give up her right to come and go from the Quaker Café as she pleased.

"We should go back there and sit with them," Sadie said after the colonel was out of earshot. "Just to mix things up."

"We could, but then you'd be sitting between the colonel and Helen Truitt."

In recent weeks, Helen had made a point of moving up from her corner table in the room to sit next to the colonel. Sadie loved it. "That's probably his greatest challenge at meals now—having Helen yakking in his ear."

The front door opened and at first a few heads turned and then one table at a time ceased conversation. It was unusual for a stranger to stumble into the Quaker Café and when one did, everyone took note.

Her skin was the color of chocolate, as clear and unblemished as Sadie had ever seen. She was slim and tall, in some ways Caren Drake's dark skinned double, but with a greater level of sophistication. Class dripped off of her like melted gold. If one had to guess, they'd probably assume she had an advanced degree in the arts. Marketing would be beneath her.

"I'm looking for Sadie Baker," she said. "The pharmacist told me to check here."

Cliff put some weight on his cane and rose to his feet. "You found her," he said nodding at Sadie. "Care to join us?" All eyes were on them now.

"May I have a moment of your time?" she asked.

"You may have as much of my time as you'd like," Cliff said. "As for Sadie, you'll have to ask her."

What an old flirt, Sadie thought. She'd have to remember to tease him about it later. "What can I do for you?" Sadie asked.

The woman glanced around the room seemingly oblivious to the stares. "Could the three of us talk someplace privately?" she said.

Cliff did an informal head count of the PROs in the café.

"Order up," Miss Ellie said as she placed hamburgers and fries on the table. She acknowledged the woman who had just entered. "Can I get you anything, hon?" she asked.

"Would you mind if we ate in the back room?" Sadie shifted her eyes to the hallway.

"Of course not." Miss Ellie picked up the two platters and headed towards the back. Sadie grabbed her sweet tea and silverware and motioned the woman to follow.

"Excuse us, Billie, won't you?" Cliff said.

"Don't worry about me," Billie said. "I can always find good company. You three take care of business." Sadie knew Billie would be all over her as soon as the woman left to get the details.

Cliff steadied his cane and moved with unprecedented speed, obviously enjoying the attention and intrigue of the moment.

"Well, who does she think she is?" Helen Truitt said with some exasperation from the VIP table.

The woman seemed to have a very clear picture of who she was. The colonel pivoted to the side of his chair. A beautiful woman. A beautiful *black* woman. "Something's up," he said. He turned to Helen. "Go tell Caren Drake to get down here right away."

*****

While Sadie and Cliff pulled three of the folding chairs up around the table and after Miss Ellie left, the woman began. "My name is Audrey Garner, I grew up here. My father is Edward Garner. He lives just outside of town. You know him, I believe?"

"Of course, we know Ed," Sadie said. "Your dad butchered hogs and had a smoke house at one time. He's a regular in our store. We were sorry when your mother passed."

"Thank you," Audrey said, all business. She had yet to smile. "I've been following what's going on with this hazardous waste incinerator. I got involved with the issue when Granville County was the target and I assumed that Cedar Branch would join hands to oust the company the same way other counties have. Then I read—incredulously, I might add," her eyes and nostrils flared slightly, "that the town board had *invited* the company to build practically on top of my father's property. Obviously, the board has been bribed."

"We can't prove that," Cliff put his hand up. "We think you're probably right, but we only know for sure that one town board member had plans to sell land. She has since withdrawn her offer."

"She should resign. That's outrageous—a blatant conflict of interest," Audrey said without mincing any words. "Do you know Dr. Markus Sanders?"

Sadie stared at Cliff in hopes he did. Before either had a chance to respond, Audrey continued. "He's President of the The American Negro Churches Association. He also has a degree in chemistry. He worked on the study called *Toxic Waste and Race*. Ever heard of that?"

"As a matter of fact," Sadie spoke, "Beth Elmore mentioned the report to us."

"Have you read it?"

"Not yet," Sadie said. "There's so much to read."

"You should. This county fits all of the demographics." She reached down into her leather attaché case. "Do you know that race proved to be the most significant variable for placement of all commercial waste facilities? Three out of every five black and Hispanic Americans live within communities with uncontrolled toxic waste sites."

"We'll read the study," Sadie said.

"Here, my gift." Audrey pulled out two copies. She waited a minute while Cliff and Sadie each flipped through the report.

"I know Dr. Sanders personally," she said not waiting for them to look up. "I've already talked to him. He'll fly down from Cleveland if you invite him. I'm willing to pay for his travel."

Sadie and Cliff stopped fingering the pages and looked at her. "That would be great," Sadie said.

"One condition," Audrey said. "I want to be involved in the arrangements. This man has done a lot to expose injustices to the African American communities on a national level. People need to know who he is and appreciate the fact that he's a highly educated and knowledgeable man."

After more discussion and looking at a calendar, Audrey handed them each a business card. "You can contact me at the Blue Cross Blue Shield Corporate Office in Durham. I'm often out training staff, but leave a message and I'll return your call at the end of the day. After I talk with Dr. Sanders, we'll lock in a date."

Sadie and Cliff accompanied Audrey back to the front of the restaurant. Caren Drake had joined the colonel and Helen Truitt. The threesome had moved to a table next to the front door.

Caren rose and extended her hand as Audrey prepared to leave. The two women eyeballed one another. "Have we met? You look so familiar," Caren asked.

"I know who you are," Audrey said without taking Caren's hand. "Is this the mayor?"

"I am, indeed," said the colonel. He feigned a smile and did a partial bow that paid deference to beauty.

Audrey eyed him severely. "Shame on you. Shame. Shame. Shame," she said, turned and walked out the door.

Helen Truitt's eyelashes fluttered. She straightened her back and with her hand at the corner of her mouth sputtered, "Well."

*****

Caren and the colonel left the café and headed directly back to his house. Opening the backdoor he stormed through the laundry room and brushed by Millie in the kitchen, leaving Caren standing next to the clothes dryer. The smell of blueberry cobbler wafted through the air.

"What's the problem?" Millie asked as she peeked around the door.

"Another glitch," Caren said. She walked over next to her. "Could be nothing." She reached into her pocket book to pull out her Nokia cell phone. It wasn't nearly as bulky as the last one she'd had, but the reception was still a problem. She'd discovered Cedar Branch was full of dead zones. "I'm going to step outside just a moment to make a call."

"You do love that silly thing, don't you?" Amused, Millie shook her head.

Standing in the middle of the yard, Caren dialed and cradled the receiver in her hand as she spoke, "I need to know who Audrey Garner is." There was static on the line and she didn't want to have to shout into the receiver in the backyard. "She's in town and could be trouble." She paused and listened for a moment to make sure they'd heard her. "You promised money and backup. I'm expecting you to come through. This could turn into a racial issue. We need to derail it right now."

"There's hot cobbler coming out of the oven." Millie stood at the backdoor and sang out. "That should lift everyone's spirits."

Caren gave her a little wave and a toothy grin wide enough to be seen from where she stood. Millie remained an enigma to her. She took a background seat to the colonel, but Caren had a feeling she had more influence on the colonel than he'd admit.

"Coming." Caren hung up and made her way to the kitchen. Millie handed her a bowl of cobbler with vanilla ice cream on top. "Really, Millie, if you don't stop feeding me I'm going to swell up like a blowfish. I've put on five pounds already." Caren started to refuse the dessert, but knew she couldn't.

"I just worry about you, dear." Millie patted her hand. "Staying over there at Mary's. She's not much of a cook and Teensy's daily specials at the Quaker Café leave a lot to be desired."

"You know, Millie. You're the one who most women in town admire. You're compassionate and understanding. I hope you're advising the colonel when you can. He'd do well to listen to your common sense."

Millie looked back at Caren with big doe eyes and a curl in her lips. "Don't be too hard on him, dear. He's just used to being in control and doesn't quite know how to hand the reins to someone else. You're two of a kind, you know."

"I'm not short," Caren said in jest.

"No, of course, you're not, but you feel others don't take you seriously because you're a woman. Same thing."

Caren took the cobbler and forged ahead to the living room to try to calm the colonel. She knew he'd be seething. As soon as she sat down, the colonel shook his finger in her face. Her moment of empathy vanished and she wanted to grab that finger and snap it off.

"If that woman starts getting the black community riled up," he warned, "they may convince one or more of the land owners to withdraw their annexation request. That's the problem with trying to keep six people in line instead of just one."

"It didn't turn out so well with just one," Caren said, hitting a nerve. It was a mistake.

The colonel gave her a knee-jerk response. "And whose fault was that? We set you up so you're living with the woman for God's sake."

"You also set me up to disregard a flagrant violation of public trust. It was doomed from the start. You'd never get away with that in Raleigh."

"Don't give me any holier than thou talk about Raleigh. It's the governor pushing this deal through so I don't need a lecture on ethics. Come up with some solutions," he demanded. "Get on top of this. That's what you're paid to do."

Caren bit her tongue. She'd inflamed the conversation and realized she needed to soften her approach. She pulled out a legal pad and started to list things as fast as they came to mind. "We haven't done enough with the black ministers. They're a powerful group. The governor needs to meet with them. Take them to see that hazardous waste facility down in South Carolina. I'll call the Businesses for Advancing Growth and have them schedule a program for local business leaders. They can afford to wine and dine a few people. And the town is going to need a commitment for some high power legal representation in order to respond to the open meeting law charges and the restraining order."

"Now you're talking." The colonel seemed pleased with her shift in demeanor. "I'll talk to the governor. We need to get out in front of this negative publicity with some other high-profile names. I'll not be the only one with his neck on the chopping block."

"Call the governor," Caren said without another word, although she was sure his call would be relegated to someone else. The colonel's instincts were right, however. If the deal went south, it wouldn't be the governor taking the blame, and it sure as hell wasn't going to be her. The governor would leave office and walk into some cushy job where he'd get paid more for his contacts than his accomplishments. She was already thinking about how to exit this mess with her reputation and credentials intact. No sir, their sacrificial lamb would be the colonel. If they lost, he'd lose any hopes of regaining the level of respect he once had. He'd go out like fireworks on the fourth of July—a flash in the sky—then be forgotten.

*****

Audrey Garner had arranged for every newspaper, radio and television station in the area to carry the announcement that Dr. Markus Sanders would be visiting Cedar Branch. She'd set up a private luncheon in the best restaurant within twenty miles of Cedar Branch. The Quaker Café was not an option. She remembered when she was a child that her father and mother were not welcomed in the main dining room. She found a relatively new restaurant without the history.

She sent out personalized invitations to over fifty black ministers in the county. Churches flourished on every street corner. Most had less than two dozen members and built their sanctuary in a closed storefront or gas station. Some still operated out of homes with hopes to one day have enough of a following to build brick and mortar. With names like *House of the Holy Redeemer* and *The Promise of Everlasting Life*, they were led by both male and female pastors who had demonstrated a gift to bring their congregation to their feet.

Audrey hoped at least thirty-five pastors would attend her luncheon. When only five showed up, she and Dr. Sanders sat surrounded by empty chairs and an over abundance of food. "Pack it up," she instructed the caterer. "We'll take it to one of the churches to distribute."

"So what happened?" Dr. Sanders asked.

"I don't know exactly. I didn't see this coming."

"Have you got the phone numbers for these ministers?" Sanders asked.

"Yes."

"Give them to me. I'll going to start making some calls."

*****

The first call was to the Reverend Jeremiah James, a wiry man with a booming voice that filled both the inside and outside circumference of the church. Neighbors joked that they didn't have to attend the service to hear every word he preached.

"Dr. Sanders, how very good to hear from you. I'm so sorry I was unable to make your luncheon today… a prior commitment, I couldn't cancel." Reverend James sounded warm and friendly. "I hope it went well."

"Thank you, Reverend. I bring greetings from the American Negro Church Association. I missed the opportunity to speak to you. I'm hoping you have a few minutes to talk." Phone in hand, Reverend Sanders looked across the table at Audrey and nodded.

"Indeed, I always have time for you, sir."

"I'm sure you know why I'm in town. I'm sitting in Ed Garner's house right now, within a mile of where the proposed site will be for the hazardous waste incinerator. I've been studying this issue for several years and it's not a good thing for your community."

"Over there at Ed's? Why Reverend, you should come by my church. I'd love to see you. I'm here now."

"Thank you, I really appreciate that, but I only have a few more hours and I want to talk to as many ministers as possible." Dr. Sanders put his hand over the speaker and mouthed to Audrey, "Stalling."

"There's a report that the ANCA has done. I'd like for you to read it," he said into the phone.

"You know," Reverend James cleared his throat, "I've looked at that report and you raised a lot of valid concerns. The difference is that this incinerator is using much newer technology than those other places in your research. This incinerator will be monitored. I don't think we're talking about the same things."

Dr. Sanders rolled his eyes. He'd heard this argument ad infinitum. "Reverend, the people monitoring are the same people who own the company. It is not in their best interest to give accurate reports."

"Not according to what I've been told. The governor has assured us that the state will keep a close watch on things. They plan to take a health inventory of the surrounding area prior to the implementation of the facility. In addition, we'll be getting an expanded health department with a commitment to bring in another doctor and two physician's assistants within the next two years. There will be additional services for children and the elderly. Workers will qualify for an annual physical and free medical care."

Dr. Sanders took a deep breath and shook his head. "The ministers met with the governor?"

"We did."

"How long ago was that?"

"A couple of weeks. A team of experts took us down to see a similar facility in South Carolina. The facility we saw was clean. The workers spoke highly of the operation."

"I'm sure they did," said Dr. Sanders. "Reverend, did *these experts* tell you that toxic facilities were most frequently placed in communities with a majority black or Hispanic population?"

"We discussed that concern with people from the Economic Development Office, and we were assured that they worked hard to develop projects that would bring growth to underdeveloped areas of the state. There are only certain industries that are attracted to an area such as ours."

"I don't think you really believe that," Dr. Sanders said.

There was a long silence.

"I don't mean to be disrespectful in any way, Doctor, but I'm not sure you fully understand. My people work in the tobacco fields eleven to twelve hours a day getting exposed to nicotine, pesticides, and extreme heat. They work both sides of conveyer belts in cold, damp rooms with deafening machines roaring all around them as they deal with razor sharp tools to process chickens by the thousands. They develop respiratory problems from decomposing waste on corporate hog farms. They work second shifts at night as catchers loading hundreds of chickens onto trucks. We've been working in dangerous conditions all of our lives. At least with this plant, people will get a decent pay check and health insurance."

"I do know," Dr. Sanders said. "Honestly, I *do* know. I understand what parents have to do to put food on the table when they struggle to stay afloat from day to day. I'm asking you to help your congregation see the long term consequences." He looked at Audrey and frowned. He was losing the argument.

Reverend James' voice had become more defiant. "You think growing up without food on the table is less dangerous than growing up in the vicinity of an incinerator? ICS is offering starting salaries at eight dollars an hour. That's twice as much as most of my church members get paid now. Do you know what that might mean for many of my families? They wouldn't have to work two jobs. Mothers could stay home with their children. They could buy fresh fruit, more vegetables. They could go to the doctor when they're sick—see a dentist. I'm sorry, Dr. Sanders, but I'm having a difficult time understanding why this is more important to you than all the other risks we take to make a living."

"It's not more important, Reverend. It's one of many concerns that I have. I just feel as if the state government and local officials are making promises to you they won't keep."

"Don't think we haven't discussed that."

At this point Dr. Sanders knew that their discussion had ended. They'd both made their points. In a last ditch effort to find some middle ground he added, "I'll be speaking at a public meeting in Cedar Branch tonight, I'd be honored if you'd come and hear me."

"Thank you, sir. I'll try to make it and I do appreciate your call. May I, in turn, ask you for a favor?"

"Of course."

"There are six families in my congregation who have just been offered the opportunity of a lifetime. If this plant goes through, they stand to gain hundreds of thousands of dollars each. Their lives will be transformed. These are good people. There are more than thirty children and grandchildren who would benefit. Better education. A new start." He stopped. Then in a voice that was a plea more than a request he said, "Don't ruin it for them Dr. Sanders. Don't call on them to make that sacrifice."

"God bless you," Dr. Sanders said. "These are difficult decisions for everyone. You're all in my prayers."

"And you, sir, are in mine."

*****

Dr. Sanders talked with twenty other pastors that afternoon, conversations that turned out to be quite similar to the one he'd had with Reverend James. Reverend James did not come to his presentation that evening. Three of the ministers he'd spoken to that afternoon showed up, but it was a predominantly white crowd. He was preaching to the choir.

Chapter Eleven

Sadie hardly slept anymore. Every hour that she didn't juggle phone calls or try to put out fires, she was either with Cliff and Billie talking strategy or at Phil's planning for CAP meetings. Committee meetings occurred two to three times each week. She worried about Phil. He needed to be in his fields. Spring planting was underway and he was already two weeks behind.

Superior Court Judge Hassell had dismissed the petition brought by the Cedar Branch citizens to stop the annexation process. He ruled that the plaintiffs, as private citizens, had no standing involving voluntary annexation and that the court lacked jurisdiction in the case. Shortly after Hassell's ruling, the town board met for exactly five minutes. They set the date for the public hearing for May 22, 1996, at 7 pm, and adjourned.

"We're losing momentum." Cliff worried. "Everyone hoped we'd win the case in the courts and be done. We've got to ramp things up again. We've become old news."

Sadie, Cliff and Betty Tesh sat around Billie's kitchen table folding flyers to go out in a bulk mailing. Betty had realized they could mail to the entire county for the same price as individual stamps on letters to Cedar Branch residents. They'd scheduled a balloon launch for the weekend. Billie reviewed the final plans. Cinnamon buns and coffee mugs graced the center of the table.

"I've called every radio and television station in the state, plus all of the newspapers," Betty said. "Hopefully we'll get some good press. They keep asking for action photos. They're bored with a room full of people and a speaker at a podium. This will give them something different."

"I think we should hang the governor in effigy," Cliff blurted out suddenly. He twisted in his chair, got up to stretch his bad leg and leaned on the kitchen counter. "A balloon launch is lame. We need to turn some heads in a hurry… up the ante."

"I don't know." Billie wrinkled her nose and stopped folding flyers. "That's a bit harsh, don't you think. People might perceive it as a threat."

"As well it should be," Cliff said. "I think Sadie nailed it when she used the word *rape*. The state government gives the town board five thousand dollars of taxpayer money for *educational purposes* that exclude anyone who wants to speak against it and then they pay Caren Drake three thousand dollars a month as a consultant. On top of that Mary Law gets our tax money to provide room and board for the consultant. We're no dummies. We all know what Caren's being paid to do with our money. Everyone's howling about us bringing in outsiders, but no one's complaining about the governor using his vast tax-funded assets to ram this down our throats. He's the predator in this game. I say let's lynch him."

Sadie got up from her chair and walked over to Cliff. She took his hand in hers. "Hey, Lone Ranger," she said. "We're all tired. Let's take a break."

Cliff closed his eyes and dropped his chin. Sadie gave him a slight tug. "Come on, let's get some fresh air." Sitting in the corner, Smokey immediately came to attention. "You too, Smokey…outside," she said.

When the door closed behind them, Betty looked up from her pile of folded flyers and watched the two of them sit down in the rockers on the porch. She could see Sadie rubbing Cliff's arm and talking to him. "Sooooo, something going on there I don't know about?" she asked.

"They're together a lot these days," Billie said.

"They go way back, you know," Betty said. "Were best buddies through high school."

"Boyfriend—girlfriend?" Billie asked.

"Nope, just good friends. They had a lot of laughs together, liked to play pranks on one another, the kind where you put salt in the sugar bowl or hide their books until just before class—silly stuff. Sadie dated several guys. Met Coen at a football game her senior year in high school and they became a couple. Cliff joined the army after graduation and we didn't see much of him after that. He married a nurse up north. Has one son who lives in New York City and plans to stay there."

Billie pulled out a pink magic marker and started drawing little smiley faces next to the return address on the flyers. "It's good to know old friendships last," she said.

Betty looked at the artwork and raised an eyebrow, but said nothing. She let Billie do her thing. Billie always got results and if she wanted to add a bit of sunshine to an address label, then why not?

"I hope this balloon launch is a pick-me-up for everyone," Betty added, her attention back to the flyers. "It should be fun—balloons going up, barbeque and Brunswick stew, a bake sale and some music."

"It'll be good," Billie assured her. "Everyone's ready for a good time."

"Anyone heard any more from Mary Law?" Betty asked.

"Not a word," Billie sighed. "I've tried to call. Her daughter came into town shortly after the last meeting and took her to Edenton. She's screening all of Mary's phone calls and won't let anyone talk to her about the incinerator. We don't even know whether Rod and Lucy will still vote against the annexation. They're getting a lot of pressure. Caren Drake is still at Mary's house. Doesn't answer the phone. Only uses that silly cell phone she totes around."

The side door opened and Smokey bounded through, jumping up and pawing at Billie. He'd learned she had dog treats she kept in her pocket for her own dog and if he begged, he'd get one. She pulled out a mini milk bone. Cliff and Sadie walked back in, closing the outside door behind them.

"Cliff and I are going to set up a strategy committee within CAP to help plan…what did you call it, Cliff… silly capers?"

"Covert operations," Cliff corrected her. "Operations that are confidential. Just the people involved will be privy to the plans."

Billie stared at Sadie. "Nothing illegal?"

"Nope," Cliff looked somewhat annoyed. "I'm a former cop. I'm not about breaking any laws."

"Just silly capers," Sadie emphasized. "No one gets hurt…nothing damaged."

"No one gets hurt," Cliff repeated. "Just like the coffin at the public meeting. Something to get attention and annoy our opponents. We'll meet separately from CAP."

Betty still looked doubtful. "Are we going to tell CAP members about this committee?" she asked.

"Hell no. That defeats the purpose. This is all hush hush… under the table so to speak. The fewer people who know about it, the better off we are," Cliff said.

"I like it," Billie said in a sudden flare of excitement. "I want in."

"You'd have to keep quiet about whatever gets planned. Can you do that?" Sadie asked.

"Scout's honor," Billie said and raised two fingers in a mock salute. "It just sounds like too much fun to miss."

*****

Sadie smiled in relief when Ada Lynn called and asked her to come help at the store. It was the sort of reprieve that all parents feel when there's been a breech in family communications and no one's quite sure who should apologize first. The blow-up over dinner six weeks before had definitely strained Sadie's relationship with her two boys. She felt she'd handled the television interviews as evenly as possible. She'd avoided the word *rape* and gave researched answers to support her opposition. Ultimately, the newsperson seemed somewhat disappointed as if he'd hoped for more emotion. Sadie had begun to realize that passions would win this fight, not facts.

Ada Lynn had an appointment on Tuesday to take Gabe to Greenville to get tested for allergies, and they needed someone at the register. Sadie went. Dutch remained cool in their interactions. Ada Lynn seemed more willing to engage in their normal chatter on her way out, but Sadie hadn't heard from Hammie at all.

She did her best to be what the pundits called politically correct, but she simply couldn't help herself as she checked out selected customers while working at the store. "Did you get the flyer? Balloon launch south of town, next Saturday at noon. Free balloons for all the kids."

Several people brightened up. Too many didn't remember seeing any flyer.

"Posters and flyers are across the street at the pharmacy."

Dutch stopped at the register to write a check for the Hostess Twinkies driver and eyed his mother. "You aren't selling anything but groceries, right?"

"Of course not," she replied, and felt guilty for lying to him. He looked more tired than usual—older. What was he…thirty-one now? Hell no. Thirty-two. An alarm went off in her head. She'd forgotten his birthday. It had been …the night they'd asked her to come over for dinner together.

The evening was supposed to have been a birthday celebration she realized, and she'd dropped in and stormed out and the whole cake deal had never crossed her mind. Oh, Lord, what else had she forgotten? She began to go over birthday dates in her mind. She'd have to think of some way to make it up to him.

When the afternoon help arrived, she offered to stay on. "Can I help with anything else?" she asked Dutch.

"Think we're good," he said. He placed some local frozen pecan pieces from the fall crop alongside angel food cakes and fresh strawberries. They'd be on special tomorrow.

"I could stock some shelves if you like."

"No, I've got it covered."

"Listen, I forgot your birthday." Sadie placed her hand on his arm. "I'm so sorry. I'd like to make it up to you. What would you like?"

"I'd like for this whole mess to disappear. That's what I'd like."

She did a lip roll. "Have you talked to Hammie lately?"

"A couple of times."

"He still upset at me?"

"He's in a tough spot, Mom. We're all looking at this differently. For me and him it involves business. For you…" he stopped and looked away for a moment. "I don't know what it's about for you."

"Dutch," she said, hurt that he couldn't see it. "It's about you, your kids, the community and what's right. It's about how a democracy is supposed to work."

"Look," Dutch said. "That all sounds good, very patriotic and all, but the bottom line is that we each have to support our families. We get a job and try to pay the bills. If that doesn't work, we get another job. I'm doing my best to make this grocery store work, but if I have to go back to the packing plant for a dependable monthly check, then I won't do that commute again. We'll move anyway, incinerator or not."

"It'll work," Sadie said. "It worked for me and your father for thirty years."

"It's not the same anymore," Dutch said. "It's not just this small town grocery. People are willing to drive farther to get cheaper prices at the chain stores. The wholesalers expect more on their monthly contracts. My fresh produce is coming in from Florida and California instead of five miles down the road. Look at these strawberries here." He picked up a package and pointed to the fine print. "They're being shipped from Mexico, and they're cheaper than the ones I get from Westtown. It's crazy."

"Are you telling me the store is losing money?"

"Business is off. Not a big problem yet, but if it gets worse."

"And you think that's because of me?"

"I didn't say that." He shrugged her off. "It's Tuesday. I've got lots to do."

"Okay," Sadie said, knowing that nothing was okay at all.

She picked up her purse and headed past Marvin's butcher section and through the backdoor where she'd parked her car. Marvin and Teensy were sharing a cigarette break.

With a Coke can in one hand, Marvin raised it in a kind of salute. He had more gray in his hair, not so much, but enough for her to notice. His loose fitting clothes and butcher's apron gave him a boxy appearance—squared off shoulder to shoulder, knee to knee. "Mama Sadie," he nodded.

She liked the way all the employees called her Mama Sadie. It felt more equalizing. Too many in the black community addressed her as Miss Baker or ma'am, but not Marvin. She had always been Mama Sadie to him, despite the fact that there was little age difference. But the two of them had a special relationship. Whenever trouble brewed between the black and white communities, Sadie could count on Marvin to be honest and explain the subtleties that she sometimes failed to understand. She admitted she could never fully appreciate the challenges faced growing up black in a white man's world.

She expected Teensy to make some Tweedle Dee comment. Teensy only arched her caterpillar eyebrows and let the smoke drift over her head. Sadie took a whiff and wanted to climb into the middle of that toxic cloud. There used to be times she'd take a cigarette break right along with them.

"I see you're helping out today," Marvin said. "It's nice having you back in the store."

"Thanks," Sadie smiled. "I miss it." What she really missed was the normalcy of it all: opening up, stocking shelves, greeting customers, the in and out of the vendors, the predictability. How many times in the past weeks had she dreamed of having her old routine? She had underestimated how secure the daily grind made her feel.

"You're way too busy with politics now." Marvin smiled. His statement was an acknowledgement, not an affront. He threw his cigarette on the ground and rubbed it out with the sole of his shoe.

She looked down at the cigarette butt and was tempted to pick it up and throw it in the trash, but didn't. "I've been meaning to talk to you both about everything that's going on. Don't want to put you on the spot, though. I know how it is with Dutch and Miss Ellie."

Marvin reached into his pocket and pulled out his pack of Camels, offered her one. She shook her head.

"It ain't exactly a good time to be climbing on a band wagon around here." Marvin said as he lit his second. Folks at our church are keeping mighty quiet and the minister, well…he's preaching up a storm. He says that folks who are making plenty of money can afford to be concerned about the environment. Them that aren't need to be more concerned about feeding their families."

Teensy grunted. She eyed Marvin first, glanced over at Sadie and then looked to the sky as she took a long drag on the stub still between her fingers.

Sadie watched Teensy inhale and almost felt the cool menthol moving through her own lungs.

"Is that what all the ministers are saying?" Sadie asked still watching the smoke curling though the air.

"Pretty much," Marvin said. "Then of course, we know the folks who got the land options. They're our own. No one wants to stand in the way of them making a little money."

"Do you think I'm on the wrong side, Marvin?" she asked.

"No, I didn't say that." He paused, as if he were in deep thought… picked a bit of loose tobacco off the end of his tongue and flipped it on the ground.

"I've just been thinking if this was such a good thing, they'd be fighting to get it over in Durham or Greensboro or one of them big cities. Nobody would be looking our way. That's what's bothering me. If it's really all that safe and gonna bring in so many jobs, why do they want to stick it way out here away from everybody else? I get suspect sometimes."

"Marvin, I'm worried," Sadie said.

"We all worried, Mama Sadie. Hard choices for everybody right now."

"I don't want anybody to get hurt," Sadie said.

"Nobody does."

"Would you tell me if you heard about anybody planning to do anything that might hurt someone?"

Marvin took a step back, his chin down, his eyes riveted on her. "Mama Sadie. I don't know what you talking about."

"That brick that went through the front window of the town hall?" Sadie said. "They never figured out who did it. A window's one thing. Someone's car or a house is another."

"It's nobody in the black community," Marvin said appearing a bit disappointed that she'd asked. Teensy crossed her thick arms across her bosoms.

Sadie flushed slightly. "I didn't mean to imply that it was. I asked only because you and Teensy hear a lot of things that I don't. I thought maybe if you'd heard someone's name tossed around you might tell me."

There was a strained silence before Marvin spoke again. "We hear of anything we'll let you know."

"Thank you," Sadie said. "All I want to do is talk to them. People are getting pretty riled up, and we want to discourage any violence." She knew she'd already said too much. She'd broken her promise to Dutch one more time and she knew Miss Ellie would not want Teensy getting involved. "Teensy, you give those grans a hug from me." She turned to Marvin. "Please give your wife my regards." With that Sadie slipped into her car and backed away.

*****

The first thing the next morning Sadie stopped by the store on her way to the Quaker Café. Ada Lynn looked more tired and worried than usual. Sadie remembered when Dutch finished high school he had worked for eight years lifting carcasses in packing plants up in Smithfield. Ada Lynn was just out of community college and seven years his junior when they got married. That seemed like so long ago now. Dutch used the money he'd saved to put a down payment on the store and move back to Cedar Branch. She'd assumed they'd be here for the rest of her life.

Sadie picked up Gabe, squeezed him and kissed his cheek.

"Definitely allergies," Ada Lynn said. "The doctor tells me I need to do a deep cleaning of the house. Get rid of a lot of stuff." She looked at Sadie with more of a plea than a statement.

"What's that mean?" Sadie asked as she patted Gabe's back. "Deep clean?"

"The carpets and curtains probably all need to go... most of the fabric covered furniture. I'm going to need to look for another living room set. Everything probably has years of built-up cigarette smoke and dust mites, not to mention mold around the baseboard."

Sadie groaned. Ada Lynn was right. Most of the stuff in the house had been there for decades and both she and Coen had been smokers up until he'd been diagnosed with diabetes.

She'd assumed that things would stay the same for another few years. She didn't have the time or energy right now to deal with the furnishings she'd left behind.

"What do you need for me to do?" Sadie asked.

Ada Lynn sighed. "This is a bit overwhelming. The easiest thing for us to do would be to just start fresh in a new home, but we can't afford that right now."

"Of course not," Sadie said. "Wow, I haven't a clue where to put all of my stuff." *Stuff*, she thought. Thirty-five years of accumulated clutter that she'd hoped someone else might want. She'd die and the children could fight over the valuables, as if there were any, and then come in with a front loader and bury the rest. That was the American way.

Ada Lynn took Gabe from Sadie's arms. "Believe it or not, the store is actually the cleanest place of all...with a janitor and the cleaning company coming in weekly and the floors waxed every month. It's not the store that's the problem; it's my mess in the house."

"Nonsense," Sadie said. "It's mostly mine. You figure out what you want to keep and then I'll deal with the rest."

"Thanks," Ada Lynn said. Sadie thought she looked overwhelmed. She couldn't blame her. Life seemed to be piling up.

Chapter Twelve

The two lane road south of Cedar Branch ran by several small clapboard houses in advance of the fields of peanuts, cotton, and tobacco. It hadn't been too many years ago, no more than thirty, that these houses had been shacks with no heat or indoor plumbing. Lyndon B. Johnson's Great Society, the Rural Housing Service and the affordability of mobile homes improved living conditions for many.

The next twelve miles ambled south between the crops and were broken only by loblolly pines that shot up in parallel rows like arrows aimed at the sun. The timber and the pine straw produced good income of their own, encumbered only by a delayed profit of three seven-year cycles: two of thinning and then a final clear cut. The Hoole family owned a hundred acres of wooded property on the north side of town and Chase Hoole, the pharmacist, joked that he'd only taken home a check once in his lifetime on that crop. He imagined he'd be long gone and his grandchildren would all be driving new cars when the second check came in.

The majority of the black population lived outside town on either side of the ten to fifteen mile stretch between communities. Many worked in the chicken slaughter houses or at hog farms where pigs were raised by the thousands. JC Collier farmed forty acres left to him by his father and raised a couple of cows, pigs and a few chickens. He was one of the few white farmers who lived on Skinner Road. He and his neighbor Ed Garner had grown up side by side and still considered one another best friends.

Times had changed in the past ten years. The chances of making a living off a family farm with six to twelve hogs and a house with laying hens had vanished. No one bought the hogs or chickens except for the companies that had developed a vertical business to contract only with the farmers who signed on with them in the beginning.

Ed and JC were part of the aging fabric in the community: two lone widowers, one black, one white, often seen rocking on the same porch. One's family history dated back to the days of slavery; the other to a coal miner who'd been arrested in Wales and put on a convict ship to Australia. Neither of them knew exactly how their families had landed in Cedar Branch.

They grew up doing most everything together except going to school when JC got on a bus to go in one direction and Ed walked four miles in the other. In the afternoons, they came home to play basketball in the dirt yards with the naked hoop banged onto the side of a barn. Eventually, their brothers and sisters moved on to jobs and towns they hoped would offer them more opportunities. Ed and JC stayed behind and helped one another patch their roofs, feed their children, bury their parents and both of their wives. The joke between the two of them was which one would have to dig the last grave.

On this particular day they watched as the Hooles and Bennetts set up tents to shade the food, and Billie organized the balloon blow-up around the helium tanks.

Even though JC was a good forty pounds lighter than Ed, when he leaned back in the rocker, it creaked as if the slats felt the same weight of time as his bones. Basically, everything creaked once he'd reached his eighties. He had on his John Deere farm hat, would feel naked without it, but today he'd put on a flannel shirt over an open collar pin-striped shirt. Not something he usually wore. Billie had told them there might be reporters taking pictures. He took a bite out of one of the chocolate covered donuts that Sadie had brought along with a thermos of hot coffee in appreciation for allowing CAP to use their land.

Ed got up and walked over to the side of the porch. He'd always been the bigger of the two of them, even when they were kids. He wore a navy blue jacket and a white fedora. The fedora had been a gift from his daughter, Audrey, following one of her return trips from a conference in San Francisco. He loved it and since he no longer worked machinery, he wore it every place he went. It made him feel rather jaunty and people looked at him differently. Instead of a big black man with a scruffy beard, they seemed more inclined to appreciate an elderly gentleman with a cherub face and a sparkle in his eye.

Ed looked out towards the back of JC's property where the flatland gave rise to a gradual incline. "I see you finally got a stone for her."

"She deserved it," JC said. "She put up with me a long time."

"Looks nice. Can see it right clear from here," Ed said.

"Prissy's next to her," JC added. "I didn't put nothing there but a piece of wood with her name."

Ed looked back over his shoulder at JC and chuckled. "Your mule?"

"Yeah," JC nodded. "That ole mule helped me out for a lot of years. Didn't feel like I could send her off to the glue factory in the end."

Ed nodded, reached into his pocket and got out a packet of snuff, pinched off some and stuck it into the side of his cheek. JC's woman and his mule resting side by side…made sense to him.

JC waved in the direction of the would-be incinerator. "I 'bout worked these bones to death and don't see no way to make it on my own no more. Now they gonna build that smoke stack next door. Can't decide whether to fight 'em or just lie down and let the ash blow over me."

"Now lookie here," Ed tried to stand straight. He groaned involuntarily. "Audrey, she's busting down doors over in Raleigh trying to stop this thing."

"I know," JC said. "And if ever there was anyone who could do it, she'd be the one. Lucky for you she got her mama's looks and good sense."

"But it's not just her." Ed got more animated, and as he spoke he stood up straighter and the lines in his face seemed to disappear. "It's these people out yonder." He pointed to the CAP group in their field organizing the balloon launch. "It's the rest of the people in the town. It's you and me. It ain't about lying down. It's about standin' up."

*****

With Smokey on her heels, Sadie joined two dozen other CAP members on Ed and JC's property that straddled the county line. Three tall silver canisters of helium sat in the dirt driveway and an assembly line of volunteers filled the balloons and used magic markers to write *Beware ICS* on the side of each. Then they tucked them under a multicolored parachute that had been stretched out and pegged to the ground. When children came up, they blew their balloons to capacity and used a string to attach them to the children's wrists.

"Not too full," Phil warned helpers to keep the balloons to a medium size. "They'll expand as they go up and the air gets thinner. If they expand too much they'll pop. We don't want that. We want them to catch the wind and go as far as possible."

Beth Elmore had driven over from Raleigh to help out. She and Betty Tesh made their way through the crowd passing out an information sheet on prevailing winds and expected distances and directions the balloons would fly.

"Wherever a balloon lands will give you an idea of where the gases coming off of an ICS stack might end up," Beth kept repeating.

With prevailing winds of a little more than seven and a half miles per hour, they had gotten Sam O'Brien, a local crop duster, to help them figure out potential distances. They were rough guesses, but it was a publicity stunt and they crossed their fingers it might pay off.

"See if you spot any reporters." Sadie surveyed the crowd looking for anyone with a camera. Not one single news network had shown up thus far.

"They say they want a story with a photo op, and we're giving it to them. Where are they?" Cliff asked more to himself than anyone else.

Out of the corner of her eye, Sadie saw Dutch's 1990 Ford Ranger pull off to the side of the road. She watched as Ada Lynn lifted Gabe out of his car seat and walked with him towards them.

Sadie held out her arms as they got closer. Smokey spied Gabe about the same time as Gabe saw the dog and the child braced himself as Smokey came running and jumped on Gabe's chest knocking him to the ground. Instead of tears, the fall brought giggles.

Ada Lynn smiled. "He wants to see the balloons go up."

"Of course he does. Come on, sweetheart." Sadie retrieved Gabe from Smokey's greeting and carried him over to the helium tanks. "What color do you want?"

It felt as if it had been a very long time since Sadie had been outside with Gabe to enjoy an afternoon together. For the next hour they talked with friends around the snack table. Billie had arranged a fundraiser with baked goods. A cluster of men hovered over an outdoor cauldron of Brunswick Stew. As always they debated at which point each ingredient should be added. The pot included cut-up hens, broth, onions, tomatoes, potatoes, butter beans, corn and a list of secret seasoning that depended on the cook that day. When the magic happened and a majority deemed the stew done, it sold for two dollars a bowl or eight dollars a quart. All would be gone within three hours.

Friends and neighbors sat on folding lawn chairs and watched as children laughed and chased one another. Bathed in the warmth of the spring sun and a festive mood, Sadie counted about fifty people. Others arrived to buy stew or homemade cakes and then left. Sadie wanted more than ever to have the town come together like this once again.

As she watched Gabe play, she became aware that he'd start to run with the other children and then lag behind. Within the hour he was at his mother's side complaining of a headache.

"He seems winded, doesn't he?" Sadie asked.

"Allergies. It's spring time," Ada Lynn reminded her. "Maybe Smokey?"

Sadie frowned. "Smokey? You think he might be allergic to dogs?"

"I don't know." Ada Lynn shrugged. "It could be anything or everything. We're just trying to figure it out."

Gabe twisted at the string around his wrist and it slipped off. His balloon drifted up in the air.

"Well, lookie there. A run-away balloon," Sadie said in response to his cry. "That is one brave balloon. It's taking off on an adventure all alone and not waiting for his friends."

There was something hypnotic about space and flight. It never ceased to amaze her. A thought suddenly hit Sadie. They should have color coded the balloons to symbolize the different toxins coming out of ICS' stacks: one color for lead, another for sulfur dioxide, nitrogen oxide, arsenic, antinomy, beryllium, cadmium and so on.

"Come on." Ada Lynn took Gabe's hand. "We'll go get another balloon," and the two of them headed back to the helium tanks.

"I'm a Vietnam Vet." A man's voice from behind Sadie appeared to be for her ears only. Sadie felt the weight of two heavy hands on her shoulders and rough whiskers up next to her ear. She sat bottom heavy in a butterfly chair that made it hard for her to twist around to see who had spoken.

"Don't turn," the voice said. "Just listen. If ICS doesn't get out of town, I can blow up a few things. Me and my friends know how to make accidents happen."

"No, oh no, no, no," Sadie sputtered. "No violence. We don't want any violence."

By now, Gabe had a new balloon and was running to her with his arms out. The hands released her and Sadie struggled to get up as Gabe jumped into her arms. Holding Gabe she turned in time only to see the back of a dark haired man in an army jacket melt into the crowd. "Did you see who that was?" she asked Ada Lynn.

"Who who was?"

"Did you see that man who was behind me?" Sadie asked.

Ada Lynn looked confused. "There are a lot of people behind you."

Sadie's heart skipped a beat. How did the man know her? Who was involved when he said we? Did she need to report the incident to the police?

She turned again to look for someone with a beard and saw instead a reporter from the *Virginia Pilot* newspaper. "I think some folks in Virginia might pay more attention if one of these balloons lands in their back yard," the reporter said.

"We hope so," Sadie said. "Thanks for coming. Wish there were more of you."

"There's another." She pointed back to the two houses. "I saw a photographer taking pictures of Ed and JC. Didn't recognize him. He's not local."

*****

"Ladies and Gentlemen, we have a special guest with us today," Zan opened up his morning talk show. "As promised, Clifford Lyons is here in the studio in the flesh. As most of you already know, they had a big weekend out in Cedar Branch with balloons. Let me say that the event generated a lot of interest. Our switchboard is lit up."

"Good morning, Clifford," Zan continued. "Your balloon fest and that article in the *Virginia Pilot* freaked out some folks along the Virginia border just north of here. Are you willing to take some questions from our listeners?"

"You bet. Bring 'em on." A wide grin spread across Cliff's face. This was exactly the response he had hoped for.

Zan flipped the speaker and took the first caller. "Tell that son-of-a" bleep went the audio sound, "that he doesn't know his earhole from his," *bleep*. Zan disconnected and shook his head. "Well listeners that is why we have an on-off switch."

"Didn't quite catch the question there," Cliff chuckled, "but the voice sounded familiar… like maybe." He stopped. "No, no, I won't say his name on the air."

"Let's keep it clean," Zan pleaded to his fans. "This is a family show. Your Sunday School teacher may be tuning in. Next caller."

"Zan, I had one of those balloons land in my back yard."

"And where do you live, ma'am?" Zan asked.

"Up in Franklin, Virginia," she said. Cliff clinched his fist and mouthed a silent *YES*. "That's forty miles from this proposed site. What does that balloon mean to me?"

"I'm happy to respond to that," Cliff said. "It means on that particular day with those particular wind currents, the air that was traveling over Cedar Branch also came over Franklin, Virginia. If that air had been contaminated with hazardous waste fumes, then some of those fumes would also be in the air over your home."

"Is that dangerous to my children?" the woman asked.

"That depends. I'm trying to be as honest as I can. The risk factor relates to several things. Number one: what is being burned that day? If they were burning lead, heavy metals, mercury, arsenic…yes, they're all dangerous. Number two: how much they're burning that day and how much is escaping, and number three: how many days in a row it falls in your yard. Cumulative effect is much more powerful than one single dose."

"Well then, I don't want that industry to build near here," the lady said.

"No ma'am," agreed Cliff. "We don't want them to build anywhere. That's why every county that has been a possible site has opposed it."

"So why does the governor want it in North Carolina?"

"That's a very good question and the answer requires more time than we probably have today. Should I try to explain, Zan?"

"Sure, go on."

"Some companies make products using some form of toxic chemicals to produce their merchandise. What is left over goes in a sort of garbage can. At the end of the day, these companies have to do something with this excess *stuff* because this *stuff* is hazardous or poisonous to humans. They pay another company to take it off their hands."

"So a hazardous waste incinerator is one of those companies?" the lady asked.

"Exactly. ICS is one of those companies and Governor Dunnet is telling us we need to help out those other businesses in Raleigh and Charlotte and Atlanta and New Jersey and New York and all up and down the east coast by giving them some place to send their *poisonous stuff*."

The woman on the end of the phone gasped. "Well, I don't want their stuff here. Whoever created it to begin with in Charlotte or New Jersey can keep it there."

"My sentiments exactly," said Cliff. "Or, they can figure out ways to reduce the amount of hazardous waste they produce in their product. That would make the most sense."

"Mr. Lyons," the next caller asked. "Our state has a responsibility to deal with its own waste, wouldn't you agree."

"I agree," Cliff said.

"Isn't that what the governor is trying to do…find a solution for businesses in our state to responsibly dispose of the waste we create? After all, we all enjoy the products they produce."

"You're right," Cliff said. "But the reality is that North Carolina cannot restrict the flow of commerce in and out of its state borders, and hazardous waste is considered part of commerce. Because this facility is so large the only way they can make money is to import waste from other states…as much as the facility can handle…every day of the year. We could be responsible for disposing of hazardous waste from every other state in the nation that chooses to send it here."

Zan took two more phone calls which Cliff answered honestly before Zan asked his own question. "Tensions seem to be building down there in Cedar Branch. What's next on the agenda?"

"The annexation hearing is in two weeks....May 22nd. We need three of the town board members to vote against it."

"Think you've got the vote?"

"We don't know, but I heard that Dick Ever's wife has moved into the guest bedroom. Doesn't sound so good for Dick."

"Oh my God," Zan howled, "Another Lysistrata! Women of Cedar Branch unite. Practice that old Greek strategy and abandon the marriage bed until there's peace in the land once again."

Chapter Thirteen

Sadie picked up the phone and hesitated before she dialed. It'd been almost two months since she'd seen Hammie. There'd been a brief and polite exchange between her and his wife Cece that hadn't amounted to much. Sadie mentioned that she was going to clear out most of the things from her old home. She'd told Dutch and Ada Lynn to tell her what they might want. She wondered if Hammie and Cece had an interest in anything.

"I'll ask him," Cece said and that was the last she'd heard.

"Hammie, now don't hang up on me," Sadie blurted into the phone as soon as she heard his voice. "I need to ask you about some of your father's things. I just don't think Dutch should have first pick of everything."

There was silence at the other end.

"Dutch said he'd like to keep Dad's roll top desk. There's a lovely mahogany drop leaf desk and chair I thought you might want, and the poster bed that was in your bedroom. It's been in my family for two generations now. I hate to give it away but I don't have room in the duplex. Your grandfather's pocket watch is also there." She was talking at warp speed, aware of how much it sounded like gibberish.

"Of course, there's a lot of old furniture that we're getting rid of if you'd want any of that, but I do have two beautiful quilts that your grandmother made. Ada Lynn wants one. I thought I'd give Cece first pick." She finally took a breath. "Hon, are you still there?"

"I'm here, Mom."

"Is this a bad time?"

"We had one of your freakin' balloons land in our back yard last Saturday." His voice was sharp.

A chill ran up Sadie's neck.

"It spooked the hell out of Cece. I hope you got a kick out of scaring people to death. You and that reporter…writing up how many pounds of lead and heavy metals would be leaking out of the stack every year. Where did she get that crap?"

"Well, you should be a little spooked. It's not crap. That's what ICS stated in their own figures when they made their first projections for the state. You know—that's the part they want everyone to believe is steam." Sadie tried to keep her voice steady, but her lower lip started to quiver and her throat tightened up. Hammie had never spoken so harshly to her.

"That's all bullshit. How many times does Sam O'Brien fly over Cedar Branch crop dusting every summer? How many tons of pesticides do the farmers dump in their fields and let wash into the river? When the mosquitoes land, everyone is begging for the town to pull out the Malathion and spray. I blame you and that CAP group. You're a bunch of hypocrites."

"You blame ME?" She couldn't believe what he'd just said. It took a minute for Sadie to swallow the lump in her throat and regain her composure. "I'm not the one that came sneaking into town on Christmas Eve like the damn Grinch. I'm not the one bribing land owners to sell out their neighbors. I'm not the one telling lies in order to line my own pockets."

She stopped. This was senseless. She didn't want to yell at him. "I'm sorry, Hammie. I don't want to fight with you. If you don't want the bed or the desk, and Dutch tells me he doesn't have the room, I'll sell them. I'll tell Ada Lynn she can have both of the quilts unless Cece calls. We'll be clearing out the house next Saturday morning. Show up before then or assume they're gone."

*****

The sale on Saturday morning went better than Sadie had hoped. With enthusiastic help from a number of CAP members, she sold almost everything. She'd marked down all items to rock bottom prices with the objective of getting rid of them. When no realistic offer came on the poster bed, she reconsidered at the last minute and turned down twenty-five dollars.

Phil said Sadie could store the bed at his house along with the mahogany drop leaf desk and chair until she wanted them again. If Sadie didn't mind they'd make some practical use of both. She took him up on the deal in hopes that one day Hammie might have second thoughts. She'd never planned to sell the pocket watch.

"Brought everyone something to eat," Ada Lynn said holding Gabe in one arm and clutching a bag from the Quaker Café in the other. Afternoon help had arrived at the store and to Sadie's delight Ada Lynn offered to pitch in at the yard sale. Sadie knew that the idea of getting rid of a lot of clutter and improving Gabe's health were strong motivators.

"Well, if you aren't an angel," Cliff Lyons said waving his cane from the lawn chair under a cedar tree where he'd sat the entire morning. "Come on over here and give an old man whatever you got in that bag."

"How are you today, Mr. Lyons?" Ada Lynn pulled out a bag of chips and a ham sandwich.

"Sitting up and taking nourishment," he said. "And you, hon?"

"I'm doing good," she said, handing her bag of food off to Sadie and putting Gabe down on the grass. Gabe immediately headed for Smokey who sat obediently a few feet away wagging his tail.

"When's the baby due?"

"End of June," she said. "Another six weeks."

A 1995 Toyota Corolla pulled up across the street and honked. Betty Tesh emerged waving her hand frantically as she jogged towards them. "Guess what? You're never going to believe this." She looked around at the few people rummaging through what remained of Sadie's household goods and motioned Sadie and Billie closer to where Cliff sat. "CBS is sending a reporter and cameraman to the annexation hearing. We're going to get some national coverage."

"My God." Sadie sucked in a gulp of air. "How did you manage that?"

"I just did a cold call. Got a reporter on the line and told him my name was Betty Tesh and we had a mess going on in North Carolina. They needed to send down a reporter. After I explained the situation to him, he told me he'd be down to cover the annexation hearing."

"I never thought we could hook them that easily," Billie said, and then stopped. A glint came into her eyes accompanied by a crooked smile. She hadn't spent fifty years in New York City not to catch the possible connection. "Did he ask you to spell your name?" she asked.

Betty seemed confused. "No, why?"

"Tesh—Tisch," Billie broke into a howl. "The bloke thinks you're related to his CEO."

*****

"I don't expect any of the shenanigans like the ones that happened at the school," the colonel lectured Chief Meacham. "I hold you personally responsible for that screw up. Where were your men? Why didn't you have the building locked down in advance?"

Meacham looked at the colonel with the face of a combat-weary soldier. He stood in the colonel's study and eyed Caren Drake. She seemed to be glued to the colonel's hip these past two weeks. "It's a school, sir. I can't lock down a school. I have no *men*. It's just me."

"Should we be talking to the county sheriff instead of you?" Caren asked.

"I can do that," the colonel interrupted her.

"We've already been in touch," Chief Meacham said. "He'll send out six of his deputies. That's practically the entire force."

"I want a detailed plan as to how you're going to control the annexation hearing and don't give me any crap about freedom of speech," the colonel said.

"I can only do what the law allows, sir."

A vein in the colonel's temple began to twitch. Caren took control of the conversation.

"Look, Chief." Caren lowered her voice and stepped to within two feet of Andy. "I know this is a lot to ask, and I really admire all that you've accomplished for someone your age. You're a smart young man. Don't you think there should be you or someone in that building for twenty-four hours prior to the meeting?"

The color began to rise on Andy's neck and he blushed as Caren nudged inches closer. "It's on a Tuesday night, ma'am. There'll be students in the building during the day."

The colonel clicked his tongue in disgust.

"How about if they just cancel school?" Caren asked.

"That's a decision that would have to be made by the Board of Education," Meacham said.

"Damn it." The colonel grit his teeth and stood. "Enough of this la-dee-da. "Just what can you do, Meacham?"

"I will plan to be on the premises during the day and I personally will ask to inspect the upstairs and lock the stairwell after the children leave," Meacham suggested. "I think they'd let me hold the key until after the meeting."

"Do that," the colonel said abruptly.

"That would be a tremendous help," Caren added softening the rebuke. "You make sure they give you the keys. After all, you are the town law enforcement officer."

The colonel showed a flicker of agitation that she'd interrupted him. "I want men stationed at the back and front steps and protection in front of the stage. Anyone who throws anything, like those silly quarters, should be arrested. That's considered disruption of a public meeting."

"Yes sir." Meacham listened to what seemed to have become a rampage. "I'll explain that to the sheriff."

"And no microphones will be allowed in the meeting. No bullhorns, no amplifiers, nothing," Caren added almost as an afterthought.

Meacham repeated what he heard. "No microphones, bullhorns or sound systems except for the one on the stage."

"No," Caren corrected him. "No sound systems anywhere."

Meacham stopped. He frowned in an effort to understand. "No one will be able to hear you if you don't have at least one microphone."

The colonel let the silence pass between them as if the statement required no answer.

"Is there a law that says we are required to have a microphone at a public meeting?" Caren asked mischievously.

Chief Meacham raised his eyebrows, then turned and walked out.

*****

The same night close to fifty people gathered for the CAP meeting to plan for the annexation hearing. Over a thousand had contributed their two dollars for membership in the organization, proving that it was more than just a Cedar Branch issue. A few dozen showed up for weekly meetings at the Hoole

Pharmacy on Main Street. It was common to see Helen Truitt drive by to check out the gathering.

Sadie had accepted the co-chairmanship with Phil Harper. Betty Tesh and the publicity committee had just sent out a professional looking eight page flyer detailing why a hazardous waste incinerator should not be built in Cedar Branch. Chase Hoole agreed to be treasurer and his wife was in charge of the phone tree. They had a connection system where each person in turn called five people assuring all the members could be reached within thirty minutes. Billie handled fund raising.

Sadie's brief encounter with the Vietnam veteran at the balloon launch had made her nervous, but to date she'd shared the exchange with no one, not even Cliff. She worried that he might overreact and if leaked, the information might encourage someone to do something foolish. Tempers flared easily. People felt betrayed by their elected officials and Sadie feared these public meetings could turn into fist fights if they couldn't find a way to channel people's anger.

As CAP members met one last time in preparation for the meeting, cigarette smokers fogged the sidewalk entrance. Many depended on nicotine to help calm their rage as everyone stood around talking about the latest deception. Old habits ran deep, and Sadie lingered outside to breathe in two more breaths of secondhand smoke.

A tall slender man in a dark brown suit and tie wedged his way through the crowd and found a seat in back. "Who's that?" Sadie asked Phil. While Sadie didn't claim to know everyone in the room personally, someone should. She had never been big on conspiracy theories but she'd become more suspicious in recent weeks. If a PRO supporter attended their meetings, in theory they could keep the opposition updated on all their plans. Having considered this possibility, the group had decided to divide into several subcommittees that met separately and didn't always share all of their information with everyone at the CAP meetings.

"Don't recognize him," Phil said.

"I don't want to tell everyone that CBS will be at the annexation hearing until we know who that is," Sadie said.

"I'm okay with that," Phil agreed. "We'll give an update and break into committees."

Sadie stood up and went rapidly through the necessary business. "Just so we're all on the same page for next week's meeting, you all know that two board members, Lucy Woodright and Rod Palmateer, voted against the motion to proceed with the annexation at their last meeting. Mary Law's absence allowed the colonel to cast the tie-breaking vote. This meeting will be our last opportunity to stop the annexation. We do not know how Mary will vote, but assuming that she shows up there is a chance we could end this whole thing if she votes 'No'."

"Anyone been in contact with her?" a lineman asked.

"No," Sadie said. "She's isolated herself."

"How about the others?" called out the manager of a sawmill on the outskirts of town.

"We're pretty sure Rod Palmateer will oppose the annexation again. Lucy is still with us, we think."

"We need to plan on what we'll say at the meeting. I know we don't have any control over what others say, but I think it's going to be important to hit a wide variety of concerns." Sadie said. "This will actually be the first time the town board has to listen to us since they walked out on the last meeting. But in order to meet the requirements for the annexation, they have to document that they provided an opportunity for citizens to be heard."

"Are they required to vote based on how the community responds," a woman asked.

"Of course not. They only have to confirm that they held the meeting as required by law," Sadie said.

"So, why be nice?" Cliff asked. "Really?"

"Because we want to persuade Rod and Lucy and hopefully Mary to agree with us," Phil said. "We know they're having second thoughts. Let's prove to them that we've done our homework. We're good neighbors and our concerns are valid."

"Listen," said the owner of a fishing shop. "I heard that over in Rowan County they were able to get an injunction based on nineteen pregnant cows and one being a rare Red Poll."

"Did it work?" asked Sadie.

"It gummed up the process. They got some extra time."

"I think that's what we've got to be thinking of…as many issues as we can raise that will gum up the process, as you said. Will you address the fishing business?" Sadie asked and got a head nod in response.

Ideas popped up around the room as people discussed the impact on the Roanoke River, the bear trails, the peanut production industry, the children and many retirees with frail health conditions. Sadie gazed suspiciously at the suited man in the back with growing concern.

"If your committee plans to meet tonight, find a corner. Otherwise, I think we need to go home and prepare our talks. Remember, there's a three minute limit per person. Make it brief and to the point. If you need help with statistics or background to support your arguments, let me know."

Cliff rallied his people over to one side of the room. Others hung around to talk before leaving. Sadie approached the stranger. "Welcome," she said. "Haven't seen you before."

"Hello." He extended his hand with a firm shake. No calluses told Sadie he had probably never unloaded produce or dug a ditch. "And you are?" he asked.

"Sadie Baker," she said.

"It looks as if you're pretty well organized here," he said. He did a quick side to side of the room and adjusted the frames of his designer Calvin Klein glasses. He was Nordic looking, late-thirties, she guessed. Blond hair, wide shoulders, but very narrow hips. He reminded her of one of those Olympic skiers she saw on television.

Sadie had always been skeptical of men with long fingers and pampered skin. They lived in a world unlike her own, but she could be charmed out of any preconceptions by blue eyes and a steady gaze. Manners counted in her book. She hadn't yet decided on this one.

"I don't live close by and can't come to your meetings, but I heard about your cause and decided to drive down from Virginia Beach to find out what you are up to."

"You live in Virginia Beach?" Sadie asked. "That's a good two hour drive."

"Not as far if you're flying in a balloon," he said. A smile warmed his expression. "What happens here could affect me, also." He took a small step closer and she caught a whiff of cedar or something woodsy, she wasn't sure, but it was quite pleasing. A man wearing cologne. Now there was a concept that hadn't caught on in Cedar Branch yet.

"I'd like to make a donation to the cause, if I may," he said and reached to the inside pocket of his coat.

"We don't turn down money," Sadie said. The man might be worth a hundred dollar bill, she thought. They could use every penny.

He handed her an envelope.

"That's generous of you," Sadie said. "It's tax deductible. We're incorporated as a non-profit."

He barely acknowledged the comment and didn't ask for a receipt. "I'll try to send a little more later on," he said. "Looks as if you're breaking up, and I need to head back."

"Thank you," Sadie said. "Careful on the roads. They're narrow and dark at night."

As he walked out the door, Sadie eyed him suspiciously. Was he on the level or not? For all she knew, he could be one of those corporate spies out of ICS. Then she opened the envelope and counted twenty one hundred-dollar bills. Her jaw dropped. She walked over to Chase and handed him the money. "Two thousand dollars from that stranger," she said.

"We could use a few more strangers like him," Chase said appearing less enthusiastic than she'd expected. "You want to hear the bad news?"

"What now?" Sadie asked.

"My wife just called. Mary Law had a heart attack and died at the Edenton hospital about two hours ago."

Chapter Fourteen

Sadie showed up at the school building an hour ahead of the annexation hearing. Four county deputies from the sheriff's office stood like statues at the front and back entrances with their patrol cars visible along Main Street.

"My God," Sadie whispered to Betty Tesh who waited nervously under the flag pole. "You'd think we were threatening to blow up the place."

"It appears that way, doesn't it?" Betty straightened her collar and pulled her blouse down over her hips. "If I'd thought I might be on national TV, I would have lost fifteen pounds. How do I look?"

"You look fantastic, like Cinderella's fairy godmother." Sadie had developed a particular fondness for Betty. She always seemed to be able to see the overall picture in bright colors instead of grim grays. Not once had she expressed any doubt that they would win.

"Mary's death changes everything, doesn't it?" Betty said, more as a statement than a question.

"It doesn't help." Sadie nodded in the direction of a white van. "Reckon that's them?"

The van drove up onto the grass and a man, who was unremarkable enough to get lost in a crowd got out: average height, average age, average beer belly, average haircut, and average tan slacks. The only thing not average about him was a CBS insignia emblazoned on the pocket of an expensive blue polo shirt, and the fact that he was followed by a camera man.

"Shall I tell him right away that I'm not a Tisch?" Betty asked.

"Hell, no," Sadie said. "Don't volunteer anything unless he asks."

Betty approached the reporter with an extended arm and an upbeat hello. "I'm Betty Tesh," she said. "So very glad you could come. I've got a packet for you to review with background information."

"CBS has arrived," he said and shook first Betty's hand and then Sadie's. He gave the packet to the cameraman who threw it in the backseat of the van.

"Like the button," he said referring to a large circular green stick-on made out of construction paper that read, Don't Waste Me. "Can we get a close-up? That would mean zooming the camera in on the front of your blouse."

"Sure," Betty said, apparently non-flummoxed at having her generous bosoms appear on the six o'clock news. "We're handing out stickers at the door, if you want one."

"That probably wouldn't make me an unbiased reporter, would it?" He grinned, and Sadie liked him instantly.

As Betty continued to talk to the reporter, Sadie saw Hammie's black Ford Pickup pull into the parking lot. "Hammie," she called out and broke away to try to catch him. He turned at the sound of his name and stopped.

"I'm so glad to see you. It's been weeks," she said. At one time he would have bent down and kissed her on the cheek. He didn't.

"Mom, I'm here tonight to speak for the PROs. You're probably not going to be pleased with what I have to say."

Sadie tried to conceal her disappointment, but she wasn't entirely surprised. He'd already told her he was attending the PRO meetings, and she knew ICS had promised big contracts to his company.

"I want to apologize for walking out on what-was-to-be Dutch's birthday dinner," she said, not wanting to argue. "I thought maybe we could all get together again as a family and not talk about the incinerator?"

"You really think that's possible?"

"I don't know, but I'm willing to try."

Sadie watched as the hard features on Hammie's face softened slightly. It was that look that reminded her so much of Coen. Of her two boys, Hammie had his father's lean build and jutting chin that made him look so determined. Dutch, on the other hand, had his father's gentle disposition.

She didn't see her coming, but suddenly Caren Drake stood next to Hammie, her three inch heels pushing her just shy of his height. "I have you scheduled as one of the first speakers," she said to Hammie, ignoring Sadie. Simultaneously she eyed the CBS cameraman. "I see we've got some national media coverage and you'd be a good person for them to interview. Would you mind?"

Hammie looked across the grounds to the flagpole where Audrey Garner had joined Betty Tesh and the reporter. The camera was rolling.

Looking at his mother, he gave a lukewarm apology. "I'll talk to you later, Mom," he said.

*****

Four hundred people filled the auditorium to capacity and three dozen stood along the walls, mostly men in jeans and work shirts, all with baseball caps sporting the insignia of a feed company or NC State. Three deputies stood at attention below the stage. The town board members walked into a muted reception and took their places around a table. Everyone had been asked in advance to be respectful in hopes of turning three of the five votes.

Colonel Little sat at the head. Rod Palmateer and Lucy Woodright sat on the side facing the citizens and their two counterparts, Dick Evers and Wade Gorman, were opposite them with their backs to the audience. The colonel called the meeting to order, but the only sound that could be heard was his gavel as it hit hardwood.

"Can't hear you, Colonel," someone shouted.

"Tough. Go home," the colonel mumbled.

The CBS guy moved closer to the front of the room. His cameraman followed. Local news reporters fell in behind. "Do you see what they're doing?" People pointed fingers and encouraged them forward. "How can you have a public hearing if nobody can hear?"

"No microphones are allowed, sir," a deputy warned the reporters.

"I'm with CBS. Do you intend to confiscate my microphone while being filmed on national television?"

The deputy backed off. "You may stand here, sir, but not beyond this point."

Rod Palmateer eyed the press corps and began to wring his hands. Lucy dropped her head, her eyes locked on the table top in front of her. The colonel adjusted his posture, shoulders back, chin up. He mentally began to prepare remarks to give the press.

Numbers had been assigned to speakers for and against the annexation. The town clerk stood up front and held up a number to indicate each speaker's turn. She then timed their three minute limit. Only those who shouted could be heard over the disgruntled objections building around the room.

When Hammie rose to speak, Sadie pushed her way up front and slid into his vacant seat between Caren and another PRO supporter. "This is great, Kare-in," Sadie said, intentionally mispronouncing her name just to annoy her. "You're quite the fixer, aren't you? You get to break up families, divide churches and destroy friendships and then walk away from the mess you've created into some cushy job. You don't give a damn about what you leave behind."

Caren's jaw tightened. She looked straight ahead as Hammie talked about the need to provide job opportunities for the youth in the area.

As soon as the last person spoke, Dick Evers made a motion to accept the request for annexation and Wade Gorman seconded it. Lucy Woodright and Rod Palmateer voted against it and the colonel cast the tie-breaking vote in favor.

The crowd jumped to their feet. Boos filled the auditorium. Someone threw a silver quarter on stage. An onslaught of quarters followed. A rat raced out of a side vent. Lucy Woodright screamed. More rats. People pushed towards the exits. The deputies scrambled in an effort to gain control.

The cameraman captured the frantic scene, but the CBS reporter had seen something more newsworthy and motioned him to the door. "They're burning the governor in effigy outside," he shouted and ran towards the flagpole that had a straw man in a suit and the words Governor Dunnet on a wood sign around its neck. Within minutes ashes drifted through the air like black snowflakes.

CBS interviewed the colonel in front of the spectacle. "See what a bunch of renegades I'm dealing with," the colonel snapped. "If government allowed mobs to rule, then we'd still be living in a segregated country without the civil rights legislation. Think about that. The majority cannot always be counted on to make decisions that are in the best interest of the people." He pointed at the flag pole. "I'm embarrassed that this level of disrespect is on camera for the world to see. I apologize to our governor and blame it on the outside agitators who have invaded our once tranquil community."

"Why didn't you allow a microphone in the hearing?" the reporter asked.

"We've already heard it all," the colonel replied. "The fabrications, the lies, the threats and profanity." The colonel shook his head. "I decided not to force the good people of this town to listen to it again."

****

The CBS news broadcast aired three days later. Cedar Branch had a three minute spot with a picture of the green *Don't Waste Me* button, a soundbite of Sadie talking about the abuse of the democratic process and Hammie talking about jobs. The reporter emphasized that they were mother and son on opposite sides of the issue.

Included were Audrey's charge of environmental racism and the fact that there had been no microphone in the hearing. A camera shot of a rat running on stage and the burning of the governor in effigy played behind the colonel talking about the use of profanity.

A resourceful CAP member had begun to tape every public meeting from beginning to end on a private recorder. Sadie and Cliff sat in her living room reviewing the hearing. "I hear the governor is furious," Sadie said.

"As well he should be… getting burned in effigy on national TV. It's not an image a governor would be proud of," Cliff said. "Not that I care much about his legacy. I think they got exactly what they deserved. The nerve…THE NERVE to have a public hearing without a microphone. That's ludicrous." Cliff got more infuriated the more they discussed the meeting.

"I'm getting calls about our disrespect for the flag pole," Sadie said. She feared they'd stepped over the line, but she didn't know how to confront Cliff without offending him. "Tempers are on a short fuse. My phone's been ringing for two days. You know the Board of Education closed the school to inspect for rats. They may not reopen before the end of the school year. Parents are angry."

"That wasn't my committee." Cliff raised his palm to stop her. "I abided by the wishes to play it low-key out of respect for Mary's death."

"The rats?"

"Well," Cliff hesitated. "Yeah, the rats were planned, just in case the vote didn't go the way we wanted, but we held off until the end."

"The effigy of the governor?" Sadie continued.

"Not us," Cliff said, both hands in the air. "Swear to God."

"But you talked about it."

"We talked about a lot of things…letting all the air out of their tires, putting skunk oil in their cars, taking Caren Drake frog gigging and losing her in the swamp. That woman's about stepped on my last nerve."

"I don't even want to hear this," Sadie said, covering her ears. "We need to be careful about how vindictive this becomes. The goal is to get the media's attention and stall the process. No damage to personal property. No one gets hurt. Those are our rules."

"I hear you. We're on the same page."

"So who did it?" A chill ran up Sadie's neck.

"Did what?"

"The flagpole caper? If not our group, who?"

"I don't know," Cliff said. "Not everyone who is opposed to this incinerator is a member of CAP and we have no control over what other people do."

"How did they get by the sheriff's deputies?"

Cliff scratched the back of his neck and squinted. "They can't be everywhere at once. You don't have to be a genius to figure out ways around them."

"But we get blamed," Sadie said. "We can't have every Tom, Dick, and Harry pulling off whatever stunt they want and us suffering the bad press." There followed an awkward moment of silence. Sadie felt like perhaps she'd been blaming Cliff and hadn't been completely honest.

"I should tell you that someone approached me at the balloon launch and said they could make things disappear—blow them up."

Cliff stared at her in disbelief.

"He said he was a Vietnam Vet and he and his friends knew how to make bombs…and they could take care of things for us."

"Who?" Cliff demanded.

"I don't know. He spoke to me from behind and when I turned he'd disappeared."

"And you're just now telling me?"

She couldn't tell if Cliff was hurt or annoyed. "I wasn't sure if I should report it to the police. I was hoping to figure out who it was so that I could talk to them privately...stop them from making threats."

"I don't know how you do that," Cliff said. "If they're not coming to CAP meetings, we don't know what other people might be planning."

"Maybe they are at our meetings; after all, you had talked about burning the governor in effigy. Maybe you've got a committee member who's taking things into his own hands."

Cliff shook his head. "Don't make what happened sound bad. We made national news. What we've learned is that if we're proper and polite, they ignore us. When we put up a fight, suddenly people care. I'm not sorry it happened."

"But I'm worried," Sadie said. "The more people who get involved, the harder it gets to control."

"I'm sure the colonel's group has the same problem."

"I'm exhausted, discouraged and frightened," Sadie said. "I never had any intentions of starting a protest movement where people might get hurt. I honestly thought we would be able to reason with people...present the facts and they'd change their minds."

"I think we need to broaden our focus and start making trips to Raleigh." Cliff refocused. "We need a stronger connection with Ed Garner's daughter Audrey, Beth Elmore, and Stu's group in the western part of the state. We need the benefit of their experience."

"The PROs already have the governor in their pocket," Sadie said, not convinced that they'd have any pull in Raleigh. "What's the use?"

"They don't have the media in their pocket," Cliff said, thumping his cane on the floor. "And there's an election coming in six months. People across the state have fought the incinerator in other counties. We just have to remind them that the fight isn't over. We have to put it squarely in the lap of the governor and the legislators. We have to make it an election issue for more than our town board."

Sadie felt overwhelmed. Challenging a local mayor and council members seemed possible. They knew each other. They lived in the same community. Who in Raleigh gave a nickel about what happened in Cedar Branch? There weren't enough votes in the entire county to put even a dent in a statewide election.

"I'll call Beth Elmore and talk to Ed Garner and Audrey," Sadie said, but without the enthusiasm that she knew she needed. "Phil needs to call Stu. We'll have to update our action plan." She stood to leave. "See you at the funeral, I guess. Monday at eleven. Methodist Church."

"Who's taking Mary's place at the organ?" Cliff asked.

"No one. They plan to eulogize her without music."

"And I suppose they think her death is our fault?"

"Of course."

*****

The crowd jammed into the Methodist Church with standing room only. No one had intentionally arranged seating, but the CAP members sat in back giving front row seats to the PROs.

Cliff and Sadie took aisle seats on the side section. Two rows in front of her Millie Little sat between Helen Truitt and Caren Drake. "Where's the colonel?" Cliff whispered out of the side of his mouth. Sadie shrugged.

The organ had been draped in black with an arrangement of white roses and calla lilies across the top. A white finished steel casket with pearl-colored lining sat open at the front of the church. Programs indicated that several vocal pieces would replace the music normally provided by the organist. A woman Sadie didn't know stood to sing acapella "Blessed Assurance" and the worshippers rose to their feet as the family walked down the aisle. Mary's daughter led the way on the arm of her husband and Colonel Little at her other side.

"Oh, my God," Sadie muttered to Cliff. "Will he not give it a rest."

Mary's son followed with his family and all eyes immediately focused on the nine year old granddaughter wearing the navy blue hat fashionably fitted on her head. She looked so vulnerable, so young, so scared. Sadie couldn't help but wonder if the child worried about her own death and had visions of others remembering her in similar fashion.

The service felt awkward. The new minister had only known Mary briefly and failed to capture any of her personality in his eulogy. The vocalists all came from Edenton, and while their voices were pleasing, they projected little emotion. But what clouded the entire service, hung heavy like Spanish moss dripping into a black river swamp, was the silence. Everyone expected to hear the pipes…imagined the majestic echo of "How Great Thou Art" thundering out into the streets in a final farewell. Mary had always played that particular song with great gusto at the end of every funeral. The absence of the organ was heartbreaking.

As the service concluded, the ushers moved forward and began to direct the rows immediately behind the family down to the front of the church to walk past the casket. Sadie had never particularly liked this viewing aspect of her own Baptist service and she preferred the Methodist tradition of having an open casket only at the funeral home. Maybe the family had requested it. Until now, she'd assumed they were Methodist, but perhaps not. She saw someone mouth "Baptist," and nod to a neighbor.

Sadie's eyes told Cliff that she didn't want to follow the line down front, but their departure would have been obvious and no one else had escaped through a side door. As the usher approached their row, Cliff stepped out and motioned Sadie in front of him. Sadie took a deep breath knowing that the whole church was watching. She lowered her eyes and approached the casket.

Mary looked more rested than the last time Sadie had seen her. Sadie prayed that when her time came people wouldn't talk about how much better she looked dead than alive. Sadie touched the side of the coffin and gazed down at the remarkably unlined face. Amazing what they could do these days. But something wasn't right. She stood longer than expected and took a closer look. Cliff nudged her forward and Sadie whispered "Sorry, Mary. Rest in peace."

As they exited through the back door, Cliff chided her. "Why did you apologize? You have nothing to apologize for."

"Sadie Baker, I'm surprised you had the nerve to show your face today." Sadie turned to see Helen Truitt directly behind her.

"It's a funeral, Helen," Sadie said. "I knew Mary for as long as you did. She was my friend, too."

Helen turned and eyed a huddle of CAP supporters under a tree. "If you had respected her, you and your friends over there wouldn't have hounded her to death."

Sadie's first reaction was to bite back, but something inside of her put on the brakes. "Helen, let's not do this. Your good friend has died, perhaps your best friend. I'm sorry for your loss."

Sadie watched in surprise as Helen's mouth collapsed to a thin line and her eyes became moist. She tucked her chin down and turned to leave. Almost unconsciously, Sadie reached out and placed her hand on Helen's shoulder in a parting touch.

As Helen walked away, Sadie looked at Cliff in astonishment. "Thought I'd never see the day. Helen Truitt brought to tears without a comeback."

"I imagine Mary might have been one of her only true friends," Cliff said. "Let's give her space. Why don't we forgo the graveyard and reception?"

After they got into Cliff's car to drive home, Sadie said, "Is it my fault, Cliff? Did I do this to our town?"

"Good Lord, Sadie. No. You didn't start it. The colonel and the town board did."

Sadie took a deep breath and fell silent. A tear rolled down the side of her cheek. As they pulled into her drive she asked, "Did you notice something different about how Mary looked?"

"Different, other than the fact that she was dead instead of alive?"

"Her boobs. Mary had great boobs. She was always very proud of the fact that her boobs never sagged."

"Oh, come on." Cliff looked at her like she was crazy. "She was seventy-five years old. Everyone sags by seventy-five."

"How would you know?"

Cliff hesitated, "Well, I don't. But I'm not sure I know what we're talking about."

"Her boobs were just lying there. No perk to them at all. The undertaker could have fixed that…stuffed a little tissue in here and there."

"Sadie, you're unbelievable." Cliff swallowed a laugh. "Mary's dead. There's no perky when you're dead."

"Well, there damn well should be. What are you paying for, otherwise? If I go before you, Cliff, you make sure that my boobs are perky when they put me in my casket."

Cliff conceded. "Perky, it will be. I promise."

Chapter Fifteen

As Sadie drove towards Roanoke Rapids, she inhaled the sweet fragrance of recently seeded fields. The tranquil two-lane road stretched out in a straight line with sweeping views of dogwoods nestled between tall pines. They gradually faded as she got closer. Factory towns symbolized all the things she didn't want for Cedar Branch—fast food, row houses, traffic, and smoke stacks. Money and jobs came at a cost.

A logging truck overtook her and swung around to pass at ten miles above the speed limit. The noise startled her. She tightened her grip on the steering wheel as the draft pushed her car to the right. What were the estimates? Twenty-five trucks of hazardous waste every day coming through on these roads? Were people nuts? They considered that progress?

Beth Elmore had agreed to meet Sadie midway for a strategy session. Before crossing over I-95 Sadie pulled off the road into Ralph's, a popular barbeque place. It wasn't quite noon, but already two dozen cars and a Trailway Bus had unloaded hungry travelers. The restaurant offered a full buffet loaded with pork, fried chicken, rice, gravy, and an array of vegetables. Trays of mac and cheese, fried okra, collards, potato salad, and slaw, plus cornbread, and banana pudding sat crammed together on an expansive serving station. This was no soup and salad place.

Sadie spied Beth immediately. Even dressed casually, she stood out among the shorts and jeans crowd. Fashionable enough to merit the cover of *Ladies' Home Journal,* she could be a model standing on a wide veranda sipping a glass of sweet iced tea with a sliver of lime.

Sadie looked at Beth and promised herself she'd try harder to spruce up her own wardrobe. Hadn't Cliff complimented her whenever she put some effort into how she dressed?

Beth rose and waved Sadie over to a corner booth and then gave her a hug. "I know you probably feel stretched to your limits. Everybody does by now."

"I do," Sadie said. "I needed this break from Cedar Branch. Look at me. I walk around dressed like a moving target." She had on a green T-shirt that read "For a Clean Green North Carolina" on the back and a large bull's eye on the front with an incinerator crossed out by a giant X.

Beth dismissed her comment. "Are you kidding? By this point we were all lucky to be brushing our teeth every day much less finding clean clothes. Who had time to do wash?"

Beth always normalized whatever happened.

"You heard about the annexation?" Sadie asked.

"Of course. Sorry, I hoped you might slip by with an easy fix, but you did get some terrific national coverage. The publicity is worth a lot."

"You don't think we looked like a bunch of hooligans?"

"Gracious no, you looked like citizens who were fighting back. The no-microphone scam the colonel pulled…unbelievable!" Beth shook her head. "But I'm not surprised by anything anymore."

A waitress approached the table and Sadie ordered a Diet Coke with the buffet. Beth asked for sweet tea.

"So where do we go from here?" Sadie asked. "We're not sure what happens next."

"I'll walk you through it. The land is annexed so they have a specific site now. Done deal. According to law, ICS has to submit their permit application to the state. Part of the permitting process requires them to hold two public hearings for people to ask questions.

"That sounds good," Sadie said. "That should give us some time to slow things down."

"Maybe," Beth said. "Let's get our food, and then I'll explain why the deck is stacked against you."

As they approached the buffet line, a tour bus off of I-95 pulled into the parking lot and a group of fifty began to stream into the restaurant. Amidst laughter and loud chatter, they found tables and advanced on the food line like an army battalion after a month in the jungle.

A man of substantial girth saddled up next to Sadie. "What are you protesting?" he asked in a jovial tone. He tried to read the back of her shirt.

"They're trying to put up a hazardous waste incinerator in my town. I'm against it," she said, not sure how much to say.

"Oh yeah? Where abouts is that?" He piled the middle of his plate with chopped barbeque.

"About thirty miles east of here—a little town called Cedar Branch."

"Is this what they call Carolina barbeque?" he asked, paying more attention to his gastronomic demands than her answer. "It's all chopped up. I was expecting ribs."

"This is it," Sadie said. "Vinegar based. Try it on a bun with some coleslaw."

"Un-huh." He seemed earnestly intent on a culinary experience. He smiled and added potato salad and slaw until it dripped over the edges of the plate. He balanced two fried chicken legs on top along with a hamburger bun, turned and smiled. "Well, I hope your team wins."

Sadie returned to her corner booth feeling smug in her moderation. She'd plotted to secretly fatten up Caren Drake, but the few extra pounds looked good on her and Sadie had simply stopped weighing. Like clothes…scales no longer held a high priority.

"So why is the deck stacked?" Sadie asked when she and Beth settled back down.

"We're told that the governor has said in no uncertain terms that this permit will be approved. No excuses. People on the inside who used to give us information a year ago have shut us out. They feel as if their jobs are on the line and they don't want to be caught aiding the enemy."

"I thought we paid their salaries. Now we're the enemy?" Sadie asked.

"Sadly, yes," Beth said. "Once you get power, the gloves come off. I guess the good news is that you're making enough noise that people in high places are feeling the pressure."

Sadie took a bite of the barbeque, but it didn't go down easily.

"As far as the permit hearings go, they are a mere formality. Regardless of the concerns raised or how many people express opposition, the permit will be approved. You have to understand that. It's a punch-the-card exercise. They are only holding the hearing because ICS is required to under the letter of the law."

The barbecue had definitely not found a comfortable landing and Sadie regretted her decision to suggest this restaurant. "But that isn't the purpose of the hearings is it? They say they will listen and respond to the public's concerns."

Beth spoke with emphasis. "Right, *to listen and to respond*—not to change their minds. They'd like to change your mind, but they have no intentions of letting you change theirs."

Sadie put her fork down. She no longer wanted the food. "So what are our options?"

"As before, it's a delay tactic. Delay, delay, delay. If you can get to the November election and oust the town board, you'll have more leverage to pass some environmental restrictions on ICS."

"Excuse me." A woman in a pink blouse and white slacks with a Barbara Streisand nose stood by their table. "I hate to bother you," she said in an accent that was definitely not Southern. "My friend over there told me that you're fighting against an incinerator in Cedar Branch."

"That's right," Sadie said.

"Well, I'm with an environmental group in Vermont and I saw that long article about your fight in the current issues of the *Utne Reader,* and then again that CBS report a week ago on television. I just wanted to tell you that I support what you're doing."

Sadie straightened up. "You saw an article where?"

"The *Utne Reader*. They did quite a spread about environmental racism and had some great pictures of your balloon launch."

"I haven't seen it," Sadie said.

"Oh my." The lady looked surprised. "Let me go see if anyone on the bus has a copy."

Sadie looked at Beth. "Did you know about this?"

"No, although I do know the magazine. It has a rather well-heeled following. Known for their strong articles on the environment."

"I'm surprised." Sadie said. "We only saw one reporter at the event although JC and Ed told us a cameraman had taken a few pictures."

The woman headed back to their table with a big smile on her face and a magazine in hand. "Got it," she said, thumbing through to the feature article. "See here, a nice picture of these two men together on their porch and then the balloons going up into the air. It's a wonderful picture, really…sort of defies the stereotype of Southerners."

"Well, I'll be," Sadie said, thrilled to see a large colored photo of Ed Garner and JC Collier under the title, *The New Face of Environmentalism*. "Can I have this? I'd like to give this copy to these two gentlemen."

"Sure, it's a great article."

"I'm Sadie Baker and this is Beth Elmore. Thank you so much for this. Where are you headed?"

"We're bird watchers from Vermont. Headed to Pea Island National Wildlife Refuge, just north of Hatteras. Hoping to see the peregrine falcons and piping plovers. Ever been there?"

"No," Sadie confessed. "But I'll try to before long. I hope you have fun." She started to read almost before the woman walked way.

"Terrific," Beth said, looking at the magazine across the table. "See. You're making a difference. I don't know how we missed this."

Sadie put the magazine down. "This makes me feel good."

"Photocopy it like crazy." Beth tapped her finger on the picture. "Send out copies to state legislators. Better yet, hand them to legislators. I think it's time to bring more people to the State Legislative Building to knock on doors."

Coming to Raleigh with any sizeable numbers would require a sacrifice for many people. To attend a local night meeting didn't involve a day off work, but Raleigh was a two hour drive one way. People who had jobs couldn't just take off, and senior citizens were less likely to make the trip. Sadie hesitated. "Does it really make a difference? Will the representatives and senators even take the time to see us?"

"Oh yes," Beth said. "Not all, but they'll know you've been there and some of the legislative assistants can be extremely valuable contacts. You could maybe schedule shifts—a dozen people one day, another ten people another. It's a short session this year, so we're mainly talking about the month of June. I'll see if I can pull in some recruits from other counties to join you."

Beth got more energized as she spoke, obviously having walked the halls many times herself and being rewarded for her persistence. Sadie remained apprehensive. This was new territory for her and the other CAP members.

"Look," Beth persisted, perhaps sensing Sadie's reticence. "You'll know exactly what to say when you get there. You've been responding to the same challenges from the proponents and press for the past five months and doing it well. If you can talk to CBS and make enough sense to make the evening news, you can talk to any legislator in Raleigh. Just remember they work for you. If enough people disagree with what they're doing and show up at the polls, they lose their jobs."

Sadie groaned. She didn't feel good about the confrontation mode that had become the new norm. Now they were moving to a new level. It created tension and more division within the town, but she couldn't see that they had any alternative.

"Remember what I told you at the beginning?" Beth said. "Educate. Agitate. Legislate and Litigate. You've passed the first two phases. Time to move to the third."

Sadie remembered, but she hadn't been listening at that point. Back then she had thought they could end it all within a couple of weeks. She'd believed every morning that the colonel would wake up and realize he'd made a mistake and he would abide by the wishes of the people he served.

"Why do you think the colonel's doing this?" Sadie wondered out loud for the hundredth time. "It doesn't make any sense to me. He's the only local official in the entire state who hasn't stood by his community to oppose ICS. I just don't get it."

"Who knows," Beth said. "He's getting a lot of personal attention from the governor at the moment. I imagine there's a lot of ego involved. He's someone who's been giving orders all of his life and people have done what he told them. I'm sure he's quite surprised anyone questions his judgement."

"But what does he get out of all of this in the end?"

"I don't know...a job with ICS or an appointment to one of the state waste management committees. Maybe a board position with BAG. We know their trade association has contributed money to the proposed project. There's almost always payback, but it's never in writing and never upfront. We've got a list of EPA administrators and directors who are now working full time for various waste industries throughout the country. It's disheartening."

Sadie's heart sank. Beth's assessment was discouraging and the fight ahead seemed endless. "I don't think I can keep up with the demands much longer," she confessed to Beth. "At the same time, I can't let go. I get so angry at our elected officials who patronized us. They keep telling us lies. *Steam. There's only steam coming out of those stacks*. Honestly, I can't believe they still use that line. They think we have no more common sense than a turnip."

"It doesn't help much to tell you I know how you feel." Beth placed her hand over Sadie's. "But I can assure you that others have felt the same way, and they've stuck it out and won in the end."

"Here you go." The Barbara Streisand nose was back again. "A little contribution to your cause from our bus. We each chipped in twenty dollars." She handed Sadie a wad of cash.

"Oh my gosh," Sadie's gasped. "That's really very generous of you all." She looked across the restaurant. Heads turned in her direction. She stood up and gave a partial bow of thanks to modest applause. If these people who didn't even live in Cedar Branch identified with their struggle, maybe others did too. Her despair turned back into hope.

*****

On the drive back Sadie felt a new level of energy. Her mind raced. They needed to reach out beyond their small community. They needed to broaden their media exposure and appeal to a larger support base. They needed to put more pressure on their state legislators.

She crossed over the Roanoke River, the fall line between the end of the Piedmont and the beginning of the Coastal Plains of North Carolina. In the river was a small boat with a lone fisherman. A vivid memory of Coen and her boys washed over her. On Sundays Coen would bring the boys up here to catch the shad that swam upstream from the ocean in search of their spawning grounds among the rocks. These little fish were too bony to eat, but Coen used them as bait for the rock fish.

Hammie had taken the johnny boat after Coen died. Dutch said he didn't have time to fish any more. Too bad. She always felt that some of the best father-son times came in that boat.

She reached the opposite side of the bridge and glanced down the gravel road that led to the boat slip. A black Toyota 4Runner with a boat trailer sat alongside the ramp. Sadie slowed. Was that the colonel's SUV? Surely not. Nothing distinguished his from every other 4Runner on the road. Curiosity overtook her. She drove another half mile and then made a U turn. She backtracked west over the Roanoke River again and then turned around once more. Yes, from a distance, it could be him.

What if? What if the two of them could sit together in a quiet place without the pressures of the press and a crowd cheering them on. Would reason and respect prevail? At one time she had admired the colonel. While they had not been close friends, she admitted that the colonel and Millie had worked to make their community a better place to live.

Slowly she edged her car down the gravel to the river and pulled up to the side of the boat trailer. For a minute she kept the motor running. She strained her eyes. It was him. She was sure it was him. He hadn't noticed her car yet. He sat slouched in his boat, bending over with his head in his hands. A fishing pole was locked into a rod holder.

She turned off the motor but didn't get out of her car. Several minutes passed. Did she have the right to intrude? What did she have to offer him? An apology? A compromise? She had nothing to apologize for and a compromise didn't appear to be on the table. She wouldn't settle for twenty thousand tons of hazardous waste instead of fifty thousand tons.

The colonel's back straightened. She saw him pick up his pole and reel in the line and then cast it again. He didn't look her way. Poor man, she thought. He had to be as exhausted and discouraged as she was. He had escaped to the river to get away from it all. She would be an unwelcomed intrusion on his solitude. She started her car and pulled back onto the highway

She passed Boone's Millpond and noticed the number of wells and outhouses set back from the small wooden framed homes. A wave of uncertainty crept through her. Would ICS make a difference in these people's lives? Would it give them enough money to have running water? Would her fight truly help the poorest of those in the community? How many times had the colonel driven to the river and noticed the same thing? Was his fight more worthy than hers?

The closer she got to Cedar Branch the bigger the knot in her stomach grew. She turned into her driveway and stopped abruptly. What in God's name was that? In the yard of the duplex next to her, two long stakes had been pounded into the ground with a four by six foot sign that broadcasted PRO in large red, white and blue letters. Underneath it read "PROmoting Growth in our Community. Support ICS."

Sadie couldn't believe what she saw. Her next door neighbor, a retired English teacher, had never said word one to her about the incinerator issue. Sadie had lived in the duplex next to Irene for five years and exchanged recipes and pictures of their grandchildren while they shared coffee together on their front steps. In the months since the ICS furor had begun, they'd hardly spoken, mainly because Sadie had been so caught up in CAP she no longer had time for casual chit-chat. In addition, she'd figured Irene wouldn't want to get involved and Sadie did not want to alienate her on the issue.

Sadie walked across the lawn and knocked on Irene's door. She saw the curtain in the front room push back slightly and then drop. Irene's rounded silhouette was unmistakable behind the sheers. "Irene," Sadie called, "I see you in there. Open the door and tell me what this is all about." There was no response.

"Irene," she knocked and called out again. "I didn't know I had upset you. Why didn't you come talk to me?" Still no response.

Sadie turned and walked back to her side of the duplex. That hurt. It felt very personal, more personal than her confrontations with the mayor or her disagreements with Mary Law. She just never expected Irene, of all people, to try to publicly humiliate her. Everyone in town would notice.

The more she thought about the offending sign, the more annoyed she became. Someone had put Irene up to this. She wouldn't have done this on her own. Irene hated any type of confrontation. Okay, Sadie thought. Two could play at this game.

"Smokey," she called. He'd been inside the duplex since ten that morning. As she opened her front door to let him out, he ran over into Irene's yard. Sadie considered letting him take a dump right there, but she thought better of that. Irene's little jab called for something bigger and better than dog poop.

Chapter Sixteen

The following week Sadie stood outside her duplex and stared at the two separate walkways. Irene loved lilies and had carefully added additional topsoil to provide for good drainage before gingerly inserting the bulbs. Several varieties including yellow crocus, white chrysanthemum and red amaryllis blossomed every spring like clockwork. A lovely little dogwood tree grew just to the left of the offensive PRO sign. Often she and her neighbor had helped each other weed their yards, and on more than one occasion Irene had graciously added a plant or two to Sadie's less well-groomed side.

Today, Sadie wasn't feeling quite so neighborly. She'd paid Marvin the butcher to make her an eight by ten foot whitewashed sign, just a bit larger than Irene's. It had large dark green lettering with CAP on top and underneath in smaller letters "Fighting for the Right to Decide. Let Us Vote".

Marvin had proven to be a great handyman around town and willing to do odd jobs on his days off. Between ordering everyone's meats and doing the small fix-it repairs, Marvin was welcomed in just about every home. Sadie had worried a bit about asking him to do her dirty deed, not wanting to put him at odds with Dutch in the store, but then she found out he'd made Irene's sign, too. He was a free agent he'd assured Sadie as he sunk the two two-by-fours into the ground.

Sadie viewed the finished product, saw Irene looking out her window and waved. Irene quickly disappeared and for an instant Sadie regretted that she'd let spite get the better of her.

When Sadie walked into the grocery, Dutch looked at her and shook his head. "Well, aren't you two the pair?"

"What?" Sadie said, her nerves already frazzled from the morning dig.

"I suppose next you'll both put up neon signs. It'll be like Christmas. The whole town can drive by daily to get updates on the yard wars."

Sadie threw her shoulders back and huffed, "I didn't start it."

"You realize the further this goes, the harder it will be to ever be friends again."

"That assumes I want to be her friend again." Sadie pouted.

"It's going to be hard living in this town once all the bridges are burnt."

Sadie stared at Dutch. She knew he was right but she didn't know how to stop the avalanche of spite that kept building. She awkwardly turned away. "I need to get some hamburger," she said and walked back to the meat counter.

She left the store and went next door to the café in hopes of finding Cliff. He sat in his usual spot with Phil.

Cliff brightened when he saw her. "Hey, like the new sign, Sadie."

Sadie ignored the comment. She didn't want to talk about the signs anymore. She wanted to know what Phil had learned when he met with Stu in Raleigh earlier in the week. "So, tell me. What did Stu have to say?"

"Among other things, I know that we've got to expand our campaign to state legislators just like Beth said. Stu gave me a list of folks in other counties who are willing to help. I've already passed their names on for our mailing list and phone tree."

"Anything more about the permit hearing in August?" Sadie asked.

"He warned us that approval by the state will go through regardless. Expert witness won't do us any good at this point. ICS is just checking off the boxes. Our only chance is to block them from successfully completing the public hearing requirements until after the election," Stu said.

Sadie ran her fingers through her hair, pushing the longer strands behind her ears. As of yet her curling iron wasn't getting the intended workout. She'd planned to pay more attention to her appearance, but this particular morning she'd climbed out of bed feeling worse than the night before. "So, it's back to the schoolhouse pranks again?" Sadie said, the fatigue obvious in her voice.

Phil and Cliff eyed one another. "We were just talking about that. You haven't heard?" Phil asked.

"What?"

"The Board of Education announced that no more public meetings will be allowed on school property. They also said that employees who discuss the incinerator in their classrooms or who get involved in any public protests during school hours would receive disciplinary action. Some of the teachers are unnerved—said they'd help in other ways, but won't come to the meetings anymore."

Sadie's eyes bulged. The knot in her stomach tightened like a screw.

"They're talking about closing down the Cedar Branch School permanently," Phil said.

"They can't do that. They can't close down our school," Sadie blurted out causing several heads in the café to turn.

"It would take care of the accusation that the incinerator would be too close to a school, and we sort of aggravated the problem with the rats…and the flagpole deal," Phil said.

"We didn't do that," Cliff insisted again. "Swear to God, we didn't light the match to the old man."

"If you didn't, who did?" Phil asked.

"I don't know," Cliff said. "All I know is that we helped them out by creating a diversion inside that brought all of the police into the building instead of guarding the front. That wasn't intentional, but what's done is done."

"And where's that money coming from for a new building?" Sadie asked, still focused on the implications of losing their school. "The bond issue failed two years ago."

Phil raised an eyebrow. "Where do you think? The governor has promised the Board of Education he can help with a school merger."

Sadie felt her anger building. They just kept piling it on. They'd start busing the kids twenty miles or more one way. Some children would have to be out by the road at six in the morning to be at school by seven forty-five.

"They're playing to win," Phil said, staring at his cold cup of coffee. "They've got a lot of money tied up in the game already and they're obviously willing to spend more."

Cliff was visibly aggravated. "I think we need to clean house all the way up the ladder: new town board, new school board, new county commissioners, and a new governor."

"That's a tall order," Sadie said.

"We've got six months," Phil said.

"I'm in," Sadie said. "Let's get rid of them all."

*****

The phone rang at four-thirty in the morning and Sadie rolled over still in a fog-like sleep. Reports from toxic waste hearings lay scattered across the floor. Pulling the pillow over her head, she debated whether or not to pick up. Recently the prank calls had increased as the school issue dominated the headlines. Some people blamed her. She'd started getting anonymous hate mail—a picture of a fat clown with BITCH BEWARE printed across the bottom.

She was ready to give the midnight caller a piece of her mind, when she heard the siren of the volunteer rescue squad. She bolted upright and grabbed the phone.

"Mama, we're on our way to the hospital in Westtown. Open the store for us today, will you?" The urgency in Dutch's voice was unmistakable.

"What's the matter?" Feet on the floor, she grabbed some clothes.

"Doctor McCabe is with us. I'll call later."

Sadie could hear other people's voices in the background. The phone went dead.

Westtown was twenty-five miles away. She did the calculations in her head. If she left for Westtown right away, she'd be there by five-fifteen, find out what was happening and then be back to the store by six-fifteen to open up at six-thirty. Was it Ada Lynn? The new baby? Or Gabe? They didn't ask her to come take care of Gabe. He must be with them. It was Gabe. She had to go. No sense sitting here not knowing.

She drove north on Highway 258. Still dark, the few houses and mobile homes sprouted along the road like volunteer corn stalks. A dozen cars passed her headed to work at the shipyards in Portsmouth or the packing plants in Smithfield. The open road seduced her. She hit sixty, then sixty-five and felt she should go faster.

She turned into the emergency room parking lot and pulled in next to Dutch's Ford Ranger. Only one or two people waited in the receiving area in contrast to the usual hordes that filled the room during the day. She knew activity would increase shortly.

Sadie approached the desk. "Gabe Baker?" she asked. "He came in an ambulance. I'm his grandmother."

Looking weary and ready for her shift to end, the receptionist raised one finger to give her a minute, picked up the phone and punched a couple of buttons. "Gabe Baker?" she asked. She listened for a moment and then said, "His grandmother is here."

Replacing the phone in the carriage, she looked back at Sadie. "Both of his parents are with him. No one else is allowed back at this time."

"Is he okay?" Sadie begged.

"I'm sorry I can't say. The nurse will tell his father that you're here."

Sadie turned. The room felt cold. Torn and crumpled magazines littered the pink plastic chairs molded together like a parade of flamingos. Empty soda cans and water bottles lay strewn atop the floor and chairs. She walked over to a vending machine, put in fifty-five cents and got a package of nabs. She sat—stood—and sat again.

The not knowing was the worst part. What had happened? A fall? Not in the middle of the night. It had to be that dern cold. The flu? A virus? Maybe pneumonia? Almost without thinking Sadie rose and began to pick up the bottles and snack wrappers and throw them in the garbage. She'd never been a clean freak, but she had to move. The activity helped.

"You don't have to do that, you know," the receptionist said. "The cleaning lady will be in at six."

Sadie waved her hand to indicate she was okay. "Just something to do."

The receptionist sat for another few minutes watching her. She got up and went through the swinging doors. Five minutes later she was back. "Red hair? A tike about two?" she asked.

"Yes, that's him." Sadie looked at her anxiously.

"He's fine."

Sadie found unexpected relief in the few words of reassurance. "You saw him?"

"I can usually tell by the expression on everyone's face. His mom and dad were talking to him. I saw some smiles." The receptionist seemed pleased to be able to pass along some good news.

"Thank you." Sadie fought back a tear and wiped her nose with her sleeve.

Dutch walked in moments later. "Mama, what are you doing here? I told you'd I'd call."

"Oh honey, I couldn't just sit at home."

Dutch's eyes were bloodshot, his face not yet shaved. He'd morphed into the stereotypical ER zombie: uncombed hair, wrinkled clothes, grayish skin tones under the florescent lights. He looked at his mother and gently brushed away a tear on her cheek. "He's all right. You can stop worrying."

"What happened?"

"Gabe had a restless night. He started to wheeze. We figured we'd take him to Doctor Jane this morning, but then it got worse. When Ada Lynn looked in on him around four, he was struggling to breathe. He could hardly catch his breath. She immediately called Jane who came straight to the house and called EMS. A pediatrician met us when the ambulance pulled in."

"What caused it?" Sadie had so many questions.

"Could be an allergic reaction to something, maybe pneumonia or possibly asthma? They're going to run some tests. His breathing is steady now. They've given him some medicine, and the pediatrician worked with an inhaler for several minutes."

"Are they going to keep him?"

"Maybe twenty-four hours." Dutch rubbed his unshaven cheek and his whole body sagged. "I'm not coming in today. Could you handle the store?"

"Right," Sadie said. "I'm on my way. You and Ada Lynn stay here."

"Thanks," Dutch said and started to leave.

"Dutch," Sadie said.

"Yeah?"

"I need a hug, honey. More than ever I need a hug."

Dutch leaned down and wrapped his arms around his mother. "We'll be okay, Mom."

Her eyes became moist and she fought back the tears. He had other people to worry about besides her. "You know I love you—all of you—more than you'll ever know,"

"I know, Mama. I know."

CHAPTER SEVENTEEN

In an eight by twelve foot room with four wooden chairs and no frills, Sheriff Howard sat behind his desk. He leaned back and crossed his arms over his chest. The third, fourth and fifth buttons pulled at the fabric on his uniform. He'd put on twenty pounds in the past two years requiring him to increase his blood pressure medicine.

"What made you feel that you should go to the attorney general's office before you came to mine?" he asked. His square jaw was set and he glared across the desk at Caren Drake and Colonel Little with unforgiving eyes.

He had sidewalls around his ears. He had lost most of his hair since the standoff at the Quaker meeting house not so many years ago. What had begun as a domestic dispute threatened to turn into the slaughter of a dozen innocent people. Under intense pressure with the press recording every minute, he'd made split-second decisions that still caused nightmares. And here, now, again, Cedar Branch was at the heart of another showdown. The last thing he wanted was a cavalcade of state law enforcement men whom he neither knew nor commanded invading his county. He deserved more respect.

"I thought you'd thank me," the colonel said with a snort. "I'm warning you, you're going to need help. If you don't show up with force, all hell is going to break loose at that permit hearing."

The sheriff cracked his jaw, eyes riveted on the colonel. "You're a military man, Colonel. You understand how a chain of command works."

"Of course, I do." The colonel did a partial eye roll.

"Then you should know that I am the one who puts in a request to the attorney general…not the mayors."

"I was there at the annexation hearing. Your men didn't do much of a job then."

The sheriff straightened. He had a good fifty pounds on the colonel and stood a full head taller when they both were on their feet. "I resent that."

"If I could just interrupt here a minute," Caren said in an effort to break the tension. "For better or worse, what's done is done. Let's move on. The attorney general is now involved. There are tactics that have proven to be more effective in similar situations. ICS has been through this before. We've learned a lot from past experiences."

Caren waited for some response. She knew the sheriff was offended to have been left out of the Raleigh meetings, but he would have insisted on handling the enforcement issues locally. They weren't willing to risk that.

When the sheriff didn't reply, she continued.

"One—the meeting will be held at the National Guard Armory since round-the-clock guards can be provided to guarantee that no one gets into the building prior to the meeting."

The sheriff stared at her.

"Two—local police and sheriff deputies should be posted at each door. Police should be visible up front to insure the safety of the ICS members on the platform and the speakers. Fire codes require that no doors may be locked in case of evacuation purposes, although we may restrict *entrance* through specific doorways."

Stone-faced, arms crossed; only silence came from the sheriff.

"Three—microphones are required." Caren said this quickly in an attempt to avoid any reference to the colonel's lack of providing one at the previous meeting. "ICS is responsible for the microphone systems and having someone there to operate and record the proceedings. The permit requires that ICS have on record every comment made at the public hearing. This is crucial."

"Novel idea," the sheriff said with sarcasm.

Caren ignored the comment. "Four—everyone who signs in to speak is allowed to do so, although there is a three minute limit for each speaker. ICS will work with the colonel to have a person in place to enforce the time requirement."

When nobody spoke, the sheriff said, "Is that it?"

"One more thing—ICS recommends that the participants either be seated according to their speaking order, or that those who are liable to create a disturbance be seated in different sections away from the microphones. It would be more effective if your deputies would assist in that, but…"

The sheriff's mouth twisted. He closed his eyes momentarily, learned forward and shook his head from side to side in a manner that indicated he'd had enough. "You're planning to tell people where they can sit? You expect my men to be ushers? You've already targeted who might be disruptive?"

"Yes," said the colonel, "or we'll get volunteers to accompany them to their seats."

"No," the sheriff said. We won't do that. That's not our role and you'll make folks madder."

"Control." The colonel raised his voice and Caren lowered her eyes. "It's all about control. He who sets the rules wins the war. Alone, people are not nearly as brave as they become in a larger group. Didn't they teach you that at the academy?"

The sheriff stared over their heads and exhaled slowly. Caren heard him grind his teeth. "Let me explain something to you folks," he said. "Unlike Chief Meacham, who is your town cop and hired by you, I am voted into office.I can win the election or lose the election based on how my performance is viewed by the public. We're not fighting a war here. We're supposed to be discussing the best options for our community. We're talking to our neighbors. Good decisions are reached when mutual respect is shared. What you're suggesting doesn't show respect as far as I'm concerned."

"You don't need to preach to me," the colonel said. His fear of a repeat of the two previous meetings had strained his patience with all law enforcement agencies. To his thinking, a good commander enforced discipline. He didn't politely ask for it.

The sheriff continued, "I am an elected official. The majority of the people voted me into office. In doing so they put their trust in my good judgment to make sound decisions."

The colonel burst out in a rant. "I haven't been the one hanging disparaging signs up all over town, making threatening phone calls, intimidating my neighbors. Since when do the rights of the minority become more important than they rights of the majority?"

"Our country is based on that proposition." The sheriff leaned over his desk and pointed his finger at the colonel. "The rights of the minority cannot be trampled on by the majority."

"Wake up, sheriff." The colonel stood up. Nobody, but nobody shook their finger in his face. "The lid may fly off at this meeting. You want media frenzy like you had in Cedar Branch two years ago? Last time nobody got hurt. This time you might not be so lucky."

"Last time a boy got kidnapped, a man died. I don't consider that lucky." The sheriff got up from his chair, now willing to use his size to his advantage. "Do you have anything else to say before you leave?"

"If I may." Caren did not want to end this meeting without some assurance that the sheriff was on board. She knew what ICS expected and she'd been involved in the meetings between them and the governor's office. She wanted to be sure that the sheriff understood that he was not the top dog.

"There may be a lot of media—live coverage—cameras—reporters. It won't look good for you or Cedar Branch if women are arrested, particularly older women, or if too many black people are arrested given the accusations of environmental racism. The public is more sympathetic when they see the police protecting them from an individual who looks menacing. Men appear more threatening. It has been suggested that you focus on white males, those who are being the most disruptive. Cliff Lyons for example. His monologue on that radio show has been appalling. He practically incites violence and you can be assured he will be a problem."

The sheriff had stopped beside the colonel's chair, but now he looked across at Caren in disbelief. "Now you're telling me *who* to arrest?"

"I'm just saying we, and by we I'm talking about those in high places in Raleigh." She arched both eyebrows to make sure he understood. "We hope that you will respect the need to downplay any outbursts from minority populations and the elderly."

"I don't believe what I'm hearing," the sheriff gagged. "Cliff Lyons! Do you know anything at all about him? A retired cop. Wounded in the line of duty. One of the most respected men in his department and you think he's the one who should be arrested?" The sheriff walked to the door and opened it. "This meeting is over."

"So," Caren said, "I'll tell the attorney general we had our meeting and you're willing to cooperate? Or should I tell him differently?"

"You can tell him any damn thing you like," Sheriff Howard said. "We're done."

Chapter Eighteen

Ada Lynn had never written a letter to a government official in her life, but her concern for Gabe and her yet-to-be born baby scared her. Mama Sadie encouraged her to find answers to her questions from someone outside of the local fray.

"If you're not sure about what I say, find someone you trust."

Ada Lynn did. She came across a newspaper article that mentioned the name of William Sanjour, Branch Chief of the Hazardous Waste Management Division with the Environmental Protection Agency. On the rare chance that he might actually reply, she wrote:

June 5, 1996

Dear Mr. Sanjour,

I live in northeastern North Carolina. Governor Dunnet is telling us that EPA has required our state to build a 50,000 ton commercial hazardous waste incinerator in order to meet requirements set by the EPA. I have a two year old who has recently been diagnosed with asthma. I am expecting our second child in a few weeks. We live less than two miles from where this incinerator will be built. I am writing to ask whether or not the EPA will monitor this facility so that it will not be of any health risk to either of my children. Our state government and local elected officials assure us that the EPA will protect us. My mother-in-law says that the EPA won't. I am concerned and confused.

Sincerely,
Ada Lynn Baker
Cedar Branch, North Carolina

*****

Ada Lynn delivered a beautiful baby girl on June 30, 1996, with stork marks on the nape of her neck and a red V that shot up from the ridge of her nose across her forehead every time the tiny thing screamed. Her sharp outbursts happened frequently and startled everyone into action. There was no sitting down with this one. Unlike her quiet brother, she demanded attention.

They named the baby Patricia, after Ada Lynn's mother who had died in a car accident.

Sadie began to arrive to help at their home or in the store first thing in the morning. She frequently cleaned the kitchen and straightened up the house before going next door to work the cash register until the afternoon employees arrived. Housekeeping had become easier after Sadie removed her years of clutter and she appreciated the new feel of openness in each room. For three weeks, everything else took a backseat. The change in momentum felt good… normal. She longed for *normal* again.

Sadie bowed out of going to Raleigh altogether. The trips back and forth had begun the third week in May and continued through the second Wednesday in July. They hit their peak with thirty-eight people going one day, but on the average Tuesday, Wednesday and Thursday they had about a dozen CAP members making the rounds.

A few stars were born. Audrey Garner strode the halls like an Egyptian queen and gained access to every office she entered. She successfully recruited Senator Lloyd Robbins to sponsor a bill to approve a commercial hazardous waste incinerator only if the state could prove need. Audrey's figures showed a current overcapacity.

Betty Tesh and Billie McFarland were naturals. JC Collier and Ed Garner proved to be unexpected hits. The legislative assistants loved their slow drawls and down-home demeanor. They were a breath of fresh air in stuffy offices that saw more pomp and privilege than the ordinary citizen could stuff into a laundry sack. But Stu had forewarned them that it all boiled down to the Committee of Eight. These men at the top of the totem pole decided which issues got attention and what bills went to the floor. Only when enough lawmakers felt like their re-election was threatened would they begin to pay attention.

Although Sadie kept abreast of what went on through Cliff, everyone understood when she asked for time out to help with her new granddaughter.

She needed the break. Then she discovered the letter.

She'd been cleaning out a glut of junk mail that Dutch tossed in a wicker basket at the end of every day for Ada Lynn to look through before delegating it to the trash. The hamper bulged to overflowing. Sadie quickly trashed one advertisement after another when towards the bottom the return address of the Environment Protection Agency, 1200 Pennsylvania Avenue, Washington, DC, caused her to stop. The letter was addressed to Mrs. Ada Lynn Baker and postmarked July 1, 1996. Sadie carefully laid it on the dining room table and placed a Coke can on top to insure it wouldn't move.

"There's a letter for you on the table," Sadie said when Ada Lynn came down the stairs with Trisha. The baby squawked, her face a crimson red. Ada Lynn handed her to Sadie with a sigh. Sadie reached out her arms and Ada Lynn relinquished the child.

"Gabe was so much easier," Ada Lynn said. "Am I doing something wrong? Do you think she's sick?"

"No, honey," Sadie said. "She's just wired different." Gabe immediately left Sadie's side and tugged at his mother's blouse to be picked up. Ada Lynn sat down in a rocking chair and lifted him to her lap.

Sadie couldn't stand the suspense. While cradling Trisha in her arms, she walked over to the table to get the letter. "Don't know what this is about, but I'd love to," she said as she handed the envelope to Ada Lynn.

Ada Lynn raised her eyebrows when she saw the return address and slid her finger under the flap to break the seal. She immediately turned to the last page and glanced at the signature before reading. "It's from William Sanjour. He actually answered my letter."

"You wrote him a letter?" Sadie's surprise didn't escape Ada Lynn.

"You suggested I write."

"I did. You're right. I'm proud of you. Good for you."

Ada Lynn read silently.

"What did you say?" Sadie became impatient. She feared that it was likely Sanjour had written a canned response reassuring Ada Lynn that all would be fine.

"I asked how well they'd monitor the facility is all…to protect my kids."

Sadie held her breath.

Ada Lynn shifted Gabe over to her side. "Sit right here, honey," she said while I read this out loud to Mama Sadie."

June 28, 1996

Dear Mrs. Baker

I can well understand why you are concerned and confused about the possible construction of a commercial hazardous waste incinerator in your county. This would result in hazardous waste coming into the state from all over the world. My personal view is that these facilities are counterproductive to EPA's goal of reducing the amount of hazardous waste production. In the early days of the EPA hazardous waste program it was believed that by making rules for the safe management of hazardous waste, waste reduction by generators would automatically follow. This has not happened to any great extent although fourteen years have passed since the passage of federal hazardous waste management laws. Toxic wastes are still being shuttled from one medium to another, from water to land to air. Whole industries have sprung up to give hazardous waste generators a "way out" that avoids their responsibility towards waste reduction.

In my opinion, a commercial hazardous waste facility is completely incompatible with waste reduction programs. A commercial facility, be it incineration, storage, disposal or recycling, makes its money on the quantity of waste entering its gates. Any attempt to reduce the amount of waste available to them would be met with resistance and the waste management industry has demonstrated that it is capable of exerting considerable influence, both with states and the federal government. This influence is due to the close working relationships formed with government officials who are lured by the huge profits made by the waste management industry. Once a facility like this enters a state, their influence is magnified by the influence of every company and government agency that uses the facility, since once their wastes are sent there, the waste generators have a vested interest in protecting the facility. Their power is so strong that it is not always clear whether the government is controlling the facility or the facility is controlling the government.

There are many examples of the cozy relationship with the government regulatory agencies. The boldness and power of this industry is further illustrated by the fact that they were able to get EPA to attempt to strike down a law in North Carolina designed to protect its drinking water from effluent from a proposed hazardous waste facility on the grounds that this interfered with the free movement of hazardous waste.

I believe that if, after due consideration, it is felt that there is a need for off-site hazardous waste management capacity, that it should be owned and operated by the state and it should be limited to waste generated in that state. It should not be run as a business. That is precisely what's wrong with the commercial hazardous waste management industry. As a business, income is produced by taking waste through the door. The more the better.

In answer to your initial question, of whether or not your children would suffer any negative health effects, I can refer you to the work of several leading chemists and toxicologists who will verify that there is definitely exposure to hazardous waste particles from every incinerator. How much depends on numerous factors, but you can look at studies by Dr. Paul Connett of St. Lawrence University or Dr. Paul Sacco, Director of Biological Sciences at Xavier University, among others. North Carolina's experience in Caldwell County where for years neighbors have been complaining is a prime example. Under investigation, the state discovered traces of ten dangerous metallic and organic poisons in local soils. A host of toxins, including dioxins, furans, cadmium, and lead are known to be associated with incineration. Any individuals who already have a compromised pulmonary condition would be advised to stay indoors during days when the incinerator is actively burning heavy metals. The challenge would be to know what days those were. History has proven that companies are not forthcoming with that information. The ultimate question remains: is the economic viability of the commercial hazardous waste industry of greater concern than the health and well-being of the citizens of North Carolina?

In conclusion, I would like to add that I know of no EPA claims that there is a shortage of hazardous waste management facilities. The federal law CERCLA Section 104c(9) is frequently cited as justification for these facilities, but it only requires that each state have a plan for handling its own waste. The law does not require that the waste be handled by an offsite commercial facility. There is nothing to preclude a state from requiring that hazardous waste be treated on the site where it is generated nor does it preclude a state owning and operating a facility limited to wastes generated within the state. The decision to build a huge commercial hazardous waste facility, many times larger than required by North Carolina's industries, was the state government's decision, not EPA's.

I hope I have adequately addressed your questions. Please let me know if I can be of further assistance.

Sincerely,
William Sanjour

Sadie's breathing became more rapid as Ada Lynn read. When she finished, Sadie gasped. "Oh my God, Holy Jesus. This is huge. I need a copy of that letter."

Ada Lynn hesitated. "I don't know. I need to show it to Dutch."

"Do you realize what he just said? What an EPA commissioner from the very top ranks just said? He just stated in writing that this facility was unnecessary, not required and potentially dangerous to those living nearby. He advised against any commercial siting!"

The baby had stopped crying, as if sensing the increasing heartbeat in Sadie's chest. Then as she got more agitated, the cries commenced again. Sadie jiggled her with more intensity, at the same time calculating the consequences the letter might have.

Gabe clawed at his mother, pushing the letter aside and climbing back into her lap. "What would you do with it?" Ada Lynn asked. She let the letter lie limply in her hand and put her other arm around her two year old.

Sadie rattled off the ways she could use it as fast as they flew into her head. "I'd make a thousand copies. Send one to every legislator, every newspaper in the state, every grassroots group, every television station, every citizen in the county. Two thousand," she changed her number mid-sentence. "I'd need at least two thousand copies."

The alarmed look on Ada Lynn's face told Sadie she'd come on too strong too fast.

"I don't know," Ada Lynn hesitated. "Dutch doesn't want to get caught in the middle of this. I need to talk to him."

Sadie was dumbfounded. The sudden thought that Dutch might destroy the letter sent her into a panic. "Honey, you've got a baby. You've got a two year old with asthma. You're living within two miles of the proposed site. You're smack dab in the middle of this whether you want to be or not. Please… please, let me use that letter."

"Maybe you'd take the baby for a walk in her stroller?" Ada Lynn groaned and Sadie saw her face go slack as if this letter, added to everything else, was too much to digest. "Let me think about it."

"Sure, okay," Sadie hesitated. "Would you let me talk to Dutch? Just don't do anything to the letter before I talk to Dutch."

Gabe squirmed in Ada Lynn's lap. "Come on, honey," she said folding the letter and slipping it back into the envelope. "Let's read you a book." Gabe slipped his thumb in his mouth and settled into the crook of his mother's arm. Sadie stepped onto the front porch and strapped Trisha into the stroller before gently bumping it down the steps to the sidewalk. Within half a block the baby had stopped crying and Sadie was quickly becoming obsessed with the letter. It could be the silver bullet they needed. This couldn't wait. She had to tell Cliff.

*****

By the time Sadie got to Cliff's house the baby had fallen asleep. When he opened the door, she gave him the classic "shush" sign, finger raised to her lips. She pushed the stroller over the threshold and to a corner wall. "There's a letter," she whispered.

"Yeah? What about?" he whispered back.

She sat down in one of the Lazy Boy recliners in front of the television. "It's from an official in the EPA condemning the siting of a commercial hazardous waste incinerator."

"So, let's see it."

"I don't have it."

"Who does?"

"I can't tell you."

Cliff frowned, exaggerating the hog jowls and lines running from the edge of his nose past the corners of his mouth. The morning sun tweaked through the sheers over the front window and caught stubble of gray whiskers on his chin. "So, how does that help us?"

"I don't know yet."

"It's just three weeks until the first public hearing. It would sure be nice to be able to pull a rabbit out of the hat when all the news media are there," he said.

"I know," Sadie said. "I'm trying to think of a way we can release the letter, if they won't give it to me."

"Why won't they give it to you?"

"They're divided between their loyalties. It's complicated."

Cliff raised both eyebrows waiting for a further explanation. When none was forthcoming he guessed and didn't push for more.

"I was thinking..." Sadie paused.

"What?"

"Well, if the governor knew about the letter and had a copy of it, we could request a copy through the public records laws. We could force him to release it."

"Are you kidding? If the governor knows, he'll do everything he can to quash it."

"He'll share it with others. We'd get it from him or someone else," Sadie said. Already she had a plan. It involved Helen Truitt.

Chapter Nineteen

"What is it, Helen?" The colonel hesitated to invite her in. He and Caren had a meeting that afternoon in Raleigh with the governor's chief of staff and ICS representatives. They needed to leave shortly.

"I came straight from the Quaker Café." Helen appeared breathless.

By the looks of it, she'd come straight from the back feed lot. Her hair was windblown, her blouse wrinkled. She'd done a hasty once over with lipstick and hadn't applied eyebrow pencil. This wasn't the Helen he knew. Was the whole town sleep deprived? Regardless, he couldn't offer her a seat. If she sat, she'd never leave.

It occurred to him that the women surrounding him had become a daily problem. It started with Sadie Baker, and then Mary Law, God rest her soul. In recent weeks Helen had become more of a nuisance, wanting daily updates and forever phoning to interject speculation and local gossip. He didn't even trust Caren Drake any more. She insisted on driving alone to the meetings in Raleigh, and often stayed overnight in her apartment there. He suspected she had a personal agenda she was unwilling to share—possibly a romantic interest, or more troubling something else.

"This morning I was having my coffee and toast and I overheard something I think may be very important. Evidently there's a letter." Helen spit out the words as fast as she could.

"A letter? What kind of letter?" He waited to hear more chicanery.

"The CAP group has obtained something in writing from a bigwig at the EPA stating they never recommended that North Carolina build a hazardous waste incinerator and it would be dangerous for the community to do so. I overheard Sadie say that once it got out, the incinerator issue would be dead."

Now she had his attention. "Good Lord, this could be a disaster. Are you sure, Helen?" He reacted instinctively and grabbed both of her shoulders. She stiffened, as if he might shake the information out of her. "Who wrote the letter?" he demanded.

Helen caught her breath, slightly alarmed. He realized he'd scared her and let go. "It was hard for me to catch the name," she said. "After all, they were sitting at another table." She seemed a bit frightened by his reaction. "Sandford? Sandor, Sander…something like that."

The colonel jotted down a few words in a small notebook he kept in his shirt pocket.

"There's more." She tried to remember. There was so much that got tossed back and forth at the café. Eavesdropping had become daily sport. "They discussed ways to disrupt the meeting…blowing something up…maybe the transformer that runs into the building? I don't know. I couldn't hear everything."

The colonel shook his head in disgust. "Good Lord, they're anarchists. I warned the governor. They'll stoop to anything." He moved Helen to the door, eager to get his thoughts together before he left for Raleigh. "This has been very helpful. You're a great asset, Helen."

"Do you want me to report this to the governor? I'll call if it would help."

"No," the colonel stopped her. That was the last thing he needed. He didn't want to give Helen direct access to Governor Dunnet's office. "I'll talk to him. As a matter of fact, we're meeting today." He looked at his watch. "So I need to get going."

Helen had her wits about her again and the idea that she could provide the details for some important information piqued her desire to be more involved. "As a county commissioner, I really should talk to him, don't you think. I represent the entire county, not just a town."

"Thank you, Helen. This is a private meeting, and I shouldn't have told you about it. Highly confidential. I can trust you to keep it between us, can't I?" He tried to usher her out the door.

Helen did a quick jerk of her head and her voice had an edge. "I think as a matter of principle, in fact, I insist that I be included. How can I tell my constituency that discussions went on at the highest levels in the state concerning our county and I was excluded?"

The colonel swore under his breath. He didn't have time for this. "Helen,

I can't put it more plainly than what I've said. The governor will know how much you've assisted him in this project." He opened the front door, and with his hand on her back, he gently guided her to the steps. "Trust me, Helen. When we have the grand opening of ICS, I promise you'll have a place on the platform and we'll recognize your contributions."

Although she followed his lead, she seemed reluctant. He remained long enough to give her a peck on the cheek in hopes of soothing her hurt feelings and then closed the front door. Back at his desk he added Helen's information to the memo he'd prepared. He didn't intend to share the limelight with anyone, Helen or Caren Drake. He had sustained a frontal attack from the media. Now it was time for the governor's office to realize that he could save their ass.

*****

The attorney general began without acknowledging the absence of Sheriff Howard. He sat next to the governor's chief of staff Ron Abernathy on one side of the table facing Caren and Colonel Little on the other. Two representatives of ICS sat at the end and a couple of assistants took notes behind them. "I have informed your sheriff that protection for the upcoming public hearing will be handled by the state," he said.

Caren felt a rush of satisfaction. She knew Sheriff Howard would be furious but it proved she had more clout.

The attorney general guaranteed full protection from the highway patrol. Ron Abernathy assured the colonel that the permit hearing would proceed as required by law.

"I have an issue of some urgency," the colonel said after the first two agenda items had been cleared. "There's a letter. Evidently someone in an influential position at the EPA is telling the opponents that a hazardous waste incinerator would never be monitored properly by the EPA and would be a threat to the health of the residents."

Caren sat up and stared at him. Unbelievable, she thought. Where did this come from? Why hadn't he told her?

"Goddamnit! Where's the letter?" Abernathy, the chief of staff, blurted out a string of profanities. "Who's the son-of-a-bitch who wrote that shit?" He seemed far more upset about the potential damage of such a letter than the prior discussion about sophomoric antics of a few unruly protesters.

"Who told you that?" Caren asked, but the colonel ignored her.

"We don't have it. It was written by a Sampson, Sandor, Sanders…?"

"William Sanjour," one of the assistants interjected. "He went to a rally in Pender County last year and made the newspapers by saying that the incinerator wasn't needed. I was down there at the time, but it didn't get much traction in the media. He focused primarily on the need for more reduction methods."

"All right." The attorney general looked at his watch to indicate he needed to be someplace else. "Abernathy, if you'd tell the governor about this. We'll track down the letter."

*****

Two days later after requesting and receiving a copy of the letter from the EPA director, Governor Martin Dunnet fired back in the return mail.

Dear Bill,

Under your leadership, the Environmental Protection Agency has encouraged, supported and pressured my administration to meet our responsibility for siting and permitting a hazardous waste incinerator. Recently, I spoke with a group of citizens from Cedar Branch who invited InCinoServe to build a facility there, provided I could arrange for additional incentives. These good people have been terrorized by extremists posing as 'environmentalists'. One of your officials in the Solid Waste Division has been active in stirring up this chemophobia. His name is William Sanjour. As I attempted patiently to explain to these constituents that our proposal has the support of the EPA, and that your agency endorses such an incinerator, I was shown a letter from Mr. Sanjour on EPA stationery which disputed my argument. Your immediate attention is required.

Sincerely, Martin

Senator Ian Lasker's office was not as politically correct. He instead forwarded a handwritten letter which read: "Action is req'd to remove Sanjour from his position with the EPA. This country is being destroyed by so called environmental experts who don't know their ass from a hole in the ground. Please advise what action has been taken to remove Sanjour from his well paid position."

Sadie called William Sanjour's office to invite him to come speak at the public hearing in two weeks to get him on record repeating what'd he'd written in the letter. He regretfully told her his travel had been restricted by the EPA director. "I'll be filing a lawsuit, though," he added. "Best of luck to your group. Keep up the fight."

Chapter Twenty

Cliff's dirty tricks committee gradually degenerated into a raucous group of beer-drinking, cigarette-smoking adolescents with no censorship on what got thrown into the mix. Cliff thrived on this sort of brainstorming. Sometimes the best ideas came from offshoots of exaggerations and joviality. As Cliff took notes, the rest of those in the room stood, cajoled and emboldened the others to get even more outrageous. Cliff quickly scanned the list and crossed out anything related to kidnapping, theft, or destruction of property. Then they got to work.

The men included a lineman, the manager of a saw mill, two construction workers, one college professor, two farmers, a pharmacist, a high school counselor, a crop duster, a dentist, and a young man who would soon be making more money than any of them in a sprouting new industry called computer technology. No women attended, although Cliff shared most of what they discussed with Sadie.

The public hearing was ten days away. They had three goals: first to insure that no one got physically hurt; second to create enough havoc to force ICS to reschedule the hearing; third to get as much publicity as possible. Arrests would be inevitable. In fact, arrests would work in their favor as long as it gained them sympathy. The media has a habit of rooting for the underdog.

Ultimately four schemes were hatched in hopes that at least three of them would work. Men were appointed to put their teams together and review their plans with Cliff when they had everything in place.

"The fewer involved, the better," Cliff forewarned. "We want the element of surprise. We're not itching to bury 'em, just derail 'em."

Back at her duplex, Sadie made phone calls to several people she trusted. Her first call was to Billie McFarland.

"Billie, we're making plans to disrupt the public hearing. We're going to create a disturbance. Would you be willing to get arrested if it comes to that?"

"What would I have to do?"

"It wouldn't be anything that is a felony. You might get fined."

"Would I go to jail?"

"They might take you to jail and file a complaint. We'd have someone there to post your bail."

"What's the plan?"

"We're keeping it a secret. We'll tell you the morning of the meeting."

"Can I opt out at that point?"

"Of course you can. If at any time you don't want to participate, you just stop. No one will hold it against you. This isn't for everyone. We recognize that."

"Any chance of getting hurt?"

"I certainly hope not, but I can't guarantee what the police will do. They might use tear gas or handcuffs." What Sadie didn't say was that there could be a nutcase in the crowded room who'd come at them unexpectedly. There were hotheads on both sides who were wired by a jackleg electrician. Nobody had a clue what they might do.

"Why are you asking me?"

"Because you're an attractive woman with balls who would grab the attention of the camera crews."

"Camera crews?" Billie's voice went up half an octave.

"We're hoping for some national coverage."

"Well then, I'm in."

Not everyone was as enthusiastic about being *in* as Billie. That was okay. Sadie was selective about the women she asked and she didn't want anyone faint-hearted or with loose lips.

*****

Sadie continued to bring up Sanjour's letter with her son and daughter-in-law. "Ada Lynn, honey, have you and Dutch made a decision about whether you're willing to release the letter from Sanjour?"

"Mama Sadie, Dutch thinks the letter would turn a lot of people against us."

Sadie didn't understand their logic. It boiled down to the health of their children, but as exasperated as she'd become, she restrained from pushing harder. She feared they would destroy the letter to end the controversy.

"I think," Ada Lynn paused. She looked out of the corner of her eye at Sadie. "I think Dutch believes you can stop the whole thing without our help."

Sadie didn't think so, but pride swelled up within her. She had his confidence. Maybe they had turned a corner together. "I wish I could," she said, "but things are very unpredictable."

Ada Lynn smiled. "That's basically life, isn't it?"

Chapter Twenty-one

Suspecting that Helen Truitt had taken the bait and gone to the colonel with rumors about a damaging letter from the EPA, Sadie alerted Audrey Garner. Under the Freedom of Information Act, Audrey requested copies of correspondence between the Waste Management Board, the governor and the EPA during the past thirty days. The governor's office stalled. It would take a while. They'd be back in touch.

The days ticked down one at a time and the tension in Cedar Branch escalated from a constant simmer to a slow burn. The August sun blistered the grass to shades of brown and the air conditioner at the Quaker Café labored, broke down, got fixed, and chugged away again like a Tonka Toy. The café had become the only place in town where both CAPs and PROs entered on civil terms and swallowed their animosity. No one dared not come. Diners had a special relationship with the café including their right to belong. The café was their second home, part of a comfortable routine that reminded them of how things should be.

Every morning the café filled with the two camps sitting a few tables apart and they blatantly eavesdropped on one another. The least snippet of new information sent committees on both sides scurrying into battle mode for a counterplan. It became difficult to decipher the red herrings.

"I hear Greenpeace is sending in hundreds to lie down in the roads and block traffic," Helen Truitt warned the colonel.

"I've overheard the crop duster is going to spray the town with itching powder."

"I heard it was sneezing powder," someone corrected.

"They're planning to kidnap the ICS executives, bomb the Armory, and dump a ton of manure on the platform."

"A ton of manure on the stage?" Cliff chuckled when Billie told him what she'd heard. "That's good. We hadn't thought of that one."

The colonel talked daily to the attorney general's office. Caren knew he had begun to keep her out of the loop. Inwardly she seethed. On Monday, three days prior to the scheduled hearing, she got in her car and drove to Raleigh, took the 440 beltway to Glenwood and parked her car in front of a pub called O'Malley's. It was still early. She claimed one of the few wooden booths with the high back for a bit of privacy.

"Hi Caren," a college kid in an O'Malley's t-shirt and a green apron across his jeans flipped open an order pad. "Where you been hiding?"

"Work," she said, thrilled to hear her name pronounced correctly for the first time in months. "I'm waiting for someone, but I'm starved. Still doing the Elvis?"

"You bet."

"How about give me one without the whipped cream and a cup of coffee."

"You got it," he said. "Haven't seen you with your friends in weeks."

"Bogged down. I need to get out more." As seriously as she took her job, she used to leave plenty of time for nightlife. She missed O'Malley's. Her apartment was only a ten minute drive and this was a favorite spot. She'd spent many early evenings over a beer on the patio and late evenings with a former male colleague. The end of that relationship and the beginning of her job in Cedar Branch had coincided. Her sex life had vanished at the same time. She watched the waiter walk away. Nice toosh, she thought.

"Miss Drake?" The man was taller than she'd expected, maybe even taller than her. She wasn't standing, so he had the advantage for the moment. On the phone he'd spoken in a bass, which implied, however erroneously, that he would be a large man with dark hair. He was neither, instead quite slender with blond hair that appeared to have been fluffed dry.

She nodded and he extended an arm. His hands were graceful, fingers long and thin, like those of a violinist. She noticed he wore no rings.

"I appreciate your willingness to talk to me. Interesting place." He looked around the pub. She couldn't tell whether he approved or not, as if it mattered. He'd specifically said *a place of your choosing*. "May I?" he said, indicating a desire to join her.

"Of course," she replied. "It's your meeting."

This was unusual for her to meet a man she didn't know, but it was midday in a public place. When he called he'd said that he represented a company that was interested in her. A headhunter, she immediately determined. Actually, she was flattered to be recruited in such a manner and interested in what he had to offer.

He looked at the wooden seat and hesitated. She thought for a moment he might pull out a handkerchief and a bottle of sanitizer, but he gave her a tight-lipped smile and slid in. A whiff of cedar floated across the table—outdoorsy smell, she thought, although he certainly wasn't a logger…perhaps part of a rowing team?

"How's it going?" he asked.

"That depends," she said, as of yet undecided as to whether she'd trust this man. Just because he smelled good didn't mean he wasn't a plant—maybe someone from CAP sent to throw her off guard. To be honest, she didn't think they were that smart. Besides this guy dressed too well. She knew something about clothes and the Carnali Sienna Contemporary navy suit he wore impressed her. He could possibly be from corporate at ICS.

"The Elvis," the waiter said sliding a plate onto the table with a warm banana muffin that had peanut butter dripping off the edges. Alongside, he plopped down a fruit salad. "You sir, what can I get you?"

The man eyed Caren's choice with amusement and then scanned the menu and quickly ordered their special. "An open faced roast beef with a cup of coffee and extra napkins." When the waiter left, he pushed his wire rim glasses up the bridge of his nose and suppressed a smile. "The Elvis?"

Caren couldn't decide whether he was humoring her or being condescending. The last thing she needed was another pompous male who needed someone to massage his ego. She responded sharply, "So, what's up?"

"I intended to ask you the same thing," he said.

"As in?"

"Why is an attractive woman like you wasting her time and talents in a nothing little town like Cedar Branch? You've got everything to lose and nothing to gain."

An attractive woman? She didn't think he was ICS corporate. "If I pull it off, then I'll be in line for a nice promotion," she said.

"And if you can't pull it off, your reputation is shot. You'll need to get married and start having babies."

Caren flinched. That was a low blow. Something a man would say. "We've already won," she fired back. "The state has sealed the deal."

"You think?"

"I know."

The man ran his thumb and forefinger under the rim of his glasses. Then he took them off. He looked at Caren and shook his head. "You really believe that?"

She sniffed, "I do."

The open faced sandwich arrived. "Anything else, sir?" the waiter asked.

"Some more coffee, please."

Caren took a small bite of her muffin. She was more cautious than usual. This would not be a good time to drip peanut butter down her blouse. He, in turn, speared a piece of beef and then pushed a small amount of mashed potatoes on the backside of the fork before lifting the food to his mouth. Very European.

They ate in silence. She waited, not in any hurry to press him for information. As a rule, silence worked to her advantage.

"Tell you what," he said after he'd consumed half of the food on his plate. "I'm here to make you an offer."

"What kind of offer?"

"In marketing with my company."

"And that company is…?"

He didn't even look at her, but speared another piece of meat and continued. "It would start immediately. I'd have to know that you were ready to leave your current job before I could give you more details."

Caren looked at him like he was from outer space. This was the craziest job offer she'd ever heard of. "You're kidding?"

"Nope. Dead serious. It would include a respectable sign-on bonus and any moving expenses that you might incur."

"It's not in Raleigh, then?"

"No."

Caren threw back her head and laughed. "Mister…" she stopped. "I don't even know your name."

He cocked his head to one side. "Todd. You can call me Todd Wilkins, if names are important."

"Well, Mr. Todd Wilkins, if that's your real name, I don't know anything about you—who you are, what you represent, where you're from, what you think I can do. I don't even know how you got my name and tracked me down. But this isn't going any further. I can tell you right now, I'm not interested." She slid out from her side of the booth, stood and motioned for the waiter.

"Oh, please," he said. "Let me pay for the Elvis."

The tone of his voice annoyed the devil out of her. She wished she'd ordered the rib eye and a Bloody Mary.

"I'll be in touch," he said rather cavalier. "I don't expect it will be long before you change your mind."

Chapter Twenty-two

Sadie didn't sleep the night before the public hearing. The possibilities of things going wrong weighed heavily and the fear of someone getting hurt ate a hole in her stomach. How many people would show up? Could Cliff's committee actually pull off any of their dirty tricks? If they got arrested, how severe were the consequences? What were the PROs planning? Was there a rebel among them with a completely different agenda? It could all backfire big time.

Miss Ellie's son, who owned the old mansion on the edge of town, slipped Sadie an envelope with two thousand dollars in cash. "For bail or whatever else you need," he said in a moment when they were alone in the café. "Just between you and me." Out of respect to his mother he had remained mute on the incinerator issue, and this was the first indication Sadie had of where he stood.

Similarly, Cliff and Phil received several large contributions from donors who wished to remain anonymous. Technically, this money was illegal considering CAP's non-profit status. Sadie felt like she'd been dropped into a suspense novel. She'd never believed this sort of thing happened in real life—especially in small towns like Cedar Branch.

Sadie opened her door at seven that morning in hopes of walking off some of her anxiety. The stench of ammonia hit her full force. She coughed, caught her breath, covered her nose and stepped back into her duplex closing the door behind her. What in the hell was that? She dialed Cliff's number. No answer. She tried the Quaker Café. Miss Ellie picked up.

"Miss Ellie, this is Sadie. What's that awful smell in town?"

"A tanker truck carrying waste from one of the hog farms to a lagoon jackknifed and spilt his load."

"Where?"

"On Main Street, in front of the school. They've already got Highway Patrol on the scene detouring traffic around a four block stretch."

"Is Cliff there?"

"He's the only one here," Miss Ellie said. "Hold a second."

"You?" Sadie asked as soon as she heard his voice.

"Had nothing to do with it." He denied fault instantly. She believed him. Cliff owned up to the holes he dug. "Honest accident. Dog ran in front of the truck and the driver swerved."

"How bad?"

"A truck's already on the way for clean-up. Said it would take three to four hours. Might leave a nasty smell for a while, though." Before Sadie asked he added, "They're refusing to postpone the hearing."

"Maybe the PROs set that up. What do you think…to keep people away?" A muscle in her right temple started to twitch.

"They're blaming us, of course. Some people might stay home, but it certainly speaks to the problem of potential accidents with tanker trucks driving through our town all day. Can't see if that helps their cause. Sort of a strange coincidence."

Sadie stood still holding the phone in her hand. *Conicidence? Really?* She hung up and fixed herself a cup of coffee and tried to steady her nerves. The coffee didn't help. Sleep was out of the question. Finally she put on a clean pair of slacks, a short sleeve blue pullover, and used her curling iron for the first time in two weeks. With the chance of cameras and television coverage, vanity prevailed.

Even Smokey refused to stay outside and scurried back in after doing his business. Lord, the town smelled like an open sewage pit, not surprising since that's exactly what the spill involved.

Sadie saw Irene peeking through the front window sheers as she left at nine-thirty and called out, "Come on up to the Armory with me, Irene. We'll sit together." The curtain dropped and Irene disappeared.

A sign on the door stated that the Armory doors would open at nine forty-five. Most people remained in their cars to avoid the foul odor. Sadie climbed into a car with Phil Harper and together they scanned the automobiles and growing media caravan.

"Looks like most of our folks are showing up," Phil said. The highway patrolmen with surgical face masks over their noses directed traffic into the

Armory parking lot.

"I don't see Sheriff Howard anywhere or Andy Meacham," Sadie said.

"Word is the attorney general is handling everything through the highway patrol. I hear the sheriff is as mad as a wild boar that's just been clipped," Phil said.

To the left of the Armory, two national guardsmen stood at the entrance to a prison bus. Police dogs sniffed around the perimeter. Sadie shook her head. "You'd think we were revolutionaries," she said.

The doors hadn't yet opened when a single engine plane could be heard flying overhead. Sadie looked up to see Sam O'Brien's crop duster towing a banner behind his plane. SEND ICS FLYING! He began to loop the Armory. The press climbed out of their trucks, each coughing or pulling out a handkerchief to cover their noses in the process. They snapped photos or recorded video.

Sadie watched with amusement as the colonel stormed out of the Armory sputtering. "Didn't I warn you? Get that man out of the sky. He's going to spray the area."

At that exact moment, something began to flutter out the back of the plane. Some retreated to their cars.

Television reporters switched over to live broadcast. "We are at the Armory in Cedar Branch where the first of two public hearings are to take place as InCinoServe tries to get its permit approved to build a fifty-thousand ton hazardous waste incinerator. There has already been much activity in town beginning with the spill of a tanker carrying hog waste. We are now watching a low flying aircraft with a banner attached and there is something being thrown out of the back of the plane. It appears to be confetti… maybe pamphlets of some sort."

The reporter paused as he waited for the first swirling piece of paper to fall to the ground. "It's money. They're throwing money out of the back of the airplane. I've just had two one-dollar bills land at my feet."

"It's money!" someone screamed.

Those who had started to line up to go into the Armory broke rank and headed back outside. People who had waited in their cars jumped out. The odor now appeared to be insignificant. *Brilliant,* Sadie thought. She got out of the car and started to pick up various pieces of the paper. One out of five bills was real money. The rest were phony paper bills stamped boldly with the words *Bribe Money.*

Cars began to wheel into the Armory. Many pulled off to the side of the road into yards and raced to pick up the bills being scattered over a two block area. People exited their homes, at first confused over the excitement but quickly alarmed by the invasion of their personal property. The highway patrolmen scattered, not sure of their first obligations.

Within ten minutes the plane disappeared. Sadie surveyed the paper covering the ground. She'd known ahead of time they might have a mess. She'd gotten a permit with an agreement they'd clean up any trash, but a lot of the problem took care of itself. People grabbed at everything in hopes of getting some real money.

"I want him arrested immediately," the colonel bellowed, but the captain in charge had little time for the colonel's tirade. He was preoccupied with what they might have missed inside the Armory during the time his men had been distracted.

"There's no law against throwing money out of a plane," he said and ignored the colonel. Instead he reviewed his men's stations to make sure everything was as it should be. The ICS representatives congregated onstage, annoyed that things already seemed out of control. People had begun to stream into the hall without the desired sign in protocol. CAP members sneered at the PRO volunteers making an attempt to seat people in designated areas. A few sharp words were exchanged and two men pushed one another in a brief shoving match.

An ICS woman packaged as tightly as the layers of makeup on her face took the microphone in hand in an attempt to bring the room to order. The microphone squealed and she stiffened. Sadie thought that a well-thrown Frisbee might sever her torso and then felt ashamed of her malice. She didn't know the woman. She was just another flunky employee paid to be the mouthpiece in place of the big guns who wouldn't dare risk the exposure.

"Could we have order?" the ICS mouthpiece shouted into the microphone.

The sound system exaggerated the shrill of her voice and the room went mute for a second or two after the assault on their hearing. Thereafter they promptly ignored her.

"Please seat yourselves so we may begin." The *please* was a mild accommodation, but it didn't work either. The goal was to be as uncooperative as possible in hopes of closing down the meeting.

Caren Drake marched to the microphone reserved for speakers and turned it on. "We are asking politely that everyone take their seats. If you don't, we will ask law enforcement officials to begin to arrest protesters."

"Who in the hell does she think she is?" Sadie grumbled. "Since when does she get to decide when they will start arresting people?"

Out of nowhere, Sheriff Howard appeared and stepped to the podium. The mic was still on. "Miss Drake," he said, "this is a matter for law enforcement to handle, not you. If you would step down and take a seat, please." Those who overheard the exchange applauded.

Sadie respected the sheriff. The way he had handled that ordeal with the Devine brothers two years earlier had left an impression on her. It could have been a nightmare at the Quaker meeting house, but he had shown patience and calm during a confrontational situation. She wanted to be able to show him that their only purpose was to close down the meeting, not to be destructive in any way. As soon as they stopped the proceedings, they'd all leave quietly.

Sadie moved to the center of the sixth row from the front. The plan had been to put her in a position to give cues to other CAP members as to what to do. Cliff predicted she probably would be targeted immediately and removed from the hall. Twelve men from CAP followed, sitting on either side of her. Cane in hand, exaggerating his limp for effect, Cliff sat behind Sadie. They had agreed to be uncooperative, but not hostile if the police tried to get to Sadie.

Sadie climbed onto the folding chair so that she stood above the crowd. They'd start by showing these city folks who would control this meeting. She immediately placed her hand over her heart and began to sing "God Bless America." Those around her stood and burst into song. "God Bless America, land that I love." The ICS stage crowd looked confused, but with the press taking notes and cameras rolling, they rose to their feet and likewise placed their hands over their hearts.

As soon as Sadie stopped singing, Audrey Garner stood on a chair three rows further up and began to sing "America the Beautiful." There wasn't a soul who was going to ask Audrey to sit down, so the ICS officials and the rest of the room remained standing. "Oh Beautiful for spacious skies…" What most people in the audience didn't know is that "America the Beautiful" has eight verses. When Audrey finished, her father, Ed, moved to the middle of the aisle to take the second verse solo. And so it went verse by verse with a chorus after each stanza. Each time the PRO group would begin to take their seats, another CAP member would rise with another verse. It took a full fifteen minutes to get through it all. In retrospect, Sadie sort of regretted they hadn't started at the very beginning all over again just to see how long it would take for someone to stop them.

Billie McFarland, dressed in a snappy red, white and blue outfit for the occasion, finished singing the last verse of "America the Beautiful." Then she whipped out a banner proclaiming ICS HAS GOT TO GO. She and six others stood with it stretched out across the front of the room along with dozens of handheld signs. Again perched atop her chair, Sadie loudly proclaimed, "The invitation to invite ICS into Cedar Branch was done in violation of the open meeting laws of this state and we, the citizens of Cedar Branch, reject any part of that process that enables an illegal siting of such facility in our town. We declare this meeting adjourned and demand that citizens are allowed to vote."

A cheer went up and a loud chant began. "Hey, Hey, Ho, Ho, ICS has got to go." As the chant continued, a confab of ICS representatives, the captain of the highway patrol, Sheriff Howard, Colonel Little and Caren Drake huddled on stage. Looking out across the crowd, the colonel began to point fingers. Sheriff Howard turned a crimson shade of red, shook his head defiantly and fumed out of the building. Arrests began.

As predicted, the patrolmen went straight for Sadie. When the men on her right side remained standing and did not give way, they were arrested one by one. Following Phil Harper's model, they each simply dropped to the floor and became dead weight. No one was resisting arrest, they simply weren't cooperating. Four patrolmen, each holding onto an arm or a leg, were required to carry each individual out to the prison bus. Arresting people became time consuming.

Sadie was next in line, but she'd remained on top of the chair so when the patrolmen finally got to her she teetered a bit as if she might fall. Standing to her left, Roger Fuller, a mild and gentle giant who had never been to a CAP meeting, was unaware of the risks he'd assumed by taking a seat next to Sadie. He reached to help steady her. He was immediately put in handcuffs. Stunned and confused he turned to the patrolman and said, "What the hell?"

From the back of the room Hammie watched in dismay at the fracas that was unraveling. For heaven's sake, he thought, all his mother had done was to sing a song. She was loud and obnoxious, he knew, but really. Give these people a break. They were old. They didn't have the stamina to keep it up. After they let off some steam, they'd tire and quiet down. Now his mother was being hauled out the back door.

Hammie sprinted after her. "Hey," he called.. "HEY," he called again with stronger inflection. "That's my mom. Be careful."

"Stand back," one of the patrolmen ordered him.

Hammie stopped and then pleaded, "Just put her down. Let her walk. She's got bad knees, arthritis."

The patrolman stared down at Sadie. "Will you stand up and walk, ma'am?"

Sadie hadn't planned to, but she was touched by Hammie's concern and his attempt to intervene. She sat up and reached out a hand. Two of the patrolmen helped her to her feet.

"You okay, Mom?" Hammie asked.

She nodded. "I'm fine."

"I'll meet you at the courthouse," Hammie said.

Sadie watched as Hammie headed to his truck. Emotions ran high and as the noise around her rose to a pitch she felt unusually calm. Hammie may have come to the public hearing to speak on behalf of ICS but when it came to push and shove, he'd deserted the PROs to stand by his mother.

When the prison bus pulled off the grounds, Sadie heard the fire alarm go off inside the building and imagined the automatic sprinklers being activated.

As Cliff had predicted, the ICS reps immediately spread a tarpaulin over their sound equipment to protect it from the water while a number of people scattered from under the spray. Cliff left a room still filled with chanting and catcalls and headed for his car where he'd locked the bail money. As he was getting into the car, Marvin Reese pulled in behind him.

"Sadie in there?" Marvin called.

"She's been arrested," Cliff said. He pointed to the bus leaving the grounds.

"Dutch told me to get her. Gabe's back in the hospital. Another bad asthma attack. Said the fumes from that hog spill must have set it off this time."

"Shit." Cliff stiffened. "I'll get her there as fast as I can."

"No, sir." Marvin said. "Dutch and Ada Lynn want Sadie to read some letter at the hearing. Said 'go on, tell her to read it.' Said she'd find it in the top drawer of their bedroom dresser."

Cliff took the manila folder with the cash out of his trunk and walked back to the Armory. The sprinkler system had been turned off although the floors were wet and slippery. While the shouting and banging on metal chairs continued inside, Ed Garner and JC Collier stood outside on a cigarette break. Cliff chuckled at the sight of them. "You two loafers out here lollygagging while the women do all the work?" he mocked.

Ed smirked. "They filled up their bus and have decided to just get through it now. Not arresting nobody for nothing at this point."

"Poor Billie McFarland over yonder." JC nodded inside the room and pointed to the other side. "She's about doing cartwheels to get that patrolman to put cuffs on her. All dressed up in her red, white and blue for the evening news. This is breaking her heart. She doesn't fit the profile."

"You think there's a profile?" Cliff asked, already knowing there was. He hadn't been a policeman for most of his life to not know there's a profile.

"Damn straight," Ed said. "You didn't see no brothers on that bus, did you? My sweet daughter's shaking her finger and yelling in their face and they won't touch her. Look at all them old ladies, God bless them, with their hair brushes banging on them chairs. Not one of them's been led out and everyone's creating more havoc than Sadie did by singing Good Bless America. What a sham."

"Listen," Cliff said, "since you two aren't gonna make front page, how about driving this bail money to the court house for me. I got a message from Sadie that she wants something else on the record here today."

JC and Ed looked interested. "We could do that. What's Sadie got?"

"Don't know yet, but I'm about to find out," Cliff said as he handed them the money. "If there's not enough there, I'll be following behind you as soon as I find that letter and read it into the hearing minutes."

*****

A crowd awaited the arrival of the bus outside the courthouse as the news spread that friends and relatives were being arrested at the public hearing in Cedar Branch. One by one, applause rang out as each one stepped off the bus. They were taken into the hallway in the basement of the court house where each person was processed individually. All told, thirty-seven people were arrested: eight women and twenty-nine men, all white, and no one over the age of sixty except Sadie.

Chapter Twenty-three

Caren Drake sat on the front row with her forehead resting on her right hand. This had turned into a nightmare and was getting worse by the minute. After being sprayed by the fire sprinklers it was agreed they would forge through the comment phase by a direct link between the microphone and the recorder. The bedlam around them would have to be ignored. Caren dreaded seeing the evening news. Undoubtedly, the reporters relished the photo opts which were a gift that kept on giving: the paper money dropped from the crop duster, the local citizens hauled out by their arms and feet to a prison bus, and the sprinkler system drenching everyone on stage as they ran for cover. But it hadn't stopped there. The fact that the colonel blathered like a lunatic to any reporter who would listen didn't help things. The media got a ten second news clip from him and then rushed to film the next publicity stunt.

Audrey Garner, the golden goddess, was a prime target for every camera, and she wasted no time in launching into her diatribe on environmental racism. The fact that Senator Lloyd Robbins accompanied her had a considerable effect. Any senator worth his weight knew how to maximize a sound bite. Instead of listening to the speaker inside, reporters were outside interviewing him.

"My research has revealed that the state of North Carolina already has ample facilities to handle the hazardous waste that our industries now create." The senator paused long enough for more reporters to push their mics closer, then in a deep resounding voice, he announced, "I am submitting a bill to my fellow state legislators that unless we can show the need here in our own state for a commercial facility, that one will not be permitted." Those standing around him applauded, while the banging and chanting in the background drowned out the proponent who was making a statement into the microphone inside the building.

Henry Bennett, a highly respected farmer in the community, stepped to the podium to address the ICS officials and the chanting immediately stopped. As he spoke, a side door to a store room opened and twelve other farmers carrying burlap bags walked out to stand on either side of him. The highway patrolmen appeared startled. Where did these men come from? How had they slipped by security? There had been too many other things to distract them. They shuffled their feet and looked at each other for a cue as what to do.

"Easy fellows," Henry said. "All we got in here is peanuts. Peanuts…the main crop of this county. Did you know we raise more peanuts here in this county than any other place in the world? Ladies and gentlemen," he said facing the stage, "this county alone sold twenty-five million dollars' worth of peanuts last year. Why would anyone jeopardize that industry for a hazardous waste facility that's only going to bring in three and a half million dollars?" Loud applause.

After waiting for the room to calm, which it did for him, Henry continued. "Farmers have heard from the companies that buy their peanuts that regardless of the real effects on their crops, peanuts are a perception crop. Mothers pay attention to what is in their child's peanut butter. The peanut plant owner wrote, and I quote, 'It is our understanding that there will be some fallout from this incinerator. If such fallout creates a problem with the growing of the peanuts or the edible quality of the peanuts, then it will have severe implications for the growers in the area as well as our company.'"

Henry stopped and looked back at his fellow farmers and nodded. "Friends, we stand to lose a whole lot more money than ICS will ever put back into our county. I implore you not to trash our primary livelihood." As he concluded his sentence each of the farmers removed the burlap bag from their shoulder and began to walk to the front of the room to dump the contents at the foot of the stage. When the highway patrolmen realized what was happening, they tried to intervene, but the farmers merely stopped and dumped the peanuts in the aisle where they stood.

At the same time, the storeroom door opened a second time and six baby pigs scampered into the room along with a clutch of baby chicks. The room went wild with laughter. The ICS mouthpiece banged her gavel and yelled, "Order. Order."

The colonel looked as if he might be having a heart attack. He put his hand on his throat and his mouth opened wide, but nothing came out. Caren noticed first and rushed to him. "Colonel, are you all right? Take a breath. Breathe in deeply…that's it. Sit down." She motioned to a chair.

He began to breathe normally although his face remained deep red. "How in the hell did they get those animals in the building?"

"I don't know. Perhaps when everyone was distracted by the airplane or the fire alarm and sprinklers. There was a lot of confusion then."

"This is a three ring circus. Can't *anyone* get *anything* right? Do something. Fix it!"

"I think we just need to get through it at this point," Caren said. She tried to calm him. "They're getting what they need recorded as required."

"YOU," he said pointing at her. "You were supposed to be the wizard to smooth out the wrinkles. Are you totally incompetent?"

Caren straightened, turned and walked away. This was just the tip of the iceberg of what'd he say to her. She looked over the chaos in the room with the camera crews capturing every minute. It was then she saw that man—standing with this back against the wall in the left hand corner. Replete in a tailored suit and tie, he stuck out like a Ferris wheel in the middle of a waterpark. He had been watching her, waiting for her to turn in his direction…the man with those delicate hands and the aberrant job offer. She hated to admit it, but she was both embarrassed and at the same time relieved. He nodded in recognition and even from a distance she saw a twisted smile creep across his face. He reached into his coat pocket and removed a card. Slipping it between the first and second finger, he held it in front of his chest long enough for her to get a good look. Then he placed it on the adjacent ledge, turned and walked out the door.

Caren glanced around to see if anyone had noticed but her. Apparently not. She crossed the room ignoring the chants, the boos, the clanking of hairbrushes, the canes against metal and the fragmentary attempts to restore order. She stood by the ledge. The business card sat, blank side up. She turned it over. A phone number. No more…just a number.

*****

By the time Cliff got back to the Armory the crowd had poured out onto the tarmac. Clusters of people stood around assessing whether or not anything had been accomplished.

"They got it all recorded. That's all they were required to do," Phil Harper told one group. "As far as they're concerned, they've completed their obligation to the community."

"But it's clear the majority of people are opposed," Billie complained.

"Only the majority of those who showed up. They will respond in written form for the permit requirement and argue that those who supported them were too intimidated by our threatening antics to come."

Cliff edged his way into the middle. "Is it over? Done?"

"Over," Phil confirmed.

Billie looked alarmed. "I thought you were supposed to be at the courthouse with the bail money. Has anyone gone after our folks?"

"Yeah, Ed and JC went," Henry Bennett said. "I hear some of them are already back in town, down at the Quaker Café."

"I got this letter," Cliff blurted out. "You're never going to believe it. Straight out of the mouth of one of the EPA directors saying no one should count on the EPA to protect the environment."

"Why didn't you read it into the minutes of the hearing?" Phil said.

"I just got it. Just got hold of it *now*," Cliff repeated. "Come on. Let's go see if Sadie's back at the Quaker Café already. She's going to be so excited." Then it dawned on him why Dutch released the letter. Sadie didn't know her grandson was in the hospital.

*****

Sadie felt as if her emotions had spun through every cycle on wash, rinse and spin that day. From anxiety and fear in the morning to an endorphin high during the permit hearing and finally a let-down reflex and unusual calmness while being transported to the magistrate's office at the county courthouse.

The arrest warrant read, *Disorderly Conduct—intentionally caused a public disturbance at the Cedar Branch National Guard Armory, Cedar Branch, N.C. by using gestures and abusive language which was intended and plainly likely to provoke violent retaliation and thereby cause a breach of the peace.* To her knowledge the only time she'd heard abusive language was when Roger had uttered, "What the hell?" as he was handcuffed. Poor guy. He had been the least offensive person in the room.

A trial date was set for a month away. Someone paid her one hundred dollar bail and she was released with the stipulation that she could not return to the Cedar Branch Armory at any time on that given date. But Cliff wasn't there to meet her. Instead, the arrestees met boisterous cheers as they exited the courthouse and a convoy of trucks and cars awaited them. Hammie stood outside watching for her.

She gave him a hug and he leaned over and kissed her forehead. "You okay?" he asked.

"I'm fine. Thanks for bailing your mom out of jail. I'll pay you back."

He tucked his arm around her shoulder and led her to the parking lot. "You're welcome, but it wasn't me. Don't know who?"

"We had some money put aside from CAP," Sadie said.

"Wasn't them either. When JC and Ed got here someone had already left cash to cover everyone. Came in an envelope. Thirty-seven hundred dollars. Lady at the desk said she didn't recognize the guy."

"I guess there are angels among us," Sadie said.

As Sadie started to climb into Hammie's truck, Cliff came limping across the lot waving at them. "I got some bad news," he said. "Gabe's back in the hospital. Ada Lynn and Dutch are with him. He had another spell after that hog spill this morning. Worse than last time."

Panic seized Sadie and before she could gather her thoughts, Hammie ordered her in his truck and they were on their way to the hospital. Cliff followed. They met Ada Lynn coming out of ER with baby Tricia in her arms.

"Gabe's going to be all right," she said. "Dutch is with him. I'm taking the baby home to get her fed and put her down for a nap."

"We'll stay," Sadie said.

"No, you all go on home," Ada Lynn said. "They won't let but two people back at a time anyway."

"I'll stay at the hospital with Dutch and Gabe," Hammie said. "The rest of you leave."

"Come on, Ada Lynn, I'll drive everyone back to Cedar Branch," Cliff said. "You must be exhausted."

"We all are," Sadie said. "It's been a long day."

*****

Later that evening after spending time with Ada Lynn and getting her and the baby some dinner, Cliff and Sadie returned to her duplex. They sat together on the sofa with Smokey in Sadie's lap. Cliff poured two glasses of wine and sat with his arm around Sadie's shoulders.

"Things never got violent, did they?" Sadie asked.

"Just noisy."

"Did any of your dirty tricks work?"

"They didn't stop the meeting."

"So it's a done deal?" she sighed.

"As far as they're concerned."

"What did we accomplish, Cliff?"

"We'll make the evening news."

"What good does that do us?"

"You've got the letter from William Sanjour. You can send it out."

"I'm going to run against the colonel for mayor," Sadie said.

"Good," Cliff winked at her. "You'll win this time."

The six o'clock local news flipped on and began a video of Sadie being carried out butt first across the screen. Cliff howled. Sadie gasped. "Not funny, Cliff. Not funny one bit."

Half an hour later her phone rang. "Mrs. Baker? Mrs. Sadie Baker?"

"Yes." she braced herself for some smart-alecky remark but the caller didn't sound hostile.

"I'm calling from CBS, Eye on America. Dennis McDonald would like to speak to you. Would you hold, please?"

Sadie jerked up straight and her eyes bulged. "*Dennis McDonald*," she mouthed to Cliff. "The commentator, Dennis McDonald."

"Miss Baker, this is Dennis McDonald with Eye on America. I see that you and your cohorts are giving the governor a rough time in North Carolina."

"We're certainly trying to," she said. Her heart pounded in her chest almost to the point she thought for a moment she would faint.

"I'd like to come down sometime and do a story. What have you got coming up that's newsworthy?"

Sadie pulled herself together. Wasn't everything newsworthy? Did he think this was all a lark? "This entire mess is newsworthy, Mr. McDonald," she said. "Have you ever heard the saying, Dump it in Dixie? Well, that's what they're trying to do. The state government is trying to cram a hazardous waste incinerator down our throats because we're a rural low-income county. We'd have no control over what's shipped in."

"I understand that, Mrs. Baker, and I'd like to talk with some of your people. Actually, I'm aware of several places that have similar fights going on and I'm working on an expanded piece. I'm looking for one where I can get some good action shots. Sorry I missed today," he said. "Sounded like exactly what I needed. Have you got something else like that scheduled soon? Something that would get the public's attention?"

Sadie paused and tried to remember what angles they'd talked about at their meetings. "We've been in touch with Alice Fillmore's office," she said in reference to a national environmental activist. "There's a chance she'll fly down. She's a pretty big name. Would you be interested if we can get her here?"

Sadie was sure she heard a groan at the other end of the line. "Alice is sort of old stuff. Not all that interested, really. Anything else?"

Sadie closed her eyes and shook her head. It was just like Stu had told them. It's all about theater. *The media wants you to put on a show.* "We've got an election coming up in November at both the local and state levels. We're going to make sure that anti-incinerator candidates are elected all the way up the chain to the governor's office. I have a group of women who are prepared to stand in front of the North Carolina State Legislative Building in Raleigh draped with American Flags around their naked bodies. They will demonstrate how our rights have been stripped away from us by lowering the flags."

Sadie heard a guffaw at the other end of the line. "I love it. Let me know when you've got it scheduled and I'll be there with a camera crew."

"Are you interested in a copy of a letter from William Sanjour that states the EPA has failed to properly supervise hazardous waste incinerators in our country and he wouldn't recommend the siting of any commercial incinerator?"

"William Sanjour, Branch Chief in the Hazardous Waste Commission of EPA?"

"Yes, *that* William Sanjour. Our sources tell us that Governor Dunnet and Senator Lasker have demanded that he be fired," Sadie added.

"No kidding? I'd like to see what you've got. Could you fax that letter to me right now?"

"I'll do my best." Sadie's thoughts scrambled wondering where she could find a fax machine at this hour. She knew that Dutch had bought one for the grocery store, but she'd never used it before. Tonight she would learn how. "Give me your number," she said.

*****

Approaching midnight, Cliff and Sadie sat in the small office of the grocery store figuring out whether or not their fax had successfully gone through. As they waited for a confirmation, Cliff bit his lip to suppress a smile. "Dennis McDonald. Pretty impressive." He looked at her and chuckled. "You haven't a clue how you're going to pull this off, do you?"

Sadie took a deep breath. "Nope."

"What? You just suddenly thought you could get some women to all strip naked?"

"It got his attention, didn't it?"

"Oh, yeah, you got his attention." Cliff gave her a peck on the cheek. "Know what?"

"What?"

"I'm falling in love with you."

The color rose in Sadie's cheeks. "Oh, you silly old man." It had been a long time since she'd experienced the sensation of physical desire. She hadn't shared her bed with anyone since Coen had died. She missed those tender moments and the physical connection between two people who cared deeply for one another.

She let her lips meet his. The kiss was firm, sweet and long. It tasted like wine…just right.

*****

Saturday morning as Sadie and Cliff left her duplex to get breakfast at the Quaker Café, they caught Irene peeking from behind her curtain. Billie spoke in a hushed whisper as soon as they walked in and joined her table.

"Well, you two are quite the gossip."

"Why?" Sadie said, taken by surprise.

"Are you kidding? Cliff's car was in front of your place all night long. Helen had the colonel's ear before he took his first sip of coffee."

"Do tell," Sadie said more than just a little disgusted. "Isn't anything sacred in this town?"

*****

Sunday morning the Baptist minister preached on "Sin in the Shadow of the Steeple." Sadie skipped the service. She and Cliff drove into Raleigh to Quick Print to run off two thousand copies of William Sanjour's letter.

Chapter Twenty-four

Caren left Cedar Branch directly after the permit hearing and returned to her apartment in Raleigh. She had to get out of town and clear her head before she sat down again with Colonel Little. More importantly, she wanted him to have time to cool off. She knew she'd get the brunt of his anger. He blamed her for everything that went wrong.

She turned on the TV and watched the hearing replayed as the lead story on the state and local news. Pictures of ICS representatives diving for cover as they got drenched by the sprinkling system flashed in front of her. The cameras highlighted farmers throwing their peanuts onto the floor as baby piglets and chicks scampered around the room. The final scene showed five women being hauled onto the prison bus. Not one picture of any of the men. *Darn them*, she knew the media would play that up. Viewers didn't pay much attention to men being arrested, but they got indignant when mothers were dragged out by cops who all looked like retired football tackles.

They are all morons, she thought. From the ICS officials who drove into town threatening people to sell their land like a couple of two-bit mobsters, to the colonel who believed himself to be above everyone else. She'd been their token blonde. She might as well put on a bikini with an ICS sash across her chest and perch atop the hood of a Dodge Ram in front of the café.

Caren reached in her pocket and pulled out the phone number written across the blank card. She didn't recognize the area code…probably a mobile phone. She hesitated—went to her wine rack and pulled out her last bottle of Cabernet. Nothing in the fridge but wilted lettuce, some low-fat Italian dressing and a hunk of dried Colby cheese. She checked in the cupboard for some crackers and found a stale open roll of Ritz. For a nanosecond she missed the Quaker Café. She could eat a cheeseburger right now with French fries slathered in ketchup.

The television rambled on into national news as she poured her favorite red sedative into a glass and took the first few swallows. Then, there it was all over again, playing in front of her. My God, Cedar Branch had gotten national coverage—not much, only about fifteen seconds, but enough. Her stomach went into that death defying plunge as if she had just dropped down the other side of the summit of a roller coaster. She thought she might throw up. She needed to start work on a press release to go out first thing the next morning, but she'd lost her equilibrium. Maybe she should just quit…stay in Raleigh. Call in the morning and tell the colonel to find another sucker to manage his personal campaign. That would stink up her resume pretty quick.

She picked up the card and fingered it again. When the wine glass was empty she dialed the number.

A voice responded after three rings. "Hello, Caren. May I call you Caren?"

He had pronounced her name correctly. That immediately elevated him above the phonetically challenged numbskulls in Cedar Branch. "Just curious, Todd." She put emphasis on his supposed name, Todd. "What are you offering?"

"Dinner. I assume you're in Raleigh?"

"I am."

"You've had a rough day. Let me take you out."

She didn't respond.

"A good meal, a drink or two might help."

"Where did you have in mind?" She didn't want to give him her address, although she guessed he probably knew. He seemed to know more about her than she cared to think.

He snickered. "Caren, I don't wish to be seen with you anymore than you wish to be seen with me. It behooves neither of us to give our adversary the advantage."

"And just who are your adversaries, Todd?" she asked.

"Let's say eight o'clock. I'll give you an address. Call a cab. If you don't like the looks of the restaurant when you arrive, just tell the cabbie to take you home and I'll dine alone."

*****

Caren didn't recognize the neighborhood, one of those planned communities where the shops, churches, school, post office and library were built in a downtown square even before the lots had been sold and the houses constructed. Sidewalks, front porches all with two rocking chairs and a central playground outfitted with a bandstand and picnic shelters were in place. Old fashioned street lamps hugged the narrow roads that ran between manicured lawns. She felt as if she'd arrived in Mayberry.

The cab pulled up in front of a store window marked Apothecary. "The restaurant?" the cabbie asked.

"Yes," she said.

"It's upstairs. Steps at the end of the walk there." He pointed to a brick path between the shop and the bank building to the right.

"Oh, yes, thank you. I see," she said. She certainly felt safe. She couldn't imagine any rapists hanging around these streets. She paid the driver and stepped out. "If I need a cab back?" she asked.

"No problem. They'll call one inside."

A receptionist at the top of the stairs was expecting her. "Miss Drake?" Caren nodded. "Right this way. Your party has already arrived."

The receptionist bypassed the main dining room and led her down a short hall to an alcove. A small square table was draped in a burgundy table cloth. Matching napkins blazed forth from stemmed water goblets and a single rose in a crystal bud vase adorned the center. The waiter pulled out her chair as her dinner partner rose and gave a slight bow. A bottle of Cabernet had already been poured.

"Quaint," Caren said.

"My very favorite. I happen to be fond of Portuguese food and Fado music. I fell in love with Amália Rodrigues the first time I heard her. Does she sound familiar?"

"I don't know her," Caren admitted. She took a few moments to listen to the background music. The soothing voice accompanied by the plucked strings of a Portuguese steel guitar had a definite charm, unlike the overbearing loud sounds of country music and pop that blared throughout most restaurants.

"This is nice. Your neighborhood?" she asked.

"No," he said and raised his glass. "Just here on business…to see you. Shall we toast the success of the first public hearing?"

"Dear Lord," Caren groaned. The wine relaxed her bit by bit and it felt good to have a sympathetic ear. "It was a disaster, wasn't it?"

"Hardly. It's been recorded as *done*. They just need to get through one more and they've met the requirements."

"Whose side are you on, anyway? I'm a bit confused," Caren said, foregoing the toast.

"The winning side. I always plan to be on the winning side…and you should too."

*****

Caren arrived at eight-thirty sharp on Monday morning at the Cedar Branch town hall. She'd already sent out press releases that condemned the adolescent behavior and childish pranks of the CAP members. She highlighted that their inability to offer any credible studies to challenge ICS nullified their protest. In addition she added, "It's impossible to conduct even an ordinary town board meeting in Cedar Branch anymore. A handful of outsiders have seized the attention of the media with these ridiculous antics. Unfortunately, news organizations thrive on this type of theatrics."

The mayor was quoted at the end of the article. "I am appalled at what this is costing Cedar Branch and the state of North Carolina as we attempt to deal with these stupid demonstrators. The opposition shows a complete lack of respect for the government officials they have elected. They are an embarrassment to the law-abiding citizens of this good town. They should all be locked up."

In response to his statement one of the CAP members had the final word in the article. "Better bring twenty prison buses for the next permit hearing, because they're going to have to lock up the whole damn town."

Colonel Little walked into his office with three different newspapers under this arm, *The News and Observer, The Virginian Pilot*, and *The Daily Herald*. He threw them on his desk and looked up to see Caren waiting for him. "Where did you run off to?" he asked, his voice dripping with sarcasm. "Funny how you weren't around, but your name is all over the papers."

"I left for Raleigh. I felt like the best place to tackle the news media was on their doorsteps, not on the telephone." She didn't appreciate his tone, but she'd expected it. She'd play his game for a bit longer.

"Un-huh." He looked down and began to thumb through *The Daily Herald.* The first five pages all carried blown-up pictures capturing the chaos at the hearing. Finally he looked up. "Who's running this show, Caren? Tell me. Am I in charge or am I being played? Because if you and the governor are making plans to walk away from this and leave me looking like some crackerjack who doesn't know the difference between a honeycomb and a wasps' nest, then we need to reset the clock."

"Colonel, I'm sorry if…"

"Don't give me *sorry*." He raised his voice. "Sorry doesn't hack it in my business. Sorry costs money and lives. Nobody gets away with *sorry.* This is *my* town, *my* shift, and *my* responsibility. I don't expect anything to go out of *my* office without *my* approval, and that includes all press releases. There should be no communications between the governor, the attorney general, or the BAG lobby unless I'm a part of them. Is that understood?"

Caren considered a rebuttal. She had an overwhelming urge to tell him that he was a two-bit pawn in a very big money operation. Instead she straightened her shoulders, arched one eyebrow and looked him in the eye. "Understood," she said. If she'd had second thoughts as she drove away from Raleigh that morning, she had none now. She'd take care of number one.

Having said his piece, the colonel sunk into his chair. "CAP has the letter from that Sanjour guy. What a son-of-a-bitch. I hope they fire him. Cliff Lyons will probably be blabbing about it all over the radio."

"Let the governor's office handle it." Caren dismissed his concern. She'd seen the letter. It was damaging, but needed to be dealt with by higher-ups. "That's between them and the EPA director. They'll discredit Sanjour and have him shuffling memos within the week."

"And Sadie Baker has announced to the press she's running against me for mayor. What a joke." The colonel forced a laugh. "Ha!"

"Well, we knew someone would challenge you. That's a gift." Caren said.

"The woman's been arrested—drug out of the public hearing feet first. She's about to self-destruct. She's coming unhinged."

The colonel snorted, "I hear that Cliff Lyons spent the night at her place Friday night." He shook his head and mumbled, "That's not an image I care to think about."

"We've got a bigger problem to focus on," Caren said. "Every one of your town board members is up for re-election in November."

The colonel hunched his shoulders and grunted. "Stupid, isn't it? Never dawned on anyone to rotate the election cycle."

Caren shook her head, having the upper hand in the conversation again. "You're going to have opposition up and down the totem pole. If people get fired up, even the dog catcher will be a CAP member. Three new board members could overturn the annexation, zoning, and environmental requirements that you've put into place."

The colonel stood up and began to pace. "I thought we would have this all tied up before the election. The permit would be approved. It's a private transaction between a company and a private land owner. It's supposed to be a done deal."

"There are a lot of *ifs* in that thinking. *If* the permit is approved and then you lose the election, the company could sue the town for reimbursement of their expenses incurred during the developmental stage. Obviously, the easiest thing to do is to win the election. Then there would be no questions. You realize you have to win. The election will be seen by the citizens and the state as a referendum, which is what the opposition has asked for all along."

Chapter Twenty-five

Sadie sat down in Billie's kitchen with a cup of hot tea in front of her. Billie put four pieces of Biscotti on the table beside a dish of sugar lumps and a small silver tong. Sadie knew no one else served Biscotti and sugar lumps in Cedar Branch.

"So is it true? You and Cliff?" Billie poked Sadie and giggled.

"I came to talk about something more important," Sadie said, sidestepping the interrogation. "I need some help from a dozen brave women in town."

"To do what?"

"It has to do with taking off our clothes," Sadie said with as much suspense as she could muster. She needed to circle the wagons on this one… gradually pull Billie into her snare.

Billie didn't need a subtle tug. She switched gears as fast as a BMW 328i.

"I'm calling it the Godiva Girls Day," Sadie said.

"Are you kidding me?" Billie was all ears.

"As serious as a heart attack."

"Where is this coming from?"

"Dennis McDonald."

"Now you *are* kidding." Billie picked up her tea cup, sneered and pretended to ignore Sadie. "Don't be a tease."

"I'm serious. Dennis McDonald said he'd do a national story if a bunch of women took off all their clothes."

Billie arched her eyebrows and emphasized each word. "Dennis McDonald asked you to get women to take off their clothes?"

"Well no, not exactly, Dennis McDonald expressed an interest in doing a story if we could come up with something original. I told him a bunch of women were going to strip naked in protest."

"Sadie, when did you last stand in front of a full length mirror and take a long hard look at our double lattes?"

"It's not whether we look good or not. The point is that we're angry enough to pull such a crazy stunt," Sadie said.

"I'm not so sure I'm THAT angry, yet." Billie balked. "Do you have a plan?"

"I don't really have a plan. I was hoping you'd help me."

"Dear Lord." Billie dropped her head into her hands and closed her eyes. Slowly she opened them and made eye contact without moving her head.

"CBS evening news...national," Sadie repeated.

"It would have to be before the weather turns too cold," Billie said.

"Ahead of the next public hearing."

"In some place that's very public," Billie added.

"Advance notice to the media, but not to anyone else. If the police heard about it they would stop us before we could untie our shoes."

"The full monty, huh?" Billie shook her head.

"I was thinking with American flags either around us or in the background," Sadie said.

"There may be some backlash."

"I'm sure we'll get backlash...the point being, it will be on prime time."

"Stripped of our American rights," Billie said. "I can see the headlines already."

"See...you got it. I didn't even have to say it." This pleased Sadie immensely.

"We'd probably get arrested."

"Probably. So we'll pay the fine. I'm sure I can raise the money." This minor detail didn't bother Sadie in the least.

"We would have a statement ready for the press—something along the lines that these public hearings are a sham. The company representatives sit on the government committees that write the regulations and dictate the rules to their benefit."

"Or we could just say, 'The fix is in. The voice of the people is out.'"

Billie became more animated as she spoke. "This could be big. Really big. How many nightly viewers does CBS have? The story would be picked up and carried by the Associated Press."

"We may even get calls for follow-up interviews," Sadie added, sensing Billie was coming around.

"Where and when?" Billie asked.

"I think in Raleigh in front of the NC State Capital or the Legislative Building. We'd have to scope out where best to pull it off," Sadie said.

"Before the next public hearing?"

"Yep…" Sadie raised her eyebrows. "Think we could find some women who might be willing?"

There was a long pause with neither saying anything. "I'm thinking," Billie said. "This is going to have to be a very elite club. So elite and secretive that women are going to beg to be a part of it, because… when it's all said and done we're going to be celebrities."

"You think?"

"I know," Billie said.

Chapter Twenty-six

JC Collier and Ed Garner seated themselves on two weathered wooden crates turned vertically in order to give their knees a rest. Their long legs stretched out in front of them. Phil Harper and Henry Bennett stood next to a windswept barn where the red paint had peeled badly even though the walls remained sturdy. Phil leaned against his John Deere, one knee bent with his foot planted on the back tire for balance. Henry unconsciously broke into some of the soft peanuts he still had in his hand from the last field he'd stopped to survey. He'd plow them up in another month to let the air dry them out before the harvest at the end of September. What he needed now was a little rain, but not too much.

"How they looking?" JC asked. Farmer talk. Every conversation started with either the weather or the crop.

"Not bad. Might have a pretty good year if the ditch don't flood."

Everybody nodded. When the ditches flooded the ground was too saturated and the roots would rot. "Listen, Ed," Phil said changing the subject, "Henry and I were thinking you might be a good man to run for county commissioner against Helen Truitt."

Ed let out a guffaw, reached down in his front overalls pocket and pulled out some chaw. "Well if that ain't the damnest I ever heard," he said, took a pinch and tucked the tobacco under his lower lip.

"Seriously," Phil said. "We want to put together a slate of candidates. We'll run them together on the same ticket...the anti-incinerator ticket. You help turn out the black vote and we'll help turn out the white vote."

Ed looked suspicious.

"We gotta all be in this together," Phil said. "Can't vote down racial lines. If we split the vote, we're gonna lose."

"Plus," Henry said, "you've got so many kids and grandkids if you just got them to vote for you, you'd win."

Ed laughed.

"They got a point," JC said. "You'd be good… a-tell-it-like-it-is candidate."

"They'll laugh at me. I barely made it through high school." Ed's bottom lip stuck out in a pout.

"Hell, you got more common sense than anyone sitting on the board right now. That's what we need…a fellow with good common sense," Phil said. "You grew up in this community. You married a local girl, fed and raised good kids. Look at them. Got every one of them through school, some even went to college. By dern, that's something to be proud of. Not many folks can say that."

Henry added, "You pay your bills. You ran a reputable slaughter house. People respect you, Ed, and you talk their language."

Ed grinned. "That would tear Helen Truitt plum damn apart to be beat by the likes of me, wouldn't it?"

"It would," Henry snickered, and nodded in agreement. "But our goal isn't to tear her up, just replace her. All the commissioners, her included, knew ahead of time that a deal was being made behind closed doors. They did nothing to stop it."

"Think of what you could do for the black community," Henry encouraged Ed. "You could force the county commissioners to consider extending the water and sewer lines. You could advocate for a county recreational center that everyone could use. How many black kids need access to a good basketball court or a baseball field?"

"It would only happen if there was a majority of blacks on the board," Ed said. "Are you willing to support that…a majority black county commission?" He knew the black community had been conned in the past. *You support my man, I'll support yours*, and then when they got into the voting booth, all bets were off. "You willing to support three blacks on such a ticket?" Ed asked. "We won't have any power if it's three whites and two blacks."

Phil and Henry looked at each other.

"We were thinking maybe the butcher Marvin Reese for a town board position and Catherine Boone for another slot. She's a retired teacher. She'd be good."

"And for county commissioners?" Ed pushed. He wasn't going to let them off the hook. They were talking about the town board. He wanted to hear about the county commissioners.

"Well, we'd certainly support you and the principal of the new middle school. You give us some recommendations for a third candidate and we'll see. We're open to anyone who is on our side, and would contribute to the county in ways that are inclusive," Henry said.

Ed rubbed the stubble on his chin like he was mulling over which way to slice up the carcass of a hog. Then he spit a little tobacco juice and straightened up. "All right, all right," he hummed. "Me and JC here will talk some."

*****

Audrey Garner drove into town two days later to meet with her father. "Of course, you'll run," she stated in no uncertain terms. "The black community has an opportunity here to gain some political muscle. This is going to be an election won on one issue. Do you know what that means?"

Ed's grin revealed a missing tooth on his upper left side. "Sure," he joked, "it means whatever is good for the white man."

"Not this time, Daddy. The white folks are split down the middle. If we can swing the black vote by bargaining some of our people onto the ballot, it would be a win-win. The white people will get to replace their town council and we'll get voting power among the county commissioners. It could work."

"Course in four years, they'll vote their own back on again," Ed said.

"Maybe, maybe not. You might be able to make a few changes that benefit both races. It's hard for even the white officials to take things away from people once they've been granted."

"Auh, Audrey honey, I'm an old man. How would I begin?"

"You begin right next door, Daddy. You go sit and talk to your neighbors and ask them what things they think need to be done if you got elected. Then you go with JC and talk with his neighbors and then you go to those neighbors' neighbors. One house at a time. That's what it takes—sitting and listening in one house at a time."

*****

Over a cup of coffee at Phil's kitchen table, Henry said, "Sadie has already told everyone she's running for mayor. I wish she'd involved us in that decision before she announced, but what's done is done."

"Nobody's ever asked permission to run before, why should she?" Phil asked.

"I know, you're right, it's just that...." Henry trailed off.

"Just what?"

"Well, she lost in the last election. She's got baggage."

"But people are paying more attention. This is the vote on the incinerator that everyone's been asking for." Phil got up to get the pot of coffee off the stove. "Rod Palmateer says he's willing to run again. He's so mad at the colonel he's ready for a shootout. Lucy's backing out. She's had enough, which is for the best, I think." Phil refilled their cups.

"So that leaves four seats we'd need to grab on the town board. Marvin and Catherine have agreed to run. Now we need two white candidates. How about you, Henry? A farmer... a landowner. Someone who has a lot to lose if ICS builds here. Most of the other farmers will throw their weight behind you."

Henry hesitated. "I was thinking maybe we could talk Chase Hoole into it. He's the pharmacist. Everybody in town does business with him. He's always been a quiet and likeable guy."

"He's certainly a possibility. Let's think on it. And the school board?" Phil said.

"Oh, yeah. We're going after them," Henry said. "They're the ones who've voted to close down our school. The superintendent needs a wake-up call."

Phil and Henry continued for the next two hours making a list of people they thought were electable and willing to take action to stop the incinerator. When they'd finished Phil took a deep breath and stretched his arms over his head to relieve the ache in his back. "We need a committee from CAP to add names and make suggestions. This has got to be a joint effort or it'll never work. We're proposing some pretty radical shifts that are going to make a lot of people uncomfortable. People need to be able to talk it through."

"We've got two months," Henry said.

"And the peanuts need harvesting between now and then," Phil added.

"Well, look at it this way. If we lose this election, the famers could lose their crops, the town could lose their school, and families may move. Anything worth doing demands time. If not us, who?"

*****

Caren Drake knew that the colonel had lined up his team of candidates to file for the election. He had chosen to leave her out of the process, arrogant old fart that he was. The entire reason for her being in Cedar Branch related to her experience in managing campaigns. But if the colonel wanted to go it alone, she'd passed the point of attempting to explain to him the obvious. He'd ignore her until the nth hour and then come screaming for her to save his ass. Maybe she would. Maybe she wouldn't.

The colonel needed someone to run against Rod Palmateer, and to fill the two empty seats left by Mary's death and Lucy's withdrawal. In reality he only needed to take one more seat to hold the majority, since Dick Evers and Wade Gorman were both running again and had stood firm as his solid supporters. This would be the referendum the town had asked for and everyone knew it. Caren also knew that the colonel felt so strongly that the town would stand behind him that he would have wagered his first born in a greasy second.

*****

The last day to register to run for a local or county election was on Monday, September 30th. By noon, only three new individuals had filed for the town seats in Cedar Branch: Walt Macaffey, the owner of the hardware store, Jason Caldwell, an insurance salesman, and Jeffrey Brundage, a traveling salesman for the auto parts store in Westtown…all white males. Colonel Max Little and Sadie Baker had both filed for mayor. The colonel felt smug. Just as he'd suspected, CAP didn't have the depth to mount any opposition. They were all a bunch of blowhards. At three o'clock sharp, fifteen people walked into the office of the County Board of Elections to file for various positions.

By five o'clock the word was out. Colonel Little dismissed the challenges as misguided…a frantic last minute attempt to throw together an opposition. None of the people had ever held public office. And there was the butcher

Marvin Reese running for town board, along with Catherine Boone. Nobody knew exactly where he stood, but it didn't really matter because he didn't believe there were enough black voters registered in the town limits to make any difference. That was a serious mistake on CAPs part. As far as the county commissioners and school board went...well, he didn't care. Again, they were heavy on black candidates...most certainly a death knell. Besides, that outcome was of little consequence to him.

Chapter Twenty-seven

Dutch and Hammie stood over the outdoor grill cooking hamburgers and hotdogs. Sadie sat on one of two folding lawn chairs. She bounced the baby in her lap and enjoyed the waning hours of the sun and a soft breeze. On a Sunday afternoon, mid-October, the weather was at its peak…warm enough to still be outdoors with a sweatshirt and cool enough to enjoy direct sunlight. The oak and sycamore trees had started to lose their leaves, but color seemed all around them.

The store had closed at two and they were celebrating Hammie's thirty-fourth birthday. This time, Sadie had remembered the cupcakes.

The children played on the swings and Hammie's boys pushed Gabe as he kept calling, "Higher, higher." Everyone was on good behavior. Tempers had cooled. Somehow the letter from William Sanjour followed by Gabe's second stay in the hospital had created a temporary moratorium. They'd agreed that they could disagree, although Sadie interpreted both Dutch and Hammie's reticence to argue with her to mean they might be having second thoughts. Most assuredly, Dutch was.

"They've set the second public hearing for Monday, November eleventh. Did you know that, Mom?" Dutch asked. He flipped the burgers over.

"I heard." Sadie said cautiously. Of course, she knew it. She followed the dates of the hearings like a mouse sniffing for cheese. She didn't take the bait.

"It's the day before the election," he continued. "I think they're planning to throw you all in jail in order to keep you away from the polls."

That's exactly what Sadie thought and the discussion had been a hot one at the CAP meetings. How were they going to show their opposition at the final public hearing without being arrested? They had yet to go to trial for the charges from the first public hearing, but they didn't want a second offense. Plus, the first public hearing had been approved by the Waste Management Commission despite the outburst of public opposition. By all reports, the next public hearing would also be approved by the state regardless of protests.

"Don't expect me to come running to bail you out again," Hammie said, only half joking.

"You didn't bail me out the first time when we got arrested at the public hearing." Sadie tried to make light of his statement.

"Did you ever figure out who posted your bail?" Hammie asked.

"A Mr. Jacob Jones, at least that's the name he left. I'm told when they checked it was a phony address and phone number."

"You mean some guy left thirty-seven hundred dollars on a table and nobody knows who he is?" Dutch asked.

He'll come get his money back after the trial. Then we'll know who he was."

"I thought the trial was supposed to be in thirty days," Hammie said.

"Judge keeps postponing it."

"Why do you think?" Dutch asked.

"Maybe he's on our side. Waiting to see what happens in the election," Sadie said.

"You won't go getting yourself in any more trouble now, Mama. Will ya?" Hammie teased, but Sadie knew that he had brought it up for a particular reason. They were worried she'd be back in the middle, fanning the flames again.

Sadie got up from her chair and put the baby in her stroller. She walked over to the grill and took a deep breath. "Boy, am I hungry," she said and opened a hamburger bun for Hammie to slip in a patty. No need to answer any more questions. Best they didn't know what was in store.

*****

The majority of the work progressed in secret. The element of surprise would be their greatest strength if they were to be successful. Sadie, Phil and Henry traveled to Raleigh at least twice a week to meet with Beth Elmore and Stu Ricks. On at least one occasion Sadie had walked in to speak to a legislative assistant to find Caren carrying on a flirtatious exchange with the twenty-five year old intern. She immediately retreated in hopes that she'd not been seen.

Success rested on the careful coordination of many people to make the

Godiva Girls Day in Raleigh a success. In fact, Sadie had ended up divulging the plan to only five women she trusted in Cedar Branch. When she ran the idea by Beth and Stu, they assured her they could name ten more women off the top of their head who'd be willing volunteers. There would be less likelihood of leaks in their plans if not every participant came from Cedar Branch. Plus it would demonstrate a larger group of protestors from around the state. ICS had stirred up animosity in enough counties that there were those who were willing to go the extra mile to help send them packing for good.

Paranoia increased by the day. The local phone company had received so many complaints about wiretapping that they ultimately placed an advertisement in the paper that wiretapping was illegal without a court order. They assured their customers they had no orders to tap anyone.

Godiva Girls Day had to be before the election with enough time that if legal charges were brought, they could have everyone out of jail and ready to vote on November twelfth. They marked October twenty-second on their calendar. Most of the senators and legislators would be in their offices. Beth had lined up the schools and Stu was perfecting his magic show. Several men who were veterans from the other protests worked with Phil and Henry to add the props and sound system. On October seventeenth, Sadie called Dennis McDonald.

"About that plan I mentioned, you know the one where I promised we'd strip naked in front of the Capitol in Raleigh?"

"I'm listening," McDonald said.

"We've got a go date," Sadie said. "It's going to be in front of the NC State Legislative Building.

"I want an exclusive," McDonald said.

"I can't make promises," Sadie said. "It's too important to us. We need as much media attention as we can get."

"You're not going to pull a bait and switch on me?" asked McDonald. "This is the real deal?"

"The real deal," Sadie said, and she hoped to God they could pull it off as planned.

*****

Todd Wilkins rose with a slight bow as Caren slipped into the chair across from him. The limousine that had picked her up whenever they had dinner during the last six weeks had been Todd's idea. She found herself becoming accustomed to the finer things he provided.

The waiter smiled. "Same as last time, Senhorita?"

She nodded. "The Arroz De Pato. I think it's my favorite." She handed back the menu. She'd come to appreciate the Portuguese food that accompanied their meetings. She lifted her glass and sipped the wine.

Todd returned the toast. "I see you've changed to the Vinho de Mesa. It's more mellow than a French cabernet, don't you agree?" His fingers laced around the stem of the wine glass as if they were a part of the delicate curvature in the crafting of the vessel. "How are things going?"

"I can't be sure," Caren said. She would have preferred to be more exact, more definitive in her response but she knew the colonel had kept information from her.

"You know what you have to do?" His tone was smooth and seductive.

"Of course," she said. "I'll make it happen." He had never sounded threatening, but it did occur to her that a double-cross might reveal a side of him that she hoped never to see. In the same breath, she couldn't help but wonder if this relationship might lead to something more romantic. To date it had been strictly business accompanied by very fine meals and wine.

"Any concerns?" he asked.

"Rumors multiply daily. Everyone has a theory about what the other side is up to. Personally, I think CAP is playing a con game, trying to make us believe one thing while planning another."

"How?"

"They're focusing all of the attention on the second public hearing. A lot of whispers overheard in the Quaker Café about road blocks, a tractor convoy, even something about naked women. Have you seen the women in Cedar Branch? Good Lord, that would be painful to watch."

Todd smiled at the naked woman comment and asked, "What's the mayor saying?"

"He's freaking out. Every day he's like a raving lunatic on the phone to the governor and the attorney general. Wants them to send in the National Guard with dogs, tap telephone lines and more."

"He's cracking," Todd said. "What's the probability he can hold off the challenge to the town board?"

"You know, I think he might be able to," Caren said. "Here's why. He's got a solid backing of citizens who think the CAP folks are crazier than he is. They're running an all-white male ticket which appeals to the older crowd, and the town is mostly older and white. Then there's the jobs angle which is popular and the health issues seem to have lost steam. Everyone's so busy talking about how wacko everyone else is they've stopped arguing about mercury and lead poisoning.

"What's CAP got going for them?"

"Mostly numbers and noise. It appears they've got a lot more people, but many of those people don't live within the town limits, so they can't vote. They've got the element of surprise. I'm not quite sure what's up and they're pretty good at keeping everyone guessing. And they've got Ed and JC."

"Ed and JC?"

"Neighbors—two older men—one white, one black. Ed is running for a position as a county commissioner on a ticket that has three black and two white candidates. That's pretty controversial for this county. Gives white folks the jitters. The whites will show up at the polls. Course, it pushes up the black turnout, too. But JC and Ed are doing a door to door campaign together. Sitting down and talking to anyone who'll let them in. They're downhome, salt-of-the-earth kind of men and I hear they're changing some minds. Then of course, that black lady of the Nile, the one who made the big deal with Senator Robbins about environmental racism, that's Ed's daughter."

"That all has to do with the county, though, not the town board."

"Yes, but the blacks in Cedar Branch who may not turn out to vote in a local election are excited about the county election. They'll be at the polls."

"So will the whites."

"That's true."

The waiter returned. "Your Arroz De Pato, ma'am, and Ameljoan a Bulhao

Pato for the gentleman." He slid a plate of duck with seasoned Chorizo sausages over a bed of rice in front of Caren, then placed a large bowl of clams in front of Todd. After refilling their wine glasses, the waiter said "bom apetite" and left them alone.

They ate in silence with only the music in the background.

Towards the end of the meal, Todd slipped his fingers inside his expensive coat and pulled out an envelope. "I have a contact in the permitting office," he said. "This woman has a package for you. You'll know what to do with it."

Caren opened the envelope to find a 3x5 card with a name. In addition were ten one thousand dollar bills. She tried to appear composed, but the amount surprised her. She lowered her gaze to disguise her astonishment. She put the envelope on the table and took another sip of wine.

Todd read through her façade. "After the election next month, if all goes well, there'll be a nice bonus in addition to that." He motioned the waiter for the bill. "I think it best if we call it an evening. Shall I ask them to get your limousine?"

"Yes, thank you."

He slipped his hand over hers and gently squeezed. She realized it was more than a pat…a pat that implied "good girl" or "you're okay." It felt warm like an unspoken promise of things to come.

"It's been a pleasure dining with you," he said, "the best part of my job. You'll understand when I say I don't think we should meet again."

She nodded, feeling as if it would be inappropriate to question him further, but she didn't want to leave. There were things she'd never said. She got up. "I just want to say," she began.

He shushed her. His finger to his lips.

"I'd like to see you again," she blurted.

He lowered his eyes, then looked back up at her standing behind her chair. "There are a lot of things that have to fall into place first. Right now, you and I both have jobs we have to do."

"Of course," she said. She could feel the color rising to her cheeks. She waved the envelope in her hand. "I'll pick up the package." Then she tuned to leave.

As she stepped out of the alcove into the hall she heard him say, "I hope to see you again, too."

Chapter Twenty-eight

The first school bus from Granville County pulled to the end of the block and parked in front of the legislative building at eleven-thirty on Tuesday morning, the twenty-ninth, exactly two weeks before the election. The driver got out of the bus, took his keys and immediately walked through the front door and out the side. Five women unloaded thirty-six children. Having already received a permit to assemble, Stu Ricks, dressed as a magician, welcomed the children and ushered them over to his mock carnival stand. A boom box blared out the song "Ya Got Trouble" from the Music Man. Stu started his shtick.

"Right this way, boys and girls," Stu called out, waving a top hat and wand like a drum major. "The governor of our state says that he can make heavy metals disappear, so today…right here, right here in the capital city, right here in front of your eyes, I'm going to show you how it's done. Are you ready?"

"Yes," came a resounding shout from the children.

One of the State Capitol Policemen stopped a teacher as she walked by him towards the building. "Your class scheduled for a tour, ma'am?"

"Yes sir. I'm on my way to Senator Gulley's office right now. We set it up with his legislative assistant."

The policeman nodded as he watched Stu out of the corner of his eye.

"Now, boys and girls." Stu motioned to the third graders circled around him on the front row. "Step forward and tell me if these look like metals to you." He pulled out ten rolls of nickels and opened one for the kids to see.

A few seemed unsure, but the rest were playing along. "Yes!" they cheered, thinking rightfully that they just might have a chance to get to pick up some change.

He opened each roll one by one and dropped the contents into his top hat. "Are they heavy?" He tried to lift them above his head and groaned in fake fatigue.

"Yes!" they shouted. A few jumped up and down.

"Well, the governor of our state." He paused. "Now what is his name?"

There was stunned silence until one little girl called out "Governor Dunnet."

Stu's eyes brightened up and a squirt of water jumped out of a fake flower on his lapel sending the children into a fit of giggles. "Yes!" he yelled in recognition. "Governor Dunnet. Governor Dunnet says he can make all the metals disappear right before your eyes, and I'm going to show you how it's done."

He reached into his pocket and pulled out a can. "Here it is, boys and girls. My super-duper metal remover created by the magicians at "I Can't See It Anymore." On the side of the can was printed ICS in large letters. "It's magic stardust! Are…you…ready?"

"Yes!" the children all screamed.

Stu lifted his magic wand with little ICS stickers and waved it over the hat. Then he sprinkled a generous amount of tiny shimmering gold and silver stars and waved the wand a second time. The children ooohed and ahhed.

"So," Stu paused and looked around the circle. "How many think the metals have disappeared?"

The children were jumping up and down with excitement. A few raised their hands.

"Well, let's see. Everyone yell together, I Can't See It!"

The children let out a roar and Stu joined them as he tipped over his hat and all of the nickels rolled onto the pavement sending the children scattering to collect them.

"See?" Stu gave them a big grin. "They all disappeared." He waved his hat to show nothing was inside.

"No, no," the boys and girls screamed as they picked up the nickels as quickly as they could. "Here they are. Here they are."

"What?" Stu looked surprised. "Where did you find those?"

"Here on the ground." The children giggled.

"I must have done something wrong."

A second school bus from Pender County had pulled behind the first as Stu was performing. It was eleven-forty. Again, the driver stepped out, took his keys and disappeared. An equal number of children and adults dismounted and hurriedly joined the children who were laughing and scrambling for the loose change.

With his audience enlarged, Stu began the act again. "Perhaps I didn't use enough magic stardust? Shall I try again?" His eyes got big with wonder.

The kids shouted "Yes!" eager for the possibility of grabbing their own round of nickels.

"A tour, ma'am?" the State Capitol Policeman asked as a woman from the second bus approached him.

"Yes," she said. "Senator Ballantine's assistant, Judith is taking us. We're letting her know that we've arrived."

At eleven-fifty, two more buses rolled in behind the first two. One from Warren County and the second from Iredell County. From inside the bus, the children could see that coins were being tossed about the front of the legislative steps and they came out of the buses on the run. The drivers pocketed their keys and walked away. The five women separated as before—three remaining outside, two going into the building.

A couple of local reporters, all familiar with Stu Ricks and his on-going antics with the governor over the incinerator began to film the children when a CBS van pulled in. The two local reporters called out, "Hey, Stu. What's going on?"

"Just showing the kids how magic works." The painted grin across his mouth got bigger. "Teaching them how to make heavy metals disappear." With that he threw another ten dollars' worth of nickels into the air and another scream went up from the children.

"Did they disappear that time?" he shouted.

"NO!" they shouted back.

"Well, golly gee, shucks. What do you think I should do?"

Anxious to have more change to chase, the children screamed, "Try again. Try again!"

Another two school buses, one from Caldwell County and one from Rowan County arrived and parked. The policeman radioed the information desk and within minutes the head officer for the NC State Capitol Police arrived from his office.

"We've got six school buses out here that have unloaded children. Did someone schedule a tour for all of these at the same time?" one of them asked.

"It's just another one of Stu Rick's magic shows," the head officer reassured his jittery colleague. "He's harmless. I'll go check with the legislative assistants to make sure we get all these kids through in a timely fashion."

The captain stopped at the reception desk on the way in. "Seen any of the drivers of these buses?"

"Think they're in the cafeteria downstairs," she said.

"Well, we need to get them back up front to move their vehicles. Traffic is starting to back up."

"I'll see what I can do," the receptionist said.

The teachers who had gone inside to speak with the legislative aides now returned to the front door at exactly noon. "Children, children, they yelled. Line up in front of us. We're ready to go inside. Stay with your class."

The number of State Capitol Police had increased to three and they breathed a sigh of relief as they watched the children running to find which line they should be in…teachers waving and shouting after them: "Margaret, stay with your class," "Anna, honey, you're in the wrong line." "Johnny, keep up with June."

With all eyes focused on the main entrance, a U-Haul truck slowly pulled around behind the six school buses and parked where it couldn't be seen by the State Capitol Police. The driver got out, quickly opened the rear door of the U-Haul and helped Henry Bennett remove a ladder. They braced it up against the opposite side of the truck. The driver then pocketed his keys and walked away.

The U-Haul was a used one that Henry had bought to transport some of his produce. He had cut a hole in the roof large enough to accommodate a mock smoke stack that he pushed in place. Phil sat inside the truck and helped to brace it. The women who had stayed outside watched the children enter the legislative building with their teachers and one by one slowly drifted back around the school buses and up the ladder to the top of the U-Haul. Sadie and Billie were already there. They hooked and unfurled a banner down the outside of the truck that read: *We're being stripped of our rights. Send ICS packing.* An American Flag was draped over the third side. When all the women had climbed on top, Henry threw the ladder into the back of the U-Haul. Phil began feeding dry ice into a plastic bucket at the base of the smoke stack and pouring water over it to create the effect of smoke coming out of the stack.

At twelve ten, fourteen women each took off the outer wraps she'd been wearing and threw them down to Henry. He pitched them into the back of the U-Haul with Phil and padlocked the door. The women briefly stood until cameramen began to notice the smoke on the opposite side of the school buses and saw the bare-breasted women. Squatting down in a circle around the smoke stack, the women handcuffed themselves together and pitched the keys to Henry. He turned and calmly walked across the street looking like the cat who swallowed the canary. The CBS reporter, forewarned of what to expect, got it all. The entire setup from the first bus to arrive from Pender County to the naked women on top of the U-Haul had taken forty-five minutes. The school bus drivers returned to their buses and moved them to the appropriate parking places.

Stu carried the boom box over in front of the U-Haul and replaced his circus music with the Seekers rendition of *We Shall Not Be Moved*. He then began to pass out information flyers to the press and a growing sidewalk crowd to explain why they were there. Senator Robbins, already prepared to meet the press and snag a sound bite, walked out of the legislative building with Audrey Garner and a portable microphone. He launched into an explanation of his bill that would refuse to permit any commercial hazardous waste incinerator unless the state could prove inadequate capacity within its borders. At this moment, CAP commanded the lead story on every channel of the evening news.

*****

Inside the legislative cafeteria children swarmed in and out of the lunchroom trying to find their group. The teacher and their aides unloaded bags of lunches to distribute.

"Good Lord, what's going on?" Senator Donald Higgins asked his colleague.

"Someone must have overbooked the school tours," she said.

Within minutes, Higgins' research assistant rushed into the private cafeteria. "Dennis McDonald is out front. He's asking for a statement."

"Dennis McDonald?" Higgins did a double take. "You're kidding, CBS Dennis McDonald?"

"No, sir, I'm not kidding."

"Why is he here? Did we miss a memo?"

"There's a protest against the proposed hazardous waste incinerator going on."

"Good Lord," Higgins groaned. "A lot of people?"

"Not yet, but the camera crews are gathering quickly."

"What are the protestors doing?"

"That Stu Ricks from the Appalachian Farmers group is doing magic tricks and passing out flyers and some women have handcuffed themselves on top of a U-Haul around a smoke stack. And there's one more thing." The intern grimaced before he added, "The women on top of the U-Haul…they're naked."

*****

When Sadie and Cliff walked into the Quaker Café the next morning, their reception was mixed. The CAP contingent stood and applauded. The PROs gave them a look that would have frozen the great lakes in July. Out of the corner of her eye, Sadie could see Helen Truitt who looked as if she might climb on a broom.

Within seconds, Helen was in Sadie's face. "It's hard to believe you have the nerve to walk in here this morning. You should be in jail."

Sadie squeezed Cliff's hand. "Meet my bail bondsman."

Helen ignored Cliff. "That was the most disgusting display of indecent exposure and inappropriate behavior I have ever seen. And on national television! You're an embarrassment to the town…all of you."

"Au contraire, my lady, she's put us on the map. Everyone knows where Cedar Branch is now," Cliff said. Both he and Sadie had known that Helen would be waiting for them with her fangs bared.

Billie McFarland burst through the door to heightened applause, did a few twirls and joined Sadie and Cliff. The blood pulsated in the temples of Helen's forehead and the whites of her eyes turned pink.

"The two of you are disgusting. I'm embarrassed for the both of you," Helen said.

"Oh, come on, Helen." Billie cooed. "The cameras blacked out the good stuff. We were all sitting with only our shoulders and backs visible. They didn't show anything you couldn't see on a summer day at the beach."

"The school children. They must have been traumatized. How could you pull such a stunt using children as a decoy?"

Sadie dismissed Helen with a wave of her hand. "The children were all inside. By the time they left, the police had covered us all in blankets. We looked like a bunch of squaws sitting around a teepee."

"I have to say," Billie added, "those blankets felt darn good, too. It was getting a mite chilly up there and that metal roof nearly froze my buns off. The police could have moved a bit faster as far as I'm concerned."

"They were distracted by the scenery," Cliff said.

"I think we became a training exercise," Sadie added. "They'll be referring to the Godiva Girls for years to come."

"It was beautiful girls, just beautiful." Cliff beamed.

Helen stiffened. "Well, you won't be getting my vote, Sadie Baker. Personally, I think you made a fool out of yourself and lost any chance of being elected. They may think that kind of stunt is newsworthy in Raleigh, but I, for one, don't want an exhibitionist for a mayor who thinks prancing around naked is the way to get attention."

*****

"If you want a newspaper, we sold out the first thirty minutes after we opened," Dutch said when Sadie walked into the store. Dutch shook his head as he looked at his mother.

This was hard. Sadie didn't know what to say. Not having the approval of her children was the most painful part. "I couldn't tell you." She felt as if he deserved an apology. "You'd have gotten upset and maybe even blown our cover. I had already made up my mind, so what would have been the point?"

The silence lingered between them. Sadie fiddled with the wedding ring on her finger like a teenager might mess with a necklace to avoid the gaze of a disapproving parent.

"Look," Dutch finally said. "I'm rooting for you. I want you to win this election. I think that incinerator might make Gabe's asthma worse." He took a deep breath. "I think you just blew it, though."

"Really?"

"I think you shocked a lot of people."

"I imagine I did," she said.

"You made the news, for sure. Lots of news. People were calling Ada Lynn and me to tell us to turn on the TV. I wasn't expecting to see Dennis McDonald talking about my mom on top of a U-Haul without…" he let the words trail off.

Sadie tried to make a joke. She thought she might have caught a hint of humor. "Neither of you had to come and get me out of jail this time. Fifty-dollar fine was all. Less complicated in Raleigh than here."

"Guess they see that sort of thing a lot over there," Dutch said.

"Don't want to fill up the jail cells with naked women," she added. She hoped to get a smile.

"You're probably right." The corner of his lip turned up ever so slightly. He stopped again and this time he looked her in the eye. "You all right? Nobody hurt you did they?"

"They hardly touched me. Scared to, I think. Course, I probably reminded them of their own mother and with Dennis McDonald there and all. The police were perfect gentlemen."

"Okay, then," Dutch said, "that's good. But you've got to talk to Hammie. I'm not doing that for you."

"Agreed," Sadie said. "Are you and me straight?"

"Yeah, Mom. We're good. Just promise you won't pull any more crazy stunts, will you? I've got enough to worry about with my kids. Having to second guess which jail my mother might be in next is too much."

"Promise," she said.

Chapter Twenty-nine

Caren and the colonel sat in his living room along with the pro-incinerator candidates for the town board. Technically, it could be considered an illegal meeting with three of the five acting town board members discussing town business without public notice. Caren observed the conflict but saw no point in bringing it to their attention. That was CAP's problem, not hers. Millie served coffee and muffins and started to return to the kitchen.

"Stay with us, won't you, Millie?" Caren asked. "You're an important part of all of this. You have a lot to contribute."

The colonel looked momentarily confused but voiced his approval. "Stay, Millie. We could use your insight. Always looking for ways to get women to the polls."

Millie seemed pleased at the invitation and found a seat as others moved to accommodate her.

"I pretty much think we've won the election," the colonel said with obvious relief. His mood had improved significantly in the past week. "If the voters had any questions about Sadie's ability with her clothes on, imagine what everyone thinks now that they've seen her without them."

Dick Evers laughed and the others joined in. "I wouldn't even give Sadie Baker a car loan at this point."

"We've got the second public hearing coming up," the colonel said. "That's the last hurdle we have to get over." He dreaded the thought of a repeat of anything similar to the first. The news media blamed the fracas on him instead of focusing on the inept handling of the Highway Patrol.

"Who cares?" Homer dismissed the concern. "The governor is bringing in the National Guard. They'll be better prepared this time. It's their responsibility. If every protestor gets arrested and ends up in jail the next day, that will be fewer votes for Sadie. Let 'em make asses of themselves?"

"It's a done deal anyway," Dick interjected. "The hearing will be approved."

The colonel cleared his throat and leaned back in his chair. "It just looks bad. Looks like we don't know how to run our meetings and I'm tired of the negative press." He got up from his chair and walked to the window. The oak trees in his front yard had brilliant shades of orange and red. He loved the prolonged change of seasons in the South. "Anybody heard anything else about what they're up to?"

"Lots of rumors floating around," Wade Gorman said.

"Like what?" the colonel asked. "Let's make sure we report everything to the governor." He eyed Caren across the room to indicate his desire for her to take notes. Caren opened her hands in a non-verbal gesture to show she had neither pen nor paper with her. What was the point anyway? The colonel had already been on the phone with every rumor that slipped through anyone's lips. He in turn looked to Millie, who immediately rose and went to secure something to write on. Caren wanted to stop her, but dared not. She was so close to the end. One more week and she was out of here.

One by one they started to revisit the Quaker Café gossip. Caren's eyes began to glaze over. How many times did they need to go over the local buzz. Cliff Lyons had become notorious on the morning radio call-in. All anyone had to do was listen to him embellish the latest rumors.

"We need to get our people there," the colonel said. "That's going to be our problem. People are scared of what might happen and if only the CAP members show up, then it looks bad on TV. The media needs to see how many people are on our side."

"They're nervous," Dick said. "Don't want to get caught in the middle of what could be a very unpleasant situation."

"But we've got the vote, don't we?" the colonel asked for assurance.

"We do," everyone agreed. "Our supporters will turn out on election day. That will be your referendum to prove that you've been right all along."

"Ten more days, Colonel. You're going to come out smelling like a rose."

*****

Caren tapped her foot impatiently as she waited for the governor's chief of staff. She'd grown quite tired of the condescending attitude that Matthew

Abernathy used every time she was summoned to his office. Today Caren didn't intend to mince words. Election Day was around the corner and the Republican Party had high hopes of extending their hold on the governorship for another six years. Caren knew that she had the power to make or break that election and she wanted a deal that recognized her worth in more ways than one.

After a thirty minute wait, the secretary received a buzz on her phone and spoke in that sweet southern lilt from behind her desk. "Mr. Abernathy will see you now." She nodded towards the office door.

Caren picked up her leather satchel and walked into the palatial office, fully aware of the power play Abernathy enjoyed as he sat behind his oversized desk. He rose, that paternal look on his face, and they exchanged a stiff handshake across the mahogany expanse. "I'm not sure we have any more to say to one another, Miss Drake. As you know, your colonel is on the phone to me or the attorney general daily." He sighed. "But you seemed quite insistent."

Caren straightened her shoulders and leveled her gaze. She'd become weary of the arrogant dialogue. She sat down, her satchel on the floor beside her. "The governor has a problem," she said, "a very big problem."

Abernathy looked amused. "And that is?" he asked.

"The permit application."

"You've seen it."

"I've read it."

"I doubt that seriously." Abernathy dismissed her statement with a smug gesture. "It's over six hundred pages and hasn't yet been released."

Caren picked up her satchel and dropped it with a thud on the desk in front of him. She pulled out the stack of papers. "Not only does the permit ask for permission to site a fifty-thousand ton incinerator, it also asks for a solvent recovery plant which would bring the combined waste discharge capacity of the rotary kiln to one hundred and sixty-four thousand, eight hundred and ninety ton capacity. To keep that full and running, you'd need the waste from the entire east coast of the United States." She paused to let her words sink in. "ICS has been lying to both the governor and the public about its intentions. ICS is planning for a disposal site three times the size of what they have disclosed." She stopped to let the words sink in. "Or did you know that all along?"

The look on Abernathy's face told Caren she'd made a slam dunk.

"I don't know where you got that permit," Abernathy said after a moment's hesitation. Then with a voice that had lost the prior bravado he added, "But I am sure you're mistaken."

Caren felt an adrenalin rush. She stood. Abernathy remained seated. For a second, just a flash, Caren sensed panic. Caren wasn't about to forfeit her advantage. She pulled out three individual sheets she'd clipped together in advance.

"I'll save you the trouble of reading through the entire document," she said. "Check out pages two hundred twelve and thirteen. You add up the numbers on those pages and see if they correlate with the numbers on page two hundred and thirty-three. It's a word game as old as dirt. The company tells the same lie so many times that when the review committee gets the written material, they're fooled into believing that what the company told them conforms to what's in the permit."

Abernathy looked at the papers and picked them up. "I'd need time to study this, to verify what you're telling me is true."

Caren didn't intend to wait. "Here's the deal, Mr. Abernathy. Your office set me up in a two bit town for a year. During that time I've taken insults and degradation from a pompous ass who thinks my sole purpose is to be a pretty face and take the blame for anything that goes wrong. I've been your doormat. Not anymore. I want a guarantee that when this election is over and the mayor is tossed out, I don't end up in the ditch beside him."

"I think you're jumping the gun." Abernathy gathered his wits. "Every indication is that the mayor and his supporters will win with or without you. Frankly, Miss Drake, we've found your work to be a disappointment. The CAP organization has overplayed their hand and their gimmicks to grab the media have backfired. We'll win, not because of your skills, but because of their mistakes."

"Backfired?" Caren laughed out loud. "I'd hardly think the national attention of Dennis McDonald is a backfire. As they say in business, any news is better than no news. Personally, I'm thinking the election could still swing either way and if this report is leaked to the press prior to the election, the governor's office is going to have a lot of explaining to do. If it's withheld until after the election, well the governor-elect can deal with ICS behind the scenes to straighten out the numbers."

"All you have is an unofficial report that hasn't yet been finalized," Abernathy said. "I don't even know if this is real or not. I don't think you can get away with such an accusation."

"Oh, I can and I will. I'll simply put it in the hands of the press and let them dig up the truth. Meanwhile, the governor can spend his time in front of the camera the week before the election denying he knew anything. He'll appear to have either colluded with big business to deceive the public, or simply be incompetent." Caren sat back down and let the silence between them linger.

"Boy," she said after a full sixty seconds of nothing. "What a break for the Democrats. Guess you'll need to be looking for another job, too."

"What are you asking for?" Abernathy sat stone-faced.

"The day after the election, I want a government appointment with no less than six-figures attached and a commendation from the governor himself."

"And if that's not possible, where do you think that leaves you, Miss Drake? If the governor loses the election and you've proven yourself unable to secure the vote of a small town the size of a Cracker Jack box, no one will touch you."

"There you're wrong. You see, I'm covered either way."

Abernathy pushed back his chair and stood abruptly. "Good luck to you, Miss Drake. If you don't hear from me, then you can assume your career moves are limited."

Caren flashed an icy smile. "Twenty-four hours," she said. "Otherwise you can read the headlines in next week's papers."

*****

Sadie and Cliff left the office of the Board of Elections with five computer generated sets of names and addresses of the registered voters in the county. They distributed them among the CAP members who met daily in small teams. This was their final push.

The week before the election, the CAPs and PROs might as well have all worn garlic cloves around their neck. Suspicion cloaked the town like pollen on the first day of Spring.

Sadie was specifically interested in the five hundred and forty-two voters in Cedar Branch. In the last election, less than fifty percent had voted. They couldn't afford to have so many people stay home this time, and they needed to be pretty sure which way they'd vote before they went door to door offering to drive them to the polls.

Other members on the CAP Election Committee worked to contact voters throughout the county. They had names of sixteen thousand, six hundred and twenty seven voters. Their challenge would be to identify those opposed to the incinerator, put a list of anti-incinerator candidates in their hands and get them to turn out on November twelfth.

Betty Tesh trained the teams for the county elections. "You need five on each team. You must have at least two people from the black community to help confirm names. If you already know they're pro-incinerator people, cross their names off the list with the black marker. If they're anti-incinerator and you know it, highlight their name with a yellow marker. We want to be sure to get to every one of those houses. The hard part will be those we're not sure of. Sometimes neighbors will help tell you who's leaning which way."

JC Collier and Ed Garner worked tirelessly covering as many houses as they could in both the black and white communities. It paid off. When Sadie and Cliff hit the pavement, prepared to defend any backlash they might get over the Godiva Girls incident in Raleigh, no one mentioned it. Sadie realized she'd eliminated a lot of her critics by not visiting the known PRO voters, but she had expected a few harsh words. At most she got curiosity and even some admiration.

The fact that Marvin Reese and Catherine Boone had agreed to be on the ballot as the first black candidates to run in a town election generated the most discussion.

"Look," Sadie tried to explain, "there are more people in the black community who will be affected by the incinerator than in the white community, and they have had no say-so at all. This election is THE referendum. THIS is the chance for all of us in both races to speak up and insist that everyone has a voice in this decision."

The black ministers remained quiet. It was anybody's guess whether or not the black community would vote as a block or break rank. A lot would depend on the preaching that went on Sunday morning before the election.

In similar fashion, the Quaker community had been unable to reach consensus. This was unusual. In past elections, the Quakers could be counted on to vote progressive agendas in support of public education, healthcare services, and increased wages for the low income. Sadie had hoped they would support her candidacy despite some of her more unorthodox publicity stunts, but they remained divided. She knew the Methodist and Baptist Church members supported the colonel in general. Still, no one was sure how people would vote behind closed curtains. Rumors predicted a number of husbands and wives might cancel one another out.

If Sadie believed that things couldn't get nastier, she was sadly mistaken. Saturday's mail brought a bulk mailing to every home in the county that described her as uneducated, mentally unstable and sexually permissive. It also attacked other candidates on the CAP ticket as hypocrites who supported farmers dousing the ground in chemicals to grow tobacco, but refusing to acknowledge the safety of the controlled disposal of hazardous waste. Marvin Reese was referred to as an Uncle Tom…a black man under the thumb of the Baker family. The flyer went on to insist that the town would lose hundreds of thousands of dollars of annual revenue and up to three hundred jobs if Sadie Baker and her five feckless cronies were elected.

Sadie and Cliff had been planning to visit another twenty homes Saturday afternoon in the final three days before the election, but the vicious attack derailed her. Her legs ached. Her back hurt. Her head throbbed. "I need to go home," she told Cliff. "Take a break…a nap, maybe?"

"Sure, Babe," he said as they left the Quaker Café after a lunch she barely touched. "Save your energy. The rest of us can work this afternoon."

Even walking by Irene's sign next to her duplex felt crushing. Most days seeing it energized her, but today she looked away. She began to feel as if she might be at a breaking point. As she approached her door she noticed it was ajar. "Cliff?" She looked at him to see if he saw the same thing.

"Stay here," he said. He pushed the door open. "Anyone here?" he called but got no answer. He walked in the main room and then the bedroom and bathroom. "Smokey," he called.

"Is Smokey in there?" Sadie asked. She knew that if he were he'd be at her feet by now.

"I don't see anyone," Cliff motioned her in. "Smokey must have slipped out."

A look of panic seized her. "He didn't open the door all by himself."

"Was it locked?"

"I've never locked my door during the day," Sadie said. "Nobody in town does."

"Are you sure you closed it when you left?"

"Of course," Sadie said.

"It doesn't appear that anyone's been here that I can tell," Cliff said. "Look around and see if anything is missing. I'll go next door and ask Irene if she saw anyone."

Sadie opened the back door and called for Smokey. She went through the rooms again one by one, looking under the bed, opening closet doors, not sure why. Smokey had never hidden from her. Perhaps he was sick, curled up somewhere.

"Irene said she heard him barking around eleven, but she just assumed that you were home. She didn't see anyone else," Cliff said when he came back. "Why don't you go lie down and I'll drive around town and look for him."

"I'm going with you," Sadie insisted. "Let's go to Dutch and Ada Lynn's first. If Smokey got out, he might have headed in their direction."

Cliff drove five miles an hour, back through the few side streets that forked off the main road. There weren't too many different directions to go in unless Smokey had taken off into one of the fields or back through the swamp. And then, well, it would be anybody's guess if they didn't find him before nightfall.

Sadie became increasingly concerned. "What do you think, Cliff? Do you think someone intentionally took him? I didn't leave the door open. I'm sure."

Several times, Cliff stopped the car and they both got out and called Smokey's name while walking in different directions. Cliff didn't want to tell Sadie what he really thought. It wasn't good.

As they approached the grocery, they could see Dutch on the inside of the store plastering up posters across the front window. "What's he doing?" Sadie asked.

"Not sure," Cliff said.

"They're campaign posters," Sadie said as they pulled to a stop. "He's putting up my posters along with our list of candidates." She got out of Cliff's car and stood in front of the store staring.

Ada Lynn saw Sadie through the glass door and came out to embrace her. "Mama Sadie," she said. "That trashy flyer was so cruel. Dutch is furious. Have you got any idea who did it?"

"Smokey's gone," Sadie said, her bottom lip starting to quiver.

"What?"

"I went home to my duplex and the door was open. Smokey's gone. Is he here?"

"No....no," Ada Lynn stammered. "Let me get Dutch."

Dutch came out immediately. "When did you last see him?"

"About nine this morning when I left the house."

"Irene said she heard him barking around eleven," Cliff added.

"This whole mess has gone way too far," Dutch said. "Mama, you look terrible. Cliff, take her home and I'll go look for Smokey."

"No," Sadie objected.

"Come on, Dutch is right," Cliff put his arm around her and encouraged her to get back in the car. "After a rest, we'll all be thinking more clearly."

Dutch looked at Cliff and added, "Stay with her, okay? Just in case."

Tears began to build up in Sadie's eyes and by the time she walked inside her duplex she could hold back the sobs no longer. "They say what doesn't kill you makes you stronger, but I don't know, Cliff," she said. "I think I've about had it."

The past year had turned into a nightmare. The town had split like two opposing armies. Friends and family were pitted against one another. Religious and social groups had rearranged themselves. Every day an arsenal of threats and accusations got hurled about, and everyone blamed someone else.

Cliff plumped some pillows up on the sofa behind her head. "You know," Sadie said, "if a town of five hundred can't work through their disagreements, how in God's name can we speak in disdain of countries who can't overcome hundreds of years of wars and distrust?"

Cliff walked back to the bathroom and reappeared with some Tylenol PM. "Take a couple of these, Hon," he said. I'll make you a cup of tea and maybe you can get some sleep. We're going to find Smokey, I promise."

*****

Cliff's promise was a pipe dream, and he knew it. He feared that Smokey's disappearance was a cruel act to spite Sadie. He began to calculate who in town had the temperament to do such a thing. Whoever they were would have to know how much Smokey meant to her. What he wondered was whether they took Smokey and simply dropped him off in the countryside…a logical choice, or if they actually killed him and dumped the carcass in the woods…a vindictive choice. The second option turned his stomach.

After Sadie fell asleep, Cliff drove back to the grocery store. Marvin was at the register. "Ada Lynn took the kids in the stroller and she's walking around town looking for Smokey," Marvin said. "Dutch has the truck. Said he was going to start on the south side of town. Hammie showed up about fifteen minutes ago. Boy is he steaming mad. He's seen that flyer they sent out about Mama Sadie and when he found out about the dog, he just hit the ceiling. I suspect he's out looking for Smokey, too."

Cliff nodded. "Thanks, Marvin. I'll head out to the east side of town in case anyone asks. I hope you're not taking anything in that flyer personally."

"What? Uncle Tom?" Marvin shook his head. "I learned long ago that the only folks who know how to talk trash are pretty trashy themselves. Don't pay 'em no mind."

*****

It was Hammie who found Smokey about two hours later. He was wandering off in a field five miles west of Cedar Branch. A farmer said they'd seen a dog like Smokey cutting across their field. He was collared, so they didn't figure him to be a stray. Smokey didn't come immediately when Hammie called, but his ears perked up and he kept his distance before he recognized the voice and came running. Hammie had a jug of water in his truck and after he'd let Smokey drink his fill, he drove by the store to tell Ada Lynn and the kids. She'd pass on the good news to Cliff and Dutch when they got back. Hammie left to take Smokey home with a box of Milk-Bones tucked under his arm.

Sadie lay asleep on the couch. Hammie opened the door and let Smokey dash ahead of him and jump on top of Sadie, licking her face. Sadie's eyes slowly opened and she grinned like a Cheshire cat.

"Oh, Love," she said. She took the dog's head in her hands and scratched behind his ears. "How glad I am to see you." She saw Hammie standing at the door. "You found him?" she asked.

"Yep."

"Where?"

"Between here and Jackson."

"Thank you," she said.

Hammie closed the door behind him and sat down in the recliner that had been his dad's. "Kept his chair, huh?" It wasn't really a question. He ran his hand over the leather arm and leaned back until the foot rest popped up. "How you doin', Mom?" he asked.

"Better now," she said, rubbing Smokey as if toweling him off after a bath.

"Things have gotten pretty nasty all of a sudden," Hammie said.

"Well, not all of a sudden, exactly. They've been building. Guess I've upset a lot of people."

"Still, I think things have gone way too far."

"Oh, they think they've got cause," Sadie said, taking a deep breath and putting her hand on her forehead. The headache was gone, thank goodness. "I've embarrassed you quite a bit, I'm afraid."

"I don't care. It's not worth it anymore," Hammie said.

"You mean that?" she asked.

"I do," Hammie said. "Gabe in and out of the hospital. Cece's worried about our kids now. She's talking about taking off her clothes and running around the governor's mansion." He shook his head and cut a smile at Sadie. "And then Smokey and this." He pulled out the flyer and held it up. "I'd like to know who wrote this crap."

"Forget it," Sadie said.

"Are you kidding? I'm not going to let anybody say these things about my mama."

"A few of us have had a lapse in good manners," Sadie said.

"Good manners never stopped a runaway train."

"Guess not, if you put it that way."

*****

Cliff brought take-out and they ate chopped beef steaks, mac and cheese and baked apples for supper. "Want me to stay the night?" Cliff asked after he'd done the dishes. "I'll even sleep on the sofa if you just need someone around."

"I'll be fine now that's Smokey's back," Sadie reassured him. "What do you think happened?"

"I don't know," Cliff said. "But from now on, you lock your doors day or night, coming or going."

"Okay," she said. He gave her a peck on the cheek.

It was an hour after she'd showered and put on her night gown that she started to climb into bed. She pulled back the comforter, and there, on top of her pillow sat a large manila envelope. Sadie stared at it for a long time before she picked up the phone.

"Cliff, I need you to come back. Someone's been in my bedroom and left me something. I'm scared to open it alone."

"Don't touch it," Cliff warned. "I'll be there in fifteen minutes."

Chapter Thirty

From the very beginning Sadie, Cliff, Phil, and Henry knew that the most important day of the week would be Election Day, not the public hearing. It made no sense to create a spectacle again. People would be arrested and quite possibly detained long enough to keep them from getting to the polls. They needed every single vote. They'd learned the public hearing was a done deal. It would be approved regardless of what they did.

The election, however, was up for grabs according to their count. While Sadie may have messed up with the stunt in Raleigh, there were still five other candidates to be elected on the town board who would control what motions would pass. In the editorials, the local newspaper predicted that the CAP candidates had a good chance of winning three of the five seats. "If Sadie Baker defeats the colonel by one vote," the editor wrote, "consider it a landslide."

The public hearing was scheduled from seven to nine on Monday evening. Early that morning National Guard forces began arriving in town and lined both sides of the main roads into Cedar Branch. The Armory had been on lockdown twenty-four hours in advance, and six prison buses were parked out front. At noon, four K-9 patrol units pulled in and began to randomly stop and check cars for explosives.

The word went out on the CAP telephone tree for people not to go to the Armory, but instead show up at Phil Harper's farm at seven that evening for a massive march to the Armory. Only a few select people knew what to expect. The rest of the town felt as if they were under a military siege.

A group of men worked at Phil's farm making a cauldron of Brunswick Stew and between stirring duty they built a gigantic bonfire to light in the middle of his plowed corn field. Three days earlier the weather had turned cold for the first deep freeze of the year and afternoon temperatures hovered around the upper thirties. The temperatures were falling fast. All of the crops had been harvested and people were more than ready for the past year's upheaval to end. This year there were hopes that Thanksgiving and Christmas could be a celebration instead of another protest.

Cars and trucks pulled in and parked around Phil's property with the gigantic NO still glaring from the roof of his house. In sweatshirts with hoods over their heads, gloves and parkas, they sipped cups of hot cider and snacked on homemade donuts. Scrubbed down work benches were scattered about. Cliff passed out hotdogs off a grill as fast as he could turn them over and Billie dished up chili. Between that and the stew, an atmosphere heavy with fatigue and anxiety began to lighten. Sadie welcomed each person and thanked them for all their work. She told people to forget the public hearing. Tonight they would celebrate with a pre-election party. There would be no march to the Armory.

It didn't take the news media more than thirty minutes to realize there was nothing happening at the permit hearing. They videotaped the massive presence of law enforcement and National Guard that had been on alert throughout the day and showed an empty auditorium with fewer than forty people scattered around the room. Since ICS was required to remain in place until nine o'clock as advertised, they spent the first half hour refusing to answer questions from the press about the recent reports of problems in the permit application.

"Is it true that ICS plans to burn three times the waste limitations as originally described?" one reporter asked.

"This is not a press briefing," one official said. "We are here to listen to public concerns, not answer questions." In an attempt to spin the poor attendance, he added, "It appears there are no concerns from this community."

Not to be deterred, the reporter persisted. "So you're telling us the reports leaked to the press about overcapacity violations are incorrect?"

"Again, we are not here to address those questions. ICS representatives will meet with the Waste Management Board and the governor to resolve any misunderstandings. A press release will be forthcoming."

"After the election then?" another reporter said.

"Since the election is tomorrow, that would be a fair guess."

After the first fifteen minutes most of the audience left and ICS and state officials remained on stage staring at one another, while the National Guard Troops, Highway Patrol, K-9 Squad and explosive experts remained outside in the frigid weather.

One by one the media trucks and reporters headed over to Phil's farm where they were greeted with hot food, a warm fire, and a crowd in a festive mood.

"About the challenge to the permit capacity requests that came out on Sunday...that came from you, Sadie, right?" asked the reporter from *The News and Observer.* Other television and radio reporters crowded in behind him.

"Yes, it did."

"Can you give us your source?"

"Actually, I can't. I don't know who it was."

"So how did you get it?"

"It was left at my house, anonymously."

"You have no idea?"

"No idea at all."

"Are you sure it is accurate?"

"I'd say by the fuss it's created in the governor's office, they think it's accurate, but I'll leave the investigative work up to you guys," Sadie said. She honestly hadn't the slightest idea who had left the manila envelope but she hoped it would be a game-changer.

"Do you think you'll win?" a reporter asked.

"Tomorrow night we'll know," Sadie said.

*****

A thick layer of frost covered the ground Tuesday when the polls opened at seven o'clock. It was clear that this election would be like no other in Cedar Branch's history. The regular precinct officials included the new Methodist Church Minister and one representative from the black community and one from the white. In addition, there were four poll watchers. Each had registered and been approved by the chair of the county political party as being of good moral character. Betty Tesh and Phil Harper represented the CAPs and

Homer Liston, a Quaker who supported the incinerator, and Sadie's next door neighbor, Irene Hooper, represented the PROs. The poll watchers had two functions: to ensure that votes were cast and counted correctly and to report irregularities. Any of them could challenge a voter's right to vote if they could show cause. The law required that the challenge must be resolved one way or the other on site. Never before in the history of Cedar Branch had anyone challenged the right of anyone to vote.

Normally on an election day no more than two or three people stood in line during any given time at the Armory. They'd greet one another, sign by their name and step into the electronic voting booth. The entire process took less than five minutes.

A larger turnout could mean people who'd never voted before would show up. Unfamiliar faces and newly registered voters had the potential to confuse precinct officers who prided themselves on recognizing everyone. Tensions were high. Rumors abounded about potential fraudulent voters. Helen Truitt had requested that the county Board of Elections have a person present throughout the day.

When Sadie and Cliff pulled into the parking lot at seven a.m., there were already fifteen cars there. Ten had come to vote and five were firmly planted for the expressed purpose to count votes. Each team of two per car had a full list of the registered voters and came prepared to remain there until the final vote was cast. After Cliff and Sadie voted, they returned to the parking lot, walked over to Henry Bennett's car and leaned in the window.

"How many so far, Henry?" Cliff asked.

"We're off to a good start. Not even half past and already twenty five people have voted. I knew them all but one. Think I know how all but two voted. I've put a question mark by their names."

"I'll do a coffee run," Cliff said. Sadie slid in with Henry to wait for Cliff to get back.

At seven forty-five, Billie pulled in with her first delivery of voters from the senior center. She had two people in her Land Rover, both on walkers, and she helped them down the sidewalk and into the Armory.

Henry got out of his car to assist the ladies. "Billie," he whispered in her ear. "Do you think you should be bringing these older people out before the frost thaws?"

"Couldn't help it." Billie looked stressed. "You should have seen the cars lined up offering to drive people to the polls. It's a war out there. People fighting over who's going to get into their car. These seniors haven't been this popular since their high school prom."

Henry made sure the ladies were inside the door and then came back to the car and watched as the colonel's wife pulled in with three people in her car. He hurried over to open the car doors. "Let me help you ladies," he said.

"No, no," Millie snapped. "I can help them, Henry. Step back please."

"That's Isabelle Lane," Sadie said to Cliff who had returned with coffee and sausage biscuits. "She's got Alzheimer's. She shouldn't be voting."

"You want me to go in and challenge?" Cliff asked.

"I don't know if I'd do that," Sadie said. I think her son and daughter-in-law are on our side. We might piss them off if they think we embarrassed Isabelle in front of other people."

"Miss Isabelle," Cliff called out. "Why don't you take my cane? It would help steady you."

"Stay away, Clifford," Millie was getting flustered as the little ladies had apparently been smitten by the sudden male attention.

"Oh, a cane could be helpful, or the arm of a big strong man," Isabelle said as she slipped her hand around Cliff's elbow. "Ladies, you all remember my husband, don't you? He's just back from the war."

Cliff tipped his hat and ushered Isabelle into the front door of the Armory. Henry was right behind him and Millie was struggling with her third passenger. "Remember what we talked about in the car, ladies," she called out.

Sadie sat in the car amused at the scene playing out in front of her. Cliff and Henry had obviously enjoyed the angst they were putting Millie through. "Wonder who'll they vote for?" Sadie asked. They put a question mark by Isabelle's name and put the other two in the colonel's column.

By noon a hundred and fifty people had voted and by one-thirty they were already over the highest number of votes ever tallied in a town election. Six votes had been challenged during the morning. When Irene saw Cliff walking in with Isabelle on his arm, she'd questioned Isabelle's competency to vote and the challenge was upheld. Two couples who lived a half mile out of the town limits and had always voted in the local election were turned away. They left spitting nails. That hurt, because they farmed and Henry knew that was four lost votes.

Phil Harper's son drove home from college to vote and was challenged by Homer as no longer being a resident, which infuriated Phil, especially because Homer was a fellow Quaker. Phil's son got to vote. Two other challenges were upheld.

By one-thirty, the game was on. Now the trick was to find the people who had not voted and get them to the Armory before the polls closed that evening. Each team checked the voters' registration lists they'd been following for those they knew would vote for their side. Cliff went to pick up Teensy. She lived outside the town limits but she had a sister somewhere in town. They found her. Adam called the Pamlico Packing Company to find out where the driver was delivering seafood that day. He was a resident, and they knew he'd vote for Sadie. Cliff got his route and went to pick him up in Lewisburg and brought him back to the polls. Members of the Rescue Squad, who were to a man pro-incinerator, pulled the most daring kidnapping of all. They made a trip to the Westtown nursing home and checked out a patient on oxygen and brought him on a stretcher in the ambulance to vote.

Clifford got out of his car and saluted the squad as they rolled him in. "That's impressive," he called out. "Very impressive."

Ten minutes before the polls closed Caren Drake drove into the parking lot with four people in her car, three girls and a boy, all apparently in high spirits. As they each got out of the car, Cliff and Henry were scrambling through their lists to see who they were.

"One of them is Johnny Jenkins's boy from NC State. Johnny isn't on our side, so I didn't say anything to him about his son," Henry said. "I think the three girls are all from Meredith College. I know Amanda, Smitty's daughter. Hell, Caren's been out on the road today bringing home the voters."

"She's not planning to vote, is she?" Sadie asked.

"I hadn't thought about it, but I think she can," Cliff said. "She's been living at Mary's house since January. If she's claimed that as her residency, then she can vote."

There was a shuffling of papers and Cliff went over his sheet. "Damn, she did register, right before the deadline....here, under Lysette C. Drake. How did we miss that?"

"Because the first sheets we picked up at the Board of Elections were before the closing date on registration. Crap, so she just walked in with five votes for the colonel. Where do we stand?"

Henry shook his head as they calculated the numbers on their individual sheets. "It's going to be close, real close. I think we had damn near everyone who could vote turn out, but there are close to twenty who could have gone either way. It'll be a cliff-hanger."

*****

When Caren and her entourage departed from the Armory, she was all smiles...beaming at the gawkers and giving a thumbs up to the media. The Election Board official locked the doors. The final count was underway.

The minister turned the key on the voting machines and the numbers were tabulated. Homer popped another antacid into his mouth. Irene excused herself and went to the bathroom where she stepped into a stall and threw up.

Phil refilled his coffee cup for the ninth time that day while Betty Tesh went to the refreshment table and ate her sixth donut. As they each resumed their positions over the shoulder of the minister, the level of tension was thick enough to smell.

The Methodist minister took a deep breath and called out, "Colonel Little has 286 votes and Sadie Baker has 271. Irene let out a squeal and Homer bowed his head as if to offer a silent prayer. Phil grimaced and Betty started chewing her fingernail. That having been said, the minister proceeded with the remainder starting with the highest vote getter and going to the bottom: Marvin Reese – 299, Catherine Boone – 276, Henry Bennett – 273, Chase Hoole – 262, and Rod Palmateer – 252. That was all Betty needed to hear. She let out a shriek. The CAP candidates had swept the board. The bottom five voters had all been the colonel's PRO candidates. It wasn't a full sweep, but it was good enough.

Something didn't feel right to Phil. It didn't make sense. He stood behind the minister and reread the numbers a second time. "Reverend, would you take one more look at the mayoral race, please. I think you may have reversed two of the numbers."

The room went quiet. Everyone crowded in and strained to see. The minister seemed momentarily confused. "Let's see," he apologized. "What did I say?"

"You said the colonel had 286 votes. I believe that should be 268 votes," Phil said.

There was a long pause. Everyone pushed even closer. "Yes…yes, you're right. My mistake, the minister said. I'm sorry. I did misread that. Sadie Baker has 271 votes and Colonel Little has 268 votes.

"What?" Irene spoke first. "Are you trying to pull something over on us, Phil?"

"No, I just asked the Reverend to take another look at the numbers he read out."

Irene and Homer were practically sitting in the minister's lap by this time. The representative from the election board asked everyone to step aside and he sat down in front of the machine. Finally he said, "Phil is correct. The total number for Colonel Little is 268 and for Sadie Baker is 271. Mrs. Baker is the winner."

*****

The news ripped through the county within minutes. The headlines the next morning announced that Sadie Baker had won by three votes in a "land-slide". The election had been a clean sweep up and down the ticket. From the country commissioners to the school board and all the way up through the Democratic Party lines to the governor, the anti-incinerator candidates had won. As expected the colonel asked for a recount. Upon verification, the town clerk quit and all of the town board members except Rod Palmateer resigned. The town maintenance man stood by his duties until a new board could be sworn in and the town muddled its way into the Thanksgiving holidays.

By all accounts, Caren Drake simply vanished into thin air when she drove out of town on election night with the four students in her car. No one had heard or seen her for over a month. No one really cared. Mid December, on his way to his mom's duplex, Hammie happened to pass Caren struggling to get two suitcases in her car in front of Mary Law's house.

Hammie pulled his truck over to the side. "Can I help?"

"Oh!" Startled, she looked up. "I can get it. Not much more."

"Probably would be easier if you were dressed for the occasion," Hammie said noticing her three inch heel suede boots, short skirt and matching jacket. Her blonde hair hung loosely down her back and she was as stunning as he'd remembered. He got out and lifted the two bags into her trunk. "More inside?"

"Just two small bags. Miss Mary's family locked up the house after the election and I haven't been able to get back to town to retrieve a few things. They're here for the weekend. Cleaning out the house to get it ready to sell."

"How's the granddaughter doing?"

"They tell me the trips to Boston are working. She has more treatments scheduled, but they're optimistic."

"Good," Hammie said. "And you? How are you doing?"

"Fine, thanks."

"Back in Raleigh?" he asked.

"No, I've moved on."

"Where to?"

"I'm up in Ohio, now."

"No kidding?" His eyes opened wide. "Ohio? Wow. Hope you've got some cold weather clothes." He glanced at her bare legs.

She shrugged it off. "Well, I will pretty soon."

"Sorry this town didn't turn out to be more hospitable to you," he said. "You gotta understand. It all got very personal. My nephew has asthma, you know. Then that last flyer about my mom and losing her dog just sent me over the edge."

"Just so you know…I didn't write that flyer," she said.

"I didn't think that you had."

"And one other thing… Smokey getting out…that was an accident. I stopped by to leave something for your mom and Smokey barked and slipped by me. I was afraid Irene would see me, so I didn't hang around. Guess I should have tried to catch him."

"Oh." Hammie nodded. It didn't matter anymore. What was done was done. "So you've got a good job?"

"Really good, actually. How's Colonel Little handling everything?"

"He's pretty burned. Speculation is that he and Millie might move. Myrtle Beach, maybe. Millie's being pretty persistent. She wants to live by the water."

"Guess the Potecasi Swamp wasn't what she had in mind." Caren joked. "How's your mom?"

"Oh, she's fired up. I think this thing between Cliff and her might become permanent. They're taking a few days' vacation together before she's sworn in as mayor next month. I'm going over to pick up Smokey now."

Hammie put the last two smaller bags in her backseat. "Well, good luck to you in Ohio," he said.

"And to you," Caren said. "Hope things work out for folks in Cedar Branch."

*****

A week later on Christmas break, Smitty's daughter Amanda rushed into the Quaker Café to pick up a take-out order of burgers and fries. She saw Billie McFarland and scooted by her table. "Is Miss Sadie around?" she asked.

"Not at the moment," Billie said.

Amanda lowered her voice and whispered. "You tell her how excited I am that she won. Don't tell my daddy I said so, but I think it's time for women to run this town instead of men."

Billie raised her eyebrows. "Well, thank you, darling. I'll tell her. You know every vote counts."

"That's exactly what Miss Drake told us when she insisted we drive back with her to Cedar Branch to vote. Really, we had so much fun that day, and our votes did count, didn't they? Miss Sadie won by just three."

"They did indeed. You made a difference." Billie smiled.

*****

The first week of January after the Democratic governor-elect was sworn into office he announced that he would not consider a permit for a commercial hazardous waste incinerator unless the state could prove they had a shortfall in their capacity to meet current needs. Senator Robbins' bill went through the Committee of Eight and was passed on the floor of the Senate. The Waste Management Board was abolished.

Announcing that they no longer had the support of state or local governments, ICS withdrew its application to build in North Carolina after investing more than four million dollars in an effort to get a permit.

In February, the Nancy T. Wireman Foundation recognized JC Collier and Ed Garner as recipients of their annual award for Advocacy.

Two months later, Cliff and Sadie sat on her sofa watching the evening news when a familiar face on the screen caught Sadie's attention. "Turn up the volume, Cliff. Isn't that Andy Crew the actor? They're arresting him." A moment later she was on her feet. "Oh, my golly. Look, there's Beth Elmore and Stu Ricks beside him."

An all-too-familiar scene appeared. Sadie felt knots grow in her stomach as she watched policemen handcuff protesters and drag them into prison vans. Around them people waved signs and chanted "Hey, Hey, Ho, Ho, FLT has got to go."

Then, the CBS commentator Dennis McDonald appeared, his microphone in hand. "I'm standing here with Henrik Hoffmann, the managing director of Flammeliss Technologies, Inc. and Lysette Drake, the Vice President for Consumer Protection."

"That man," Sadie said. "I've seen him. He was at one of our meetings. Don't you remember?"

Cliff looked hard at the television. "Yeah, he was the guy in the expensive suit."

"Right…the one who gave us two thousand dollars. What's Caren doing with him and since when did she become Lysette?"

Caren brushed back her blond hair, as Dennis McDonald put the microphone in front of Mr. Hoffmann. Hoffmann spoke. "We are delighted to announce that the permit for FLT has been approved," he said. "We'll be breaking ground next month. The papers have all been signed, and we at Flammeliss Technologies, Inc. are proud to be the innovators and builders of a facility that will bring hundreds of new jobs to Ohio." Hoffmann turned to Caren. "I'd like to introduce our new Vice President for Consumer Protection. Miss Drake, please say a few words."

Caren looked poised and professional. She had on an ash grey tailored suit. The jacket opened to reveal a peach blouse with a tiered ruffle neckline that dipped low enough to create interest. She brushed a strand of hair away from her eyes and tucked it behind her ear. In her three inch peek-toe patent leather pumps she stood just shy of the six foot tall Hoffmann.

Caren faced the camera. "Mr. McDonald and all of those here, I understand your concerns. Of course, I'd be concerned too, about any organization that has received bad press similar to that fabricated against Flammeliss Technologies by environmental extremists. But if we followed every rule these outsiders want to impose, none of the ladies here would be wearing lipstick because of mercury contents or feeding children peanut butter because of the aflatoxin content. Now really! We all aren't that naïve about what could harm us, are we?"

She paused, raised her palms together at the tip of her chin prayerfully and held them there long enough for everyone to notice she wore a large diamond ring. Lowering them, she said, "We are all intelligent individuals who want what is best for our community. That is why I am here. I have been hired to be your advocate. I promise to make myself available to answer questions, to calm your fears and to investigate any concerns you may have. I want the same long-term benefits for Ohio as you do. I want to provide a healthy environment for future generations and help create good paying jobs. I am here for you."

"I remember that speech," Sadie said, feeling absolutely disgusted.

"I remember the outfit," Cliff said.

Dennis McDonald interjected. "There was quite a bit of controversy over a similar incinerator that was proposed down in North Carolina. What does FLT offer that is different?"

Caren sparkled. "Oh, there is no comparison. FLT is using a much higher quality of technology than that proposed in North Carolina. Here in Ohio, our engineers have completed a thorough review to insure the health of all citizens. For anyone who has doubts, they only need to look at this six hundred page permit and you will realize that the hard questions have been addressed. Citizens can be assured that this facility converts hazardous waste into nothing more dangerous than steam. I am proud to be the public's advocate and I am honored to be a part of this expanding business."

Cliff sat up straight. "Well, that little two-timer. She was working for the other team all along."

Sadie looked confused. "What other team?"

"FLT industries. If ICS got the contract, the company in Ohio would have lost their bid. There isn't enough hazardous waste to support both facilities. It was either going to be in North Carolina or Ohio."

"So you think FLT funneled money to support us so that we would defeat ICS and they could build up there?"

"Yep."

"The money that man handed me at the CAP meeting and the bail money when we were arrested?" Sadie's mind began to race.

"Can't prove it, but I'm willing to bet it came from them," Cliff said.

"The brick through the window at the town hall? The Vietnam Vet at our balloon launch?"

"Possibly."

"What about the overturned tanker of hog waste, burning the governor in effigy, the permit application that was left at my house? All that?"

"We'll never know for sure."

Sadie leaned back on the sofa. "That's a lot to wrap my head around," she said. "Those bastards messed-up this town for years to come. There are relationships that will never be mended. And the bottom line is that this was a horse race between two big companies trying to secure permitting rights ahead of one another."

"I think that's it," Cliff nodded.

"Well, damn," Sadie said pointing her finger at the television screen. "That woman should be in jail."

"For what?" Cliff asked. "She didn't do anything illegal. She's a player. She played the hand that guaranteed her a win."

Sadie could feel her blood pressure rising. "Oh, for God's sake, Cliff. Really. Nobody won."

"How can you say that, Sadie?" Cliff sat back and eyeballed her. "You won. Your grandchildren won. The farmers won. For the first time in this town's history we have an integrated town board and a woman mayor. We pulled together an incredible coalition of black and white, rich and poor, and working men and women from every profession in our county. For a magic moment, we appreciated one another for their individual contributions instead of what they had or the color of their skin. We learned that together we can make a difference. Hell, I'd call all of that a win."

He slipped his arm about her shoulder and pulled her closer. "It's time to let it go and move on. You have a town to run."

"A broken town," Sadie said.

"Not broken," Cliff said, "just cracked. We'll glue it back together...maybe even stronger than before." Cliff leaned over and kissed his new wife. "As for me," he said, "I've no regrets. I won the best prize of all."

Epilogue

Grassroots organizations typically form around a single issue that ignites individuals from different political sides of the spectrum. The attempted siting of a hazardous waste incinerator in North Carolina was one of those issues. Between 1985-1993 there was an effort by the North Carolina Waste Management Board to site a fifty thousand ton hazardous waste incinerator in North Carolina. The proposal was met with stiff opposition and protest groups organized. As the possible siting skipped from county to county, people became more and more creative in ways to foil the process. Most of the "theatrics" that are described took place in one form or another in North Carolina. A few of the more creative ones I was unable to work in. I always have had a great deal of respect for John Pike from Oxford, North Carolina, who sold off forty-eight acres in Granville County to sixteen thousand different people for five dollars each. In doing so he crippled the state's ability to negotiate a price with every owner and stopped the effort to build the hazardous waste incinerator in his county.

Of course, the state and the hazardous waste company doubled down on their efforts and became more cunning in ways to bypass local environmental and zoning requirements that were put in place to block them. A noncontiguous annexation was one of those attempts.

Sadie Baker and her family, Colonel Max Little and his family, Caren Drake and Todd Wilkins aka Henrik Hoffmann are all fabricated characters. Likewise, InCinoSafe and Flammeliss Technologies do not exist to my knowledge. There were a number of nationally known figures who came to the aide of the protestors. Dr. Paul Connett and William Sanjour of the EPA were two of them. Sanjour did sue the EPA for the right to respond to his constituents in an honest and straight forward manner about health issues related to environmental concerns. The suit was sparked by a letter, similar to the one in this novel, written by Jean Colston of Gaston, North Carolina, and can be referenced online. After a four year fight, the case was won in federal court in Mr. Sanjour's favor which gives employees the right to blow the whistle on their employers without having their activities restricted.

I'd like to credit Greenpeace for the stunt that I describe in front of the North Carolina Legislative Building where the women handcuffed themselves to the top of a mock incinerator. This particular event occurred in front of the White House in Washington, D.C. in May of 1993, in an effort to stop the siting of a hazardous waste incinerator in Ohio. A Hollywood actor was arrested along with fifty-eight other demonstrators including Billie Elmore, Janet Hoyle, Denise Lee and Therese Vick from North Carolina. I used my literary license and added a few more entertaining details.

It is difficult to maintain a grassroots organization after an issue is resolved. I would like to acknowledge two exceptions in the state of North Carolina: the Blue Ridge Environmental Defense League (BREDL) under the leadership of Janet Hoyle Zeller and Lou Zeller; and NC WARN, originally co-founded by Billie Elmore. I learned much of what I know through their guidance many years ago.

I have included in this book several names of individuals who are now deceased but were active in the struggle to stop the building of a hazardous waste incinerator. Their names are a tribute to their memories, although their characterization in the novel is fictionalized. Andy Crew was not a movie star and Donald Higgins was not a state senator, although both could have filled those roles in interesting ways. Included are the dearly missed Cliff Lyons, Audrey Garner who died much too young, Charlie (Ed) Garner and Clayton (JC) Collier. Ed and Charlie actually did receive the Nancy Susan Reynolds Award for Advocacy in 1992. Betty Tesh continues to work with BREDL and as a matter of fact, a CBS reporter did show up because he was confused over the Tesh and Tisch connection.

Acknowledgements

I wish to acknowledge the local reporters who followed the hazardous waste incinerator issue during the four years in North Carolina. Reading their articles again has been a helpful reminder of the controversy: Keith Hoggard and Jay Jenkins of *The Northampton News*, Lance Martin and Charles Passut of the *Roanoke Rapids Daily Herald*, Marcia Stutts and Betty Mitchell Gray of the *Virginia-Pilot*, Terry Martin of the *Winston-Salem Journal*, Stuart Leavenworth of the *News & Observer, Raleigh*, Charles Anderson of the *Wilmington Morning Star*, and Mary Lee Kerr of the *Independent Weekly*. I also referenced "Playing With Fire," A Greenpeace Report by Pat Costner and Joe Thornton, (1990), and the *Utne Reader's* article, "The New Face of Environmentalism" by Mark Dowie (July/August 1992).

Jane McCaleb, MD, and Jeanne Sumpter, RN, provided valuable insight into breathing complications in children with asthma and the possible exacerbation for those exposed to toxin emissions. Dr. McCaleb was involved in the amendment for the position paper from the North Carolina Academy of Family Physicians on December 2, 1990, that included a resolution on hazardous and toxic waste.

A thank you goes to Therese Vick of BREDL for her ongoing updates and clarifications. Others who provided critical insight included Penny Beasley, Dan Clodfelter, Eddie Tinkham, John and June Parker, Gene Bennett, Bill Futrell, Leland Slade, and my son, Nicholas, who is my resource on airplanes and proton therapy.

Again, I am deeply indebted to Kathryn Etters Lovatt who has reviewed this novel several times and made insightful recommendations. She and the Camden Writers have encouraged me throughout the writing process. My husband Bill, and good friend Martha Greenway, have helped me hunt down spelling and grammatical mistakes that seem to multiply during my sleep. Cathleen O'Brien is the best when it comes to design work, and I'm flattered that the French artist, Karen Slama, allowed her art work to be used for the cover. Catherine Drayton remains my agent supreme, always offering insightful recommendations on what to trim and how to improve my work. Thank you to everyone.

Discussion Questions for Book Clubs

This novel illustrates a common dilemma that confronts the public. At what point are jobs more beneficial to a community than the possible health or environmental repercussions? If you're without work and are unable to provide for your family, then long term consequences may seem much less threatening than immediate needs.

1. Do you think Sadie was justified in her outrage?

2. Do you think public protests accomplish anything?

3. Do you feel that the protest that Sadie and her friends led would have had the same outcome through a different approach? If so, what?

4. In your opinion, what were the real reasons behind Colonel Little's unwillingness to forsake ICS plans?

5. Do you consider Caren Drake typical or atypical of aggressive business-savvy professionals? Was she a villain or a pragmatist?

6. Do you consider yourself an activist? In what ways? What is your "tipping" point?

7. Does every product that is produced have a negative by-product? Give examples of products you think are "clean."

8. Who should be responsible for the cost of disposal of harmful by-products? The industry? The consumer? The government? Other?

9. In which of the above groups do you place the most trust? Why?

10. What changes in waste management have you seen in your lifetime?

Brenda Remmes is the author of the bestselling novel *The Quaker Café* and the sequel *Home to Cedar Branch*. Her stories and articles have appeared in *Newsweek* as well as Southern publications and Journals. She currently lives with her husband in an old family home along the shores of the Black River Swamp in South Carolina.

60494369R00156

Made in the USA
Middletown, DE
15 August 2019